THE ELEMENTS
OF DARK ENERGY

Written by Ashley V. Robinson and Jason Inman
Art by Desiree' Pittman and Becka Kinzie
Lettering by Taylor Esposito

Editing by S.M. Beiko

Bedside
PRESS

Copyright 2019 Ashley V. Robinson & Jason Inman
Front cover art by Becca Farrow
Interior artwork by Desiree' Pittman & Becka Kinzie
Interior layout by Hope Nicholson
Interior and cover design by Relish New Brand Experience
Printed and bound in Canada

LIBRARY AND ARCHIVES CANADA CATALOGUING IN PUBLICATION
Title: Science : the elements of dark energy / by Ashley Robinson, Jason Inman ;
     [art by] Desiree' Pittman; [colour art by] Becka Kinzie ; [letters by] Taylor Esposito.
Names: Robinson, Ashley Victoria, author. | Inman, Jason, author. |
     Kinzie, Becka, colourist. | Pittman, Desiree', 1983- illustrator. |
     Esposito, Taylor, letterer.
Identifiers: Canadiana (print) 20190148888 | Canadiana (ebook) 20190149043 |
     ISBN 9781988715278 (softcover) | ISBN 9781988715339 (PDF)
Subjects: LCGFT: Graphic novels.
Classification: LCC PN6733.R635 S35 2019 | DDC j741.5/971—dc23

BEDSIDE PRESS
bedsidepress.com

Guess what – this book you're about to jump into? It's a ton of fun.

Well, that's this introduction done, and... what? More?

Okay, I can do that.

Let's talk about SCIENCE!

As a concept, science is a search for the truth. You start with an expectation of how things might go and then follow the path of that expectation; winding your way through twists and turns, until you arrive at the conclusion, and you discover what's true.

That's how science works.

Fittingly, it's also how Science! – the book you're about to read – works.

We start off with a school of hyper-gifted children and a lead character with a secret. We've seen these things before and can therefore form an expectation, right?

Well now the twists start.

No one is exactly what they seem. (With the possible exception of my buddy in the rocket boots, okay, but he's clearly the control group in this enterprise.)

As this story is set in a school, you'll find all the humor and drama and romance and pressure to succeed that you could ever expect, jacked up to the nines.

As this story is filled with super-geniuses, you'll find a boatload of high concepts in every scene!

And as this story is awesome, you'll find robots! (The S.T.A.T.s are my favorite part of the book and it is to my everlasting consternation that I can't have one of my very own, no matter how much I beg.)

This team – Ashley, Jason, Dez, Becka, and Taylor have managed a fun bit of alchemy here; they've taken a little Fantastic Four, added a little Harry Potter, and mixed in a variety of flavors from across the known world to get *SCIENCE!* – a book that feels both familiar and unique, like all the best parts of pop culture do when you meet them for the first time.

I'm telling you now, Tamsin Trakroo and her classmates are gonna inspire a lot of things in their audience, not the least of which is demand for a sequel.

Which leads us back, full circle, to the beginning of this introduction.

This book is a ton of fun.

Your search for that truth is over, and with verification complete, there's nothing left to do but turn the page, enter the Prometheus Institute, and enjoy the ride.

Erik Burnham
Middle of Minnesota
July 2019

Erik Burnham is the scribe behind so many amazing IDW Ghostbusters adventures (including Transformers/Ghostbusters), as well as several of their Ninja Turtles tales as well. He has also penned Spider-Man and Scarlet Spider in his time and The Simpsons. He enjoys comic books beginning with the letter "S."

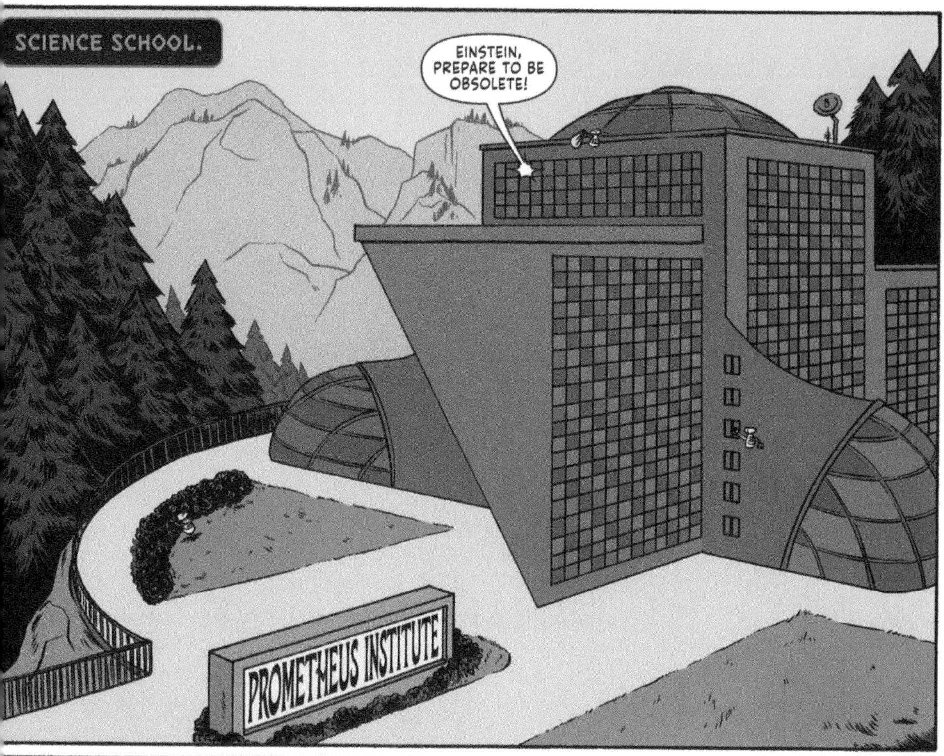
SCIENCE SCHOOL.
EINSTEIN, PREPARE TO BE OBSOLETE!
PROMETHEUS INSTITUTE

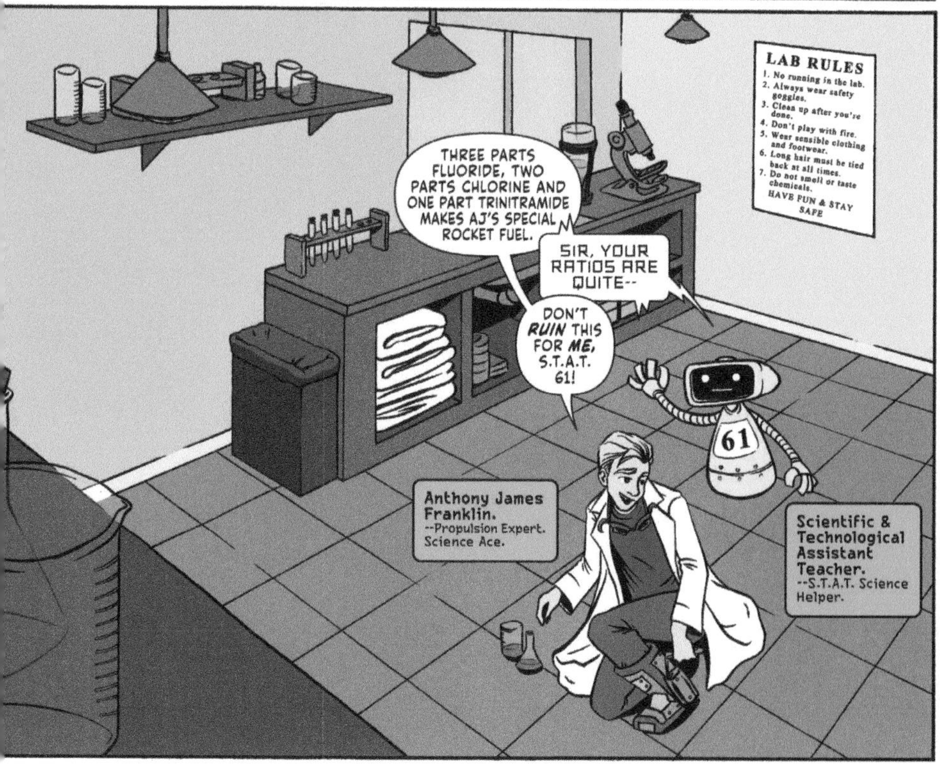
LAB RULES
1. No running in the lab.
2. Always wear safety goggles.
3. Clean up after you're done.
4. Don't play with fire.
5. Wear sensible clothing and footwear.
6. Long hair must be tied back at all times.
7. Do not smell or taste chemicals.
HAVE FUN & STAY SAFE
THREE PARTS FLUORIDE, TWO PARTS CHLORINE AND ONE PART TRINITRAMIDE MAKES AJ'S SPECIAL ROCKET FUEL.
SIR, YOUR RATIOS ARE QUITE--
DON'T *RUIN* THIS FOR *ME,* S.T.A.T. 61!
61
Anthony James Franklin. --Propulsion Expert. Science Ace.
Scientific & Technological Assistant Teacher. --S.T.A.T. Science Helper.

BLAST OFF!
BEEP
AHHHHH!
Anthony James Franklin.
--Science Idiot.
SALUTATIONS! I AM S.T.A.T. 61. YOUR ARTIFICIAL ASSISTANT THROUGH THE WORLD OF SCIENCE.
S.T.A.T. FACT: THE TRINITRAMIDE MOLECULE USED IN AJ'S ROCKET FUEL FORMULA HAS NOT BEEN PROVEN STABLE IN LIQUID OR SOLID FORM.
THEORY SUGGESTS THIS MOLECULE COULD CREATE A FUEL 20% MORE EFFICIENT THAN CURRENT METHODS. SCIENTISTS DO AGREE THIS WILL NOT BE SOLVED BY A 15-YEAR-OLD BOY.
NOW I'LL NEVER OWN A BUGATTI!
KLIK

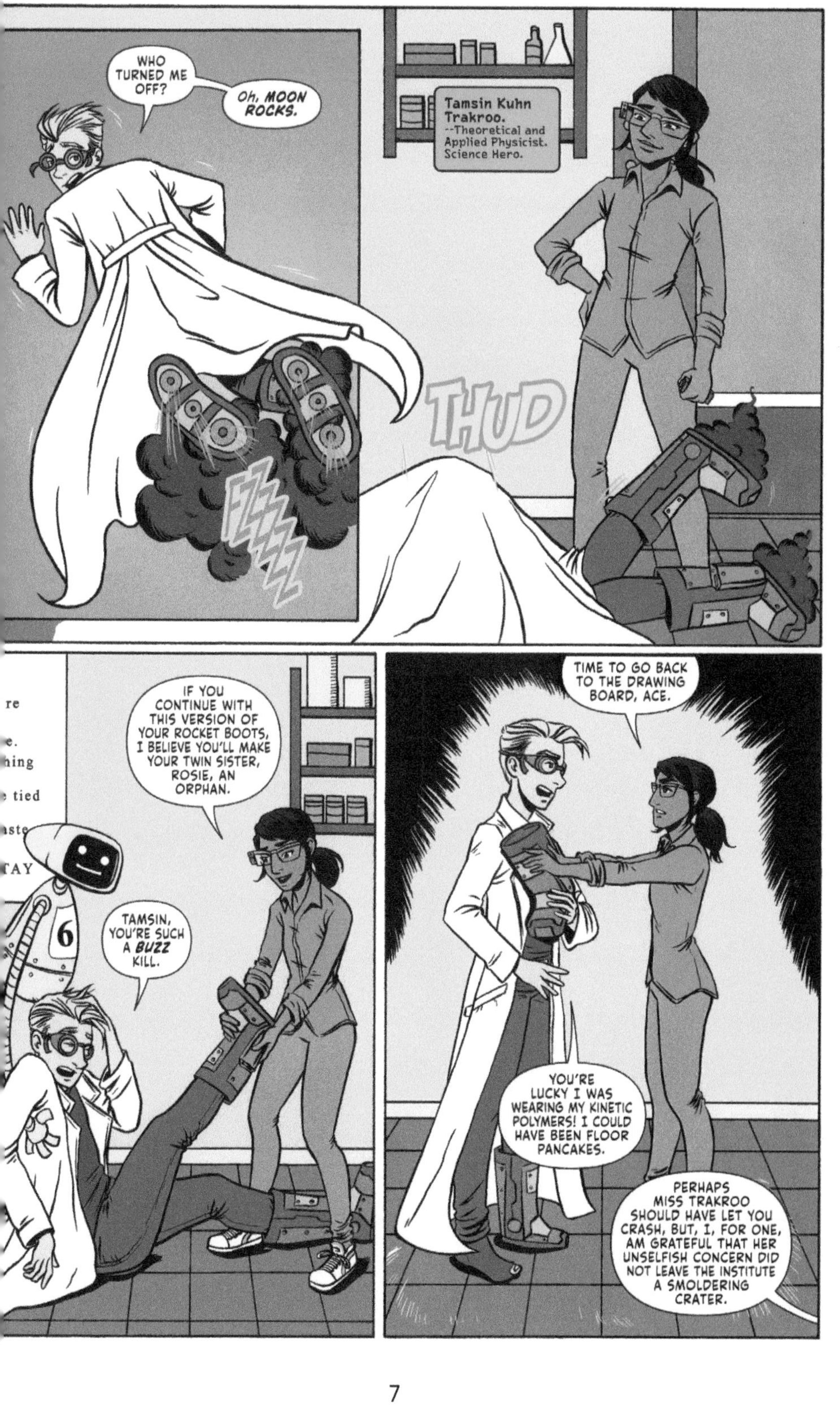
WHO TURNED ME OFF?
Oh, MOON ROCKS.
Tamsin Kuhn Trakroo.
--Theoretical and Applied Physicist. Science Hero.
THUD
FZZZZZZZ
IF YOU CONTINUE WITH THIS VERSION OF YOUR ROCKET BOOTS, I BELIEVE YOU'LL MAKE YOUR TWIN SISTER, ROSIE, AN ORPHAN.
6
TAMSIN, YOU'RE SUCH A BUZZ KILL.
TIME TO GO BACK TO THE DRAWING BOARD, ACE.
YOU'RE LUCKY I WAS WEARING MY KINETIC POLYMERS! I COULD HAVE BEEN FLOOR PANCAKES.
PERHAPS MISS TRAKROO SHOULD HAVE LET YOU CRASH, BUT, I, FOR ONE, AM GRATEFUL THAT HER UNSELFISH CONCERN DID NOT LEAVE THE INSTITUTE A SMOLDERING CRATER.

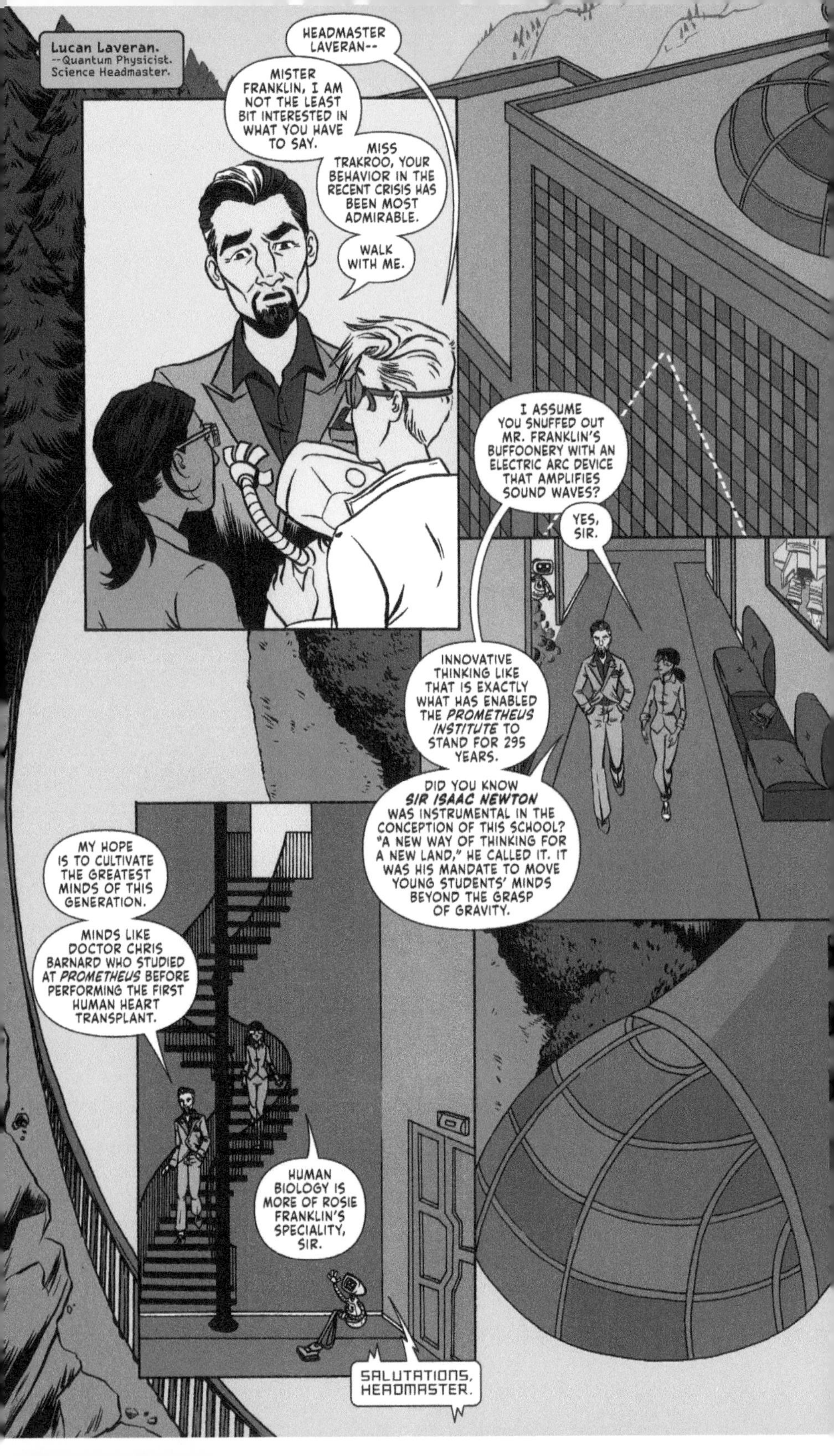
Lucan Laveran. --Quantum Physicist. Science Headmaster.
HEADMASTER LAVERAN--
MISTER FRANKLIN, I AM NOT THE LEAST BIT INTERESTED IN WHAT YOU HAVE TO SAY.
MISS TRAKROO, YOUR BEHAVIOR IN THE RECENT CRISIS HAS BEEN MOST ADMIRABLE.
WALK WITH ME.
I ASSUME YOU SNUFFED OUT MR. FRANKLIN'S BUFFOONERY WITH AN ELECTRIC ARC DEVICE THAT AMPLIFIES SOUND WAVES?
YES, SIR.
INNOVATIVE THINKING LIKE THAT IS EXACTLY WHAT HAS ENABLED THE *PROMETHEUS INSTITUTE* TO STAND FOR 295 YEARS.
DID YOU KNOW ***SIR ISAAC NEWTON*** WAS INSTRUMENTAL IN THE CONCEPTION OF THIS SCHOOL? "A NEW WAY OF THINKING FOR A NEW LAND," HE CALLED IT. IT WAS HIS MANDATE TO MOVE YOUNG STUDENTS' MINDS BEYOND THE GRASP OF GRAVITY.
MY HOPE IS TO CULTIVATE THE GREATEST MINDS OF THIS GENERATION.
MINDS LIKE DOCTOR CHRIS BARNARD WHO STUDIED AT *PROMETHEUS* BEFORE PERFORMING THE FIRST HUMAN HEART TRANSPLANT.
HUMAN BIOLOGY IS MORE OF ROSIE FRANKLIN'S SPECIALITY, SIR.
SALUTATIONS, HEADMASTER.

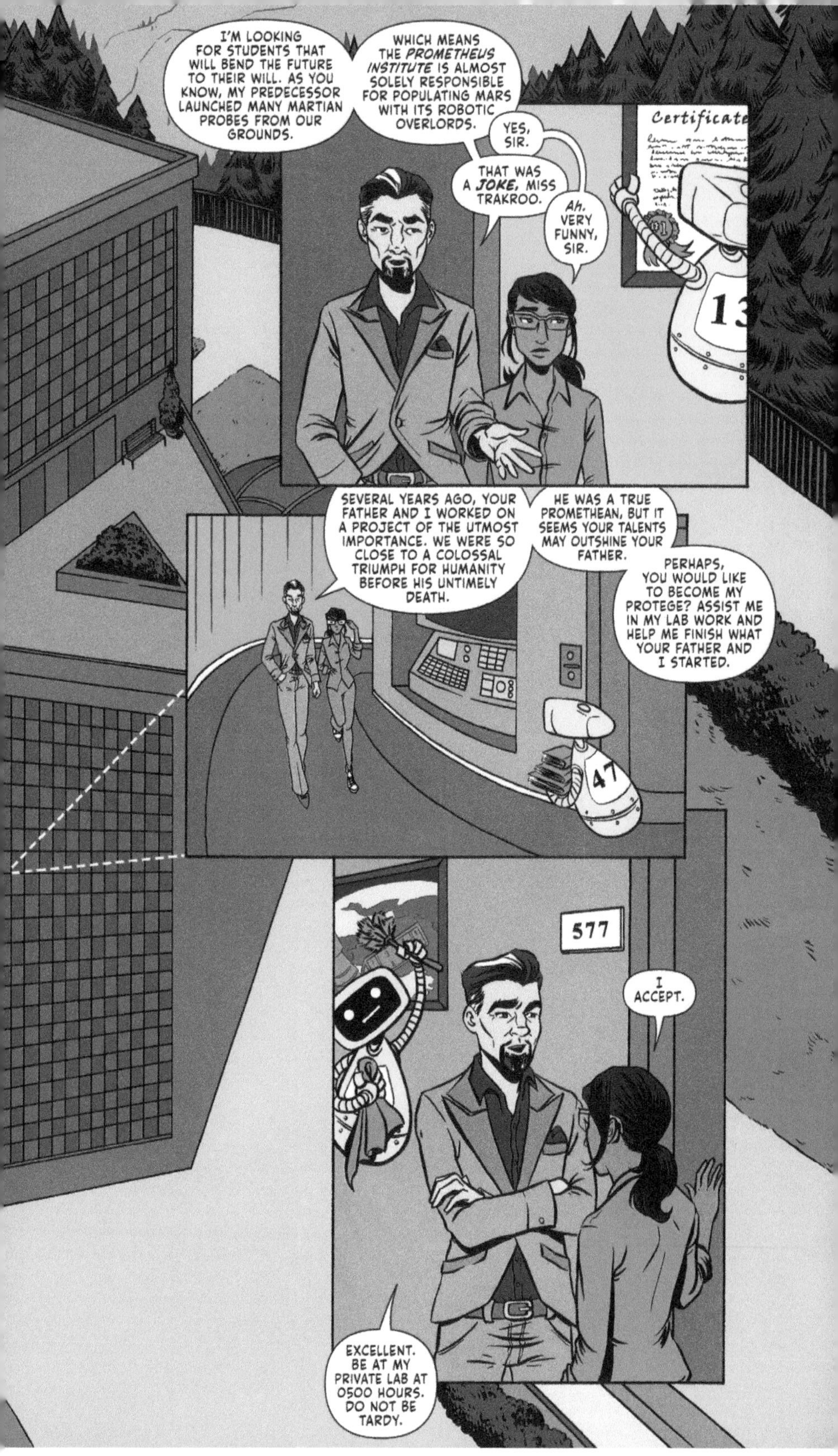
I'M LOOKING FOR STUDENTS THAT WILL BEND THE FUTURE TO THEIR WILL. AS YOU KNOW, MY PREDECESSOR LAUNCHED MANY MARTIAN PROBES FROM OUR GROUNDS.
WHICH MEANS THE *PROMETHEUS INSTITUTE* IS ALMOST SOLELY RESPONSIBLE FOR POPULATING MARS WITH ITS ROBOTIC OVERLORDS.
YES, SIR.
THAT WAS A ***JOKE,*** MISS TRAKROO.
Ah. VERY FUNNY, SIR.
Certificate
13
SEVERAL YEARS AGO, YOUR FATHER AND I WORKED ON A PROJECT OF THE UTMOST IMPORTANCE. WE WERE SO CLOSE TO A COLOSSAL TRIUMPH FOR HUMANITY BEFORE HIS UNTIMELY DEATH.
HE WAS A TRUE PROMETHEAN, BUT IT SEEMS YOUR TALENTS MAY OUTSHINE YOUR FATHER.
PERHAPS, YOU WOULD LIKE TO BECOME MY PROTEGE? ASSIST ME IN MY LAB WORK AND HELP ME FINISH WHAT YOUR FATHER AND I STARTED.
47
577
I ACCEPT.
EXCELLENT. BE AT MY PRIVATE LAB AT 0500 HOURS. DO NOT BE TARDY.

WHERE'S SALLY?

OUT. WERE YOU NEAR THE EXPLOSION?

YEAH, THAT WAS ME PREVENTING AJ'S LATEST MACHINE FROM BURNING THE SCHOOL DOWN.

YUCK, MY BRAIN CAN'T SCIENCE *ANYTHING* UNTIL AFTER NOON.

Garyn Merik.
--Quantum Mechanic
Science Rebel
Without a Cause.

I HEARD LUCAN LOSER OUTSIDE OUR DOOR. WHAT'D *HE* WANT?

I'M GOING TO BE HIS PERSONAL LAB ASSISTANT.

WHATEVER HE'S GOT WON'T BE AS AMAZING AS WHAT I HAVE COOKING IN MY PERSONAL LAB.

LAVERAN'S MIND IS STONE.

MINE IS LIKE THE WIND. MOVING CONSTANTLY TOWARDS THE TRANSCENDENT IDEA. THAT'S WHY I'M GONNA WIN *THE PROMETHEUS INSTITUTE AWARD FOR SUPERIOR SCIENCE.*

MAYBE I COULD BE YOUR LAB ASSISTANT TOO?

Oh, I DON'T KNOW IF THAT'S A GOOD IDEA. WITH YOU IN THE ROOM, I MIGHT NOT GET ANY WORK DONE.

BUT KEEP WORKING ON YOUR PITCH. I CAN ALWAYS USE SOMEONE UNDER ME.

GOTTA JET!

BZ

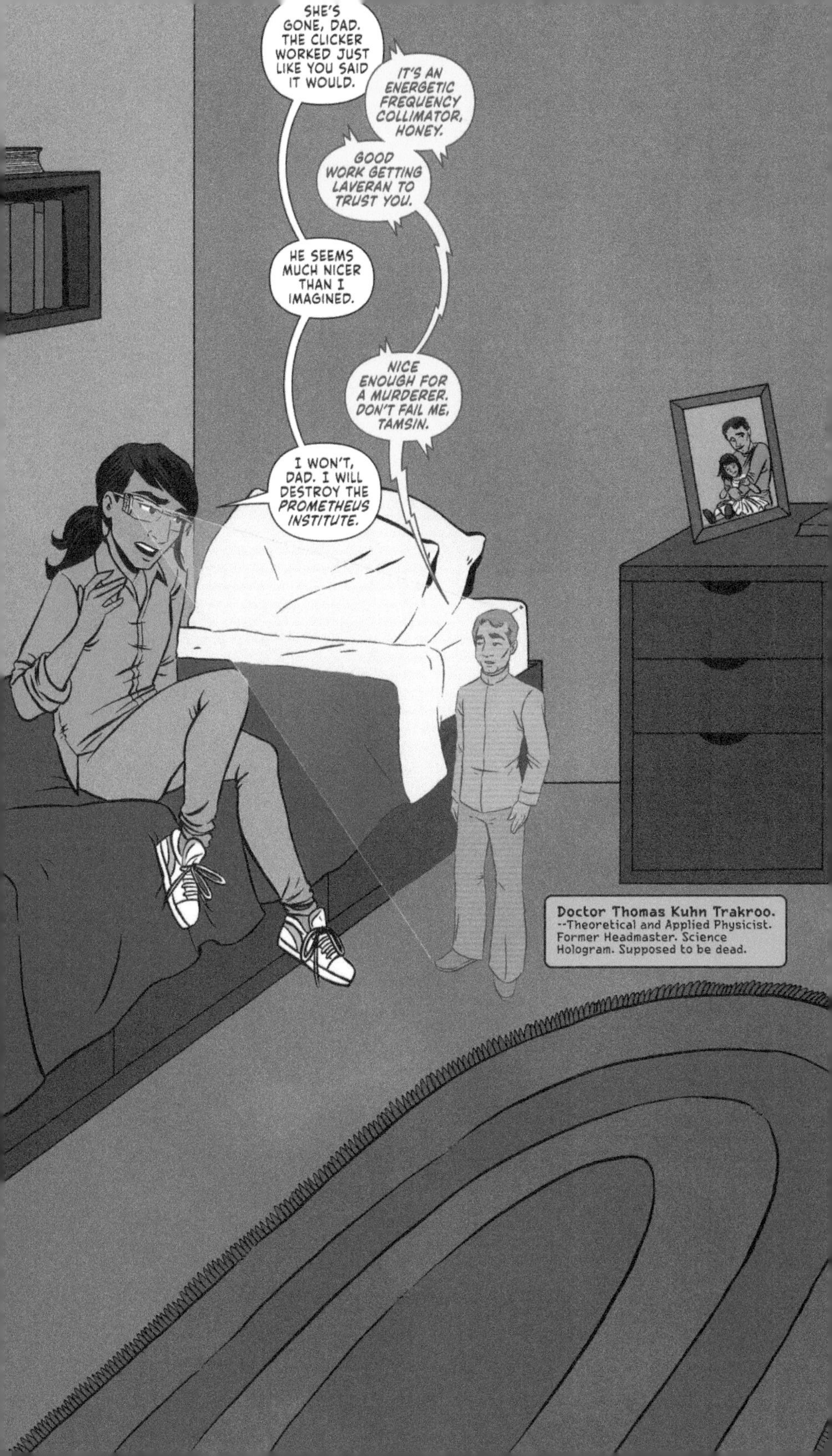
SHE'S GONE, DAD. THE CLICKER WORKED JUST LIKE YOU SAID IT WOULD.
IT'S AN ENERGETIC FREQUENCY COLLIMATOR, HONEY.
GOOD WORK GETTING LAVERAN TO TRUST YOU.
HE SEEMS MUCH NICER THAN I IMAGINED.
NICE ENOUGH FOR A MURDERER. DON'T FAIL ME, TAMSIN.
I WON'T, DAD. I WILL DESTROY THE *PROMETHEUS INSTITUTE.*
Doctor Thomas Kuhn Trakroo.
--Theoretical and Applied Physicist. Former Headmaster. Science Hologram. Supposed to be dead.

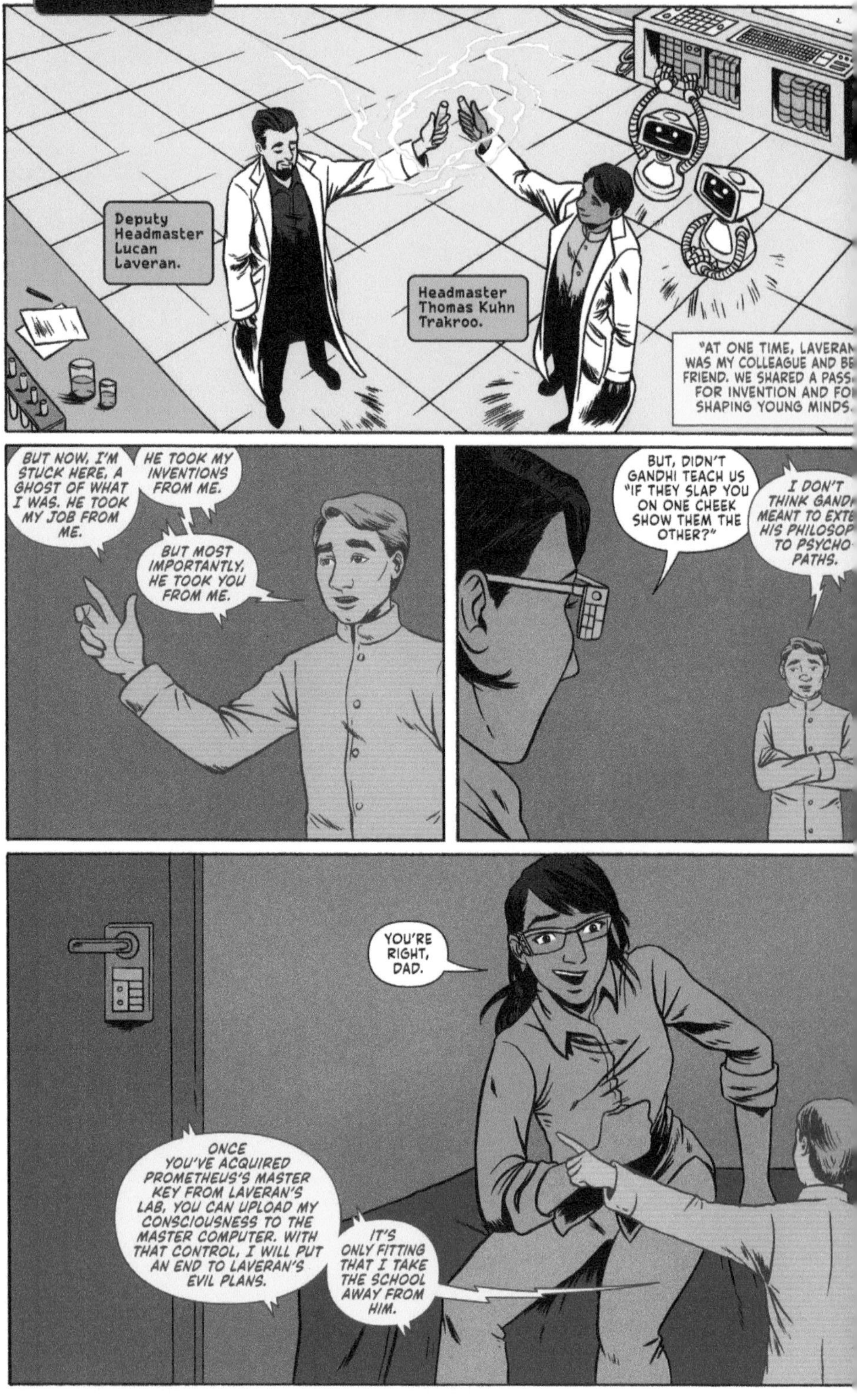
Deputy Headmaster Lucan Laveran.
Headmaster Thomas Kuhn Trakroo.
"AT ONE TIME, LAVERAN WAS MY COLLEAGUE AND BE FRIEND. WE SHARED A PASS FOR INVENTION AND FO SHAPING YOUNG MINDS.
BUT NOW, I'M STUCK HERE, A GHOST OF WHAT I WAS. HE TOOK MY JOB FROM ME.
HE TOOK MY INVENTIONS FROM ME.
BUT MOST IMPORTANTLY, HE TOOK YOU FROM ME.
BUT, DIDN'T GANDHI TEACH US "IF THEY SLAP YOU ON ONE CHEEK SHOW THEM THE OTHER?"
I DON'T THINK GAND MEANT TO EXTE HIS PHILOSOP TO PSYCHO PATHS.
YOU'RE RIGHT, DAD.
ONCE YOU'VE ACQUIRED PROMETHEUS'S MASTER KEY FROM LAVERAN'S LAB, YOU CAN UPLOAD MY CONSCIOUSNESS TO THE MASTER COMPUTER. WITH THAT CONTROL, I WILL PUT AN END TO LAVERAN'S EVIL PLANS.
IT'S ONLY FITTING THAT I TAKE THE SCHOOL AWAY FROM HIM.

TAMSIN, WHAT IS GOING ON?!

QUICK! PUT ME BACK INSIDE YOUR GLASSES!

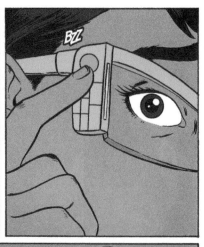

BZZ

Sarah "Sally" Dunbar.
--Mechanical Engineer.
Science Builder.

SALLY, I CAN EXPLAIN--

THAT LOOKED *RAD!* WHY DIDN'T YOU TELL ME THIS WAS YOUR PROJECT FOR THE AWARD? I LOVE HOLOGRAMS!

YES, TAMSIN. RUN WITH THIS. CONVINCE HER THAT SHE'S STUMBLED ONTO NOTHING. NO CONSPIRACY HERE.

YEAH, IT'S FOR MY PROJECT, I'M NOT EVEN SURE IF I'LL ENTER IT.

YOU DON'T HAVE TO BE MODEST! HERE, I GOT SOMETHING TO BOOST YOUR CONFIDENCE...

IT'S A MINI-TAMSIN! I KNOW YOU'RE NEWISH HERE SO IF YOU EVER FEEL LONELY, YOU NOW HAVE TWO BEST FRIENDS. MINI-TAMSIN AND YOURS TRULY!

THANKS, SALLY!

DON'T THINK THIS GETS YOU OUT OF A HOLOGRAM TALK WITH ME, MISSY! YOU HAVE GOT TO SHOW ME HOW YOU MADE THAT!

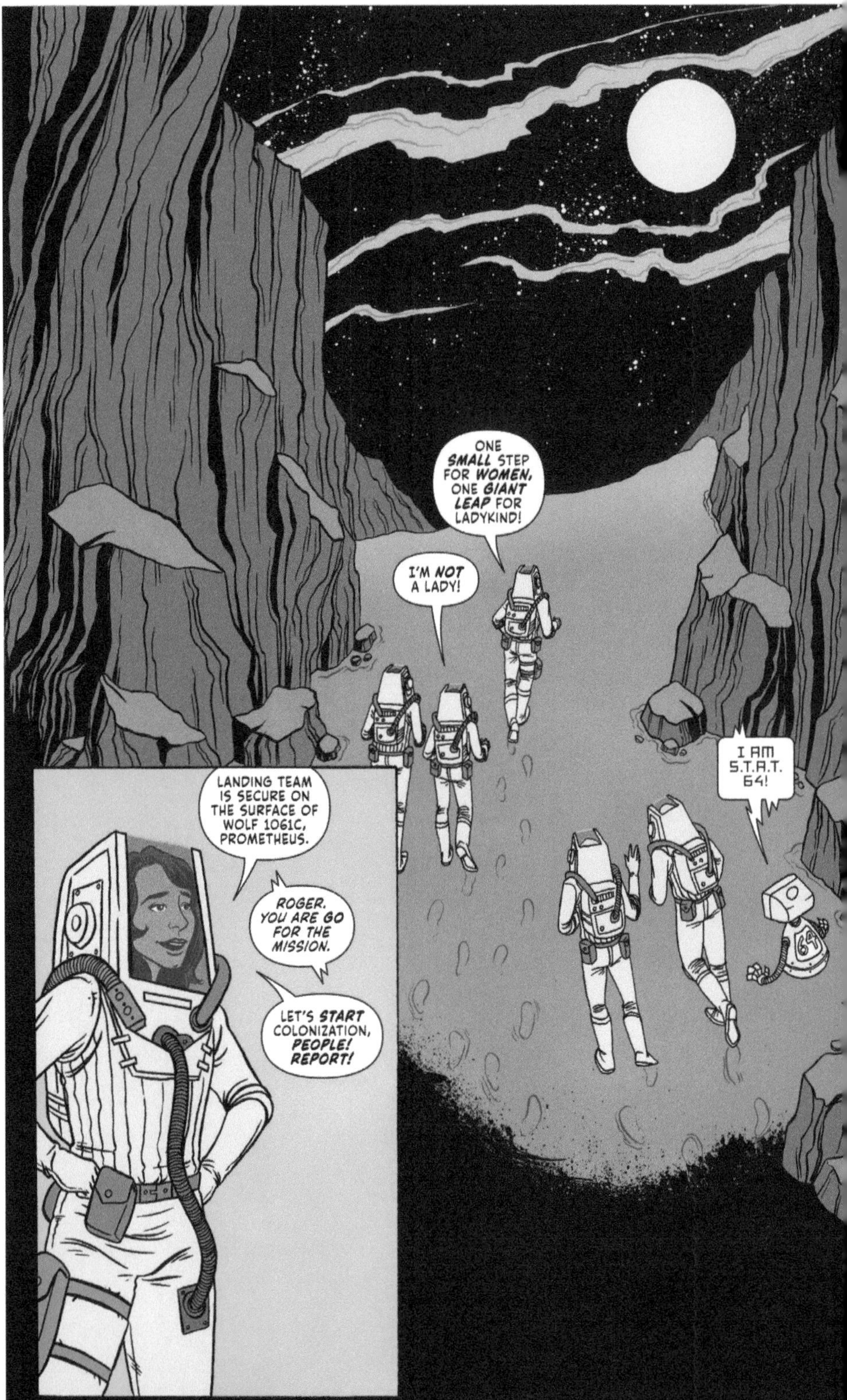

ONE SMALL STEP FOR WOMEN, ONE GIANT LEAP FOR LADYKIND!
I'M NOT A LADY!
I AM S.T.A.T. 64!
LANDING TEAM IS SECURE ON THE SURFACE OF WOLF 1061C, PROMETHEUS.
ROGER. YOU ARE GO FOR THE MISSION.
LET'S START COLONIZATION, PEOPLE! REPORT!

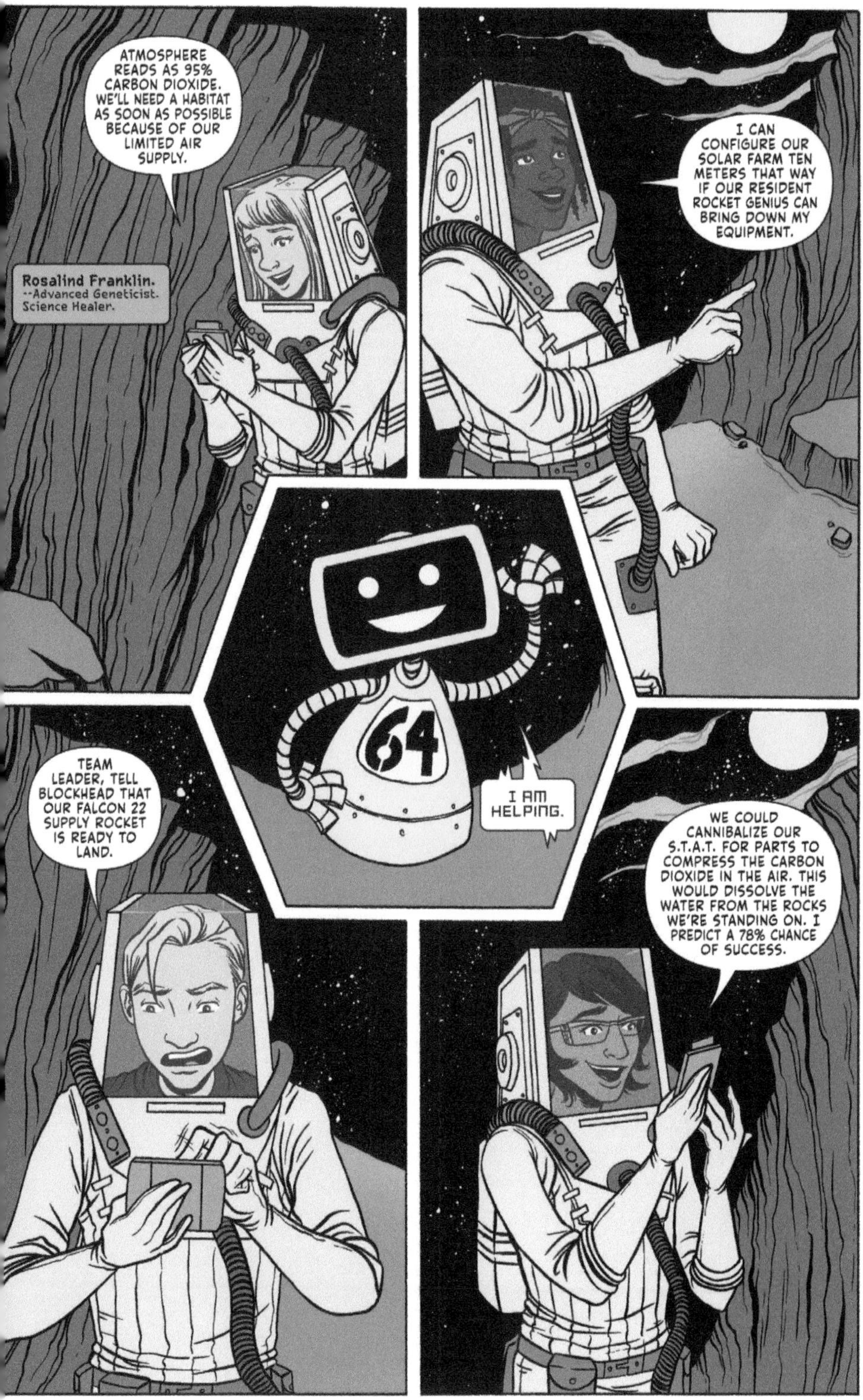
ATMOSPHERE READS AS 95% CARBON DIOXIDE. WE'LL NEED A HABITAT AS SOON AS POSSIBLE BECAUSE OF OUR LIMITED AIR SUPPLY.
Rosalind Franklin. --Advanced Geneticist. Science Healer.
I CAN CONFIGURE OUR SOLAR FARM TEN METERS THAT WAY IF OUR RESIDENT ROCKET GENIUS CAN BRING DOWN MY EQUIPMENT.
64
I AM HELPING.
TEAM LEADER, TELL BLOCKHEAD THAT OUR FALCON 22 SUPPLY ROCKET IS READY TO LAND.
WE COULD CANNIBALIZE OUR S.T.A.T. FOR PARTS TO COMPRESS THE CARBON DIOXIDE IN THE AIR. THIS WOULD DISSOLVE THE WATER FROM THE ROCKS WE'RE STANDING ON. I PREDICT A 78% CHANCE OF SUCCESS.

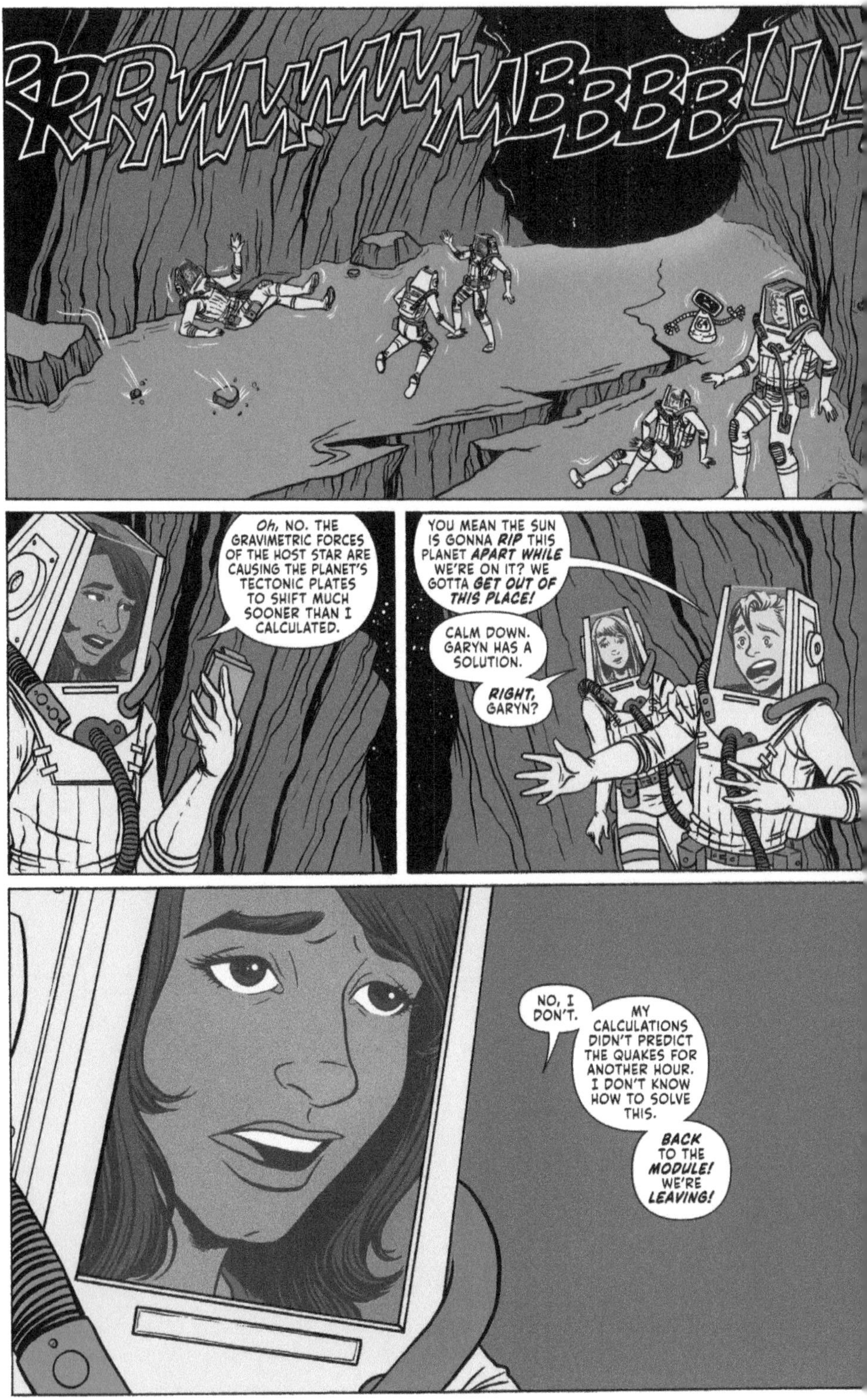
RRRMMMMMMBBBBLLL
Oh, NO. THE GRAVIMETRIC FORCES OF THE HOST STAR ARE CAUSING THE PLANET'S TECTONIC PLATES TO SHIFT MUCH SOONER THAN I CALCULATED.
YOU MEAN THE SUN IS GONNA RIP THIS PLANET APART WHILE WE'RE ON IT? WE GOTTA GET OUT OF THIS PLACE!
CALM DOWN. GARYN HAS A SOLUTION.
RIGHT, GARYN?
NO, I DON'T.
MY CALCULATIONS DIDN'T PREDICT THE QUAKES FOR ANOTHER HOUR. I DON'T KNOW HOW TO SOLVE THIS.
BACK TO THE MODULE! WE'RE LEAVING!

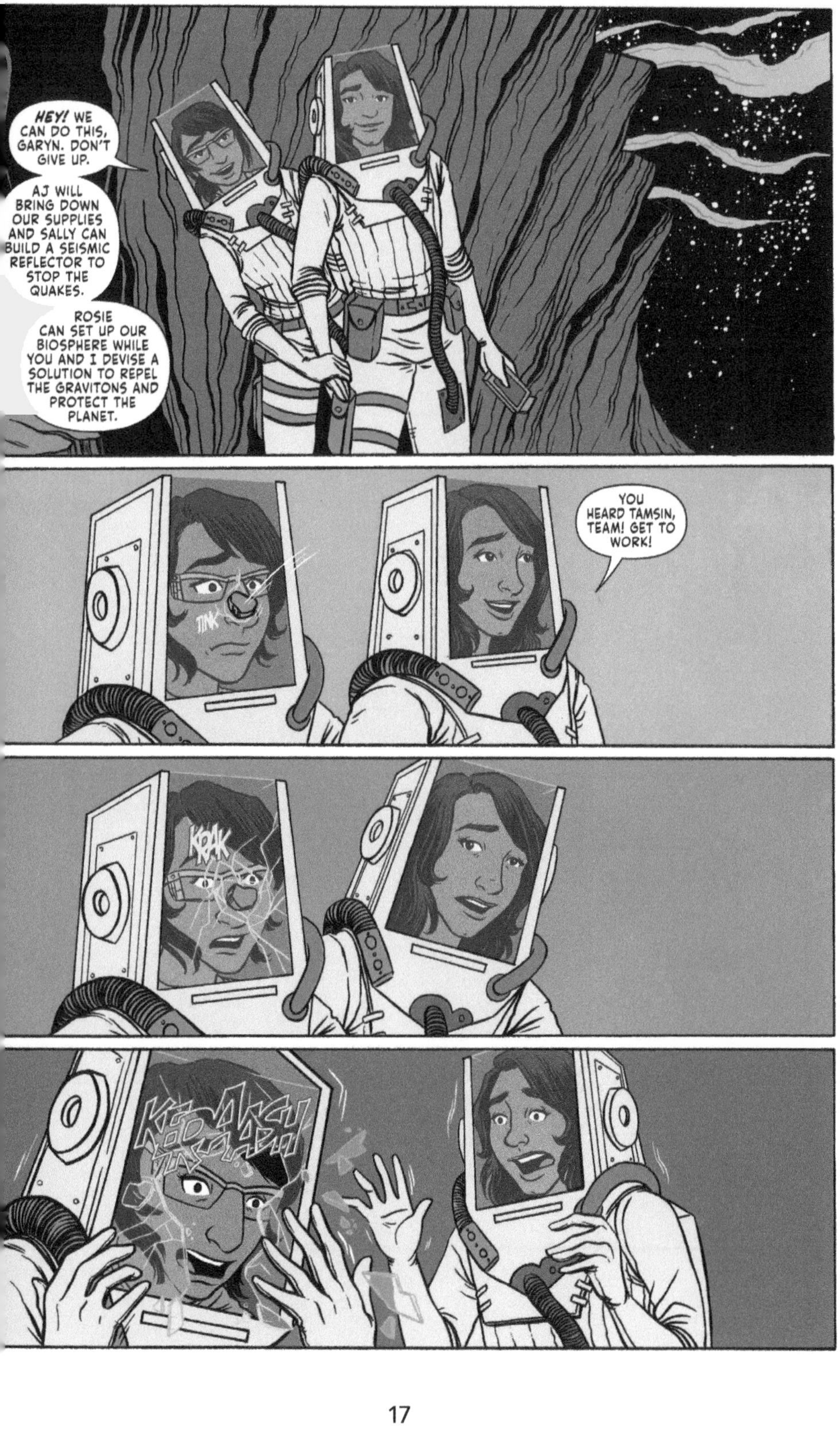
HEY! WE CAN DO THIS, GARYN. DON'T GIVE UP.
AJ WILL BRING DOWN OUR SUPPLIES AND SALLY CAN BUILD A SEISMIC REFLECTOR TO STOP THE QUAKES.
ROSIE CAN SET UP OUR BIOSPHERE WHILE YOU AND I DEVISE A SOLUTION TO REPEL THE GRAVITONS AND PROTECT THE PLANET.
YOU HEARD TAMSIN, TEAM! GET TO WORK!
TINK
KRAK

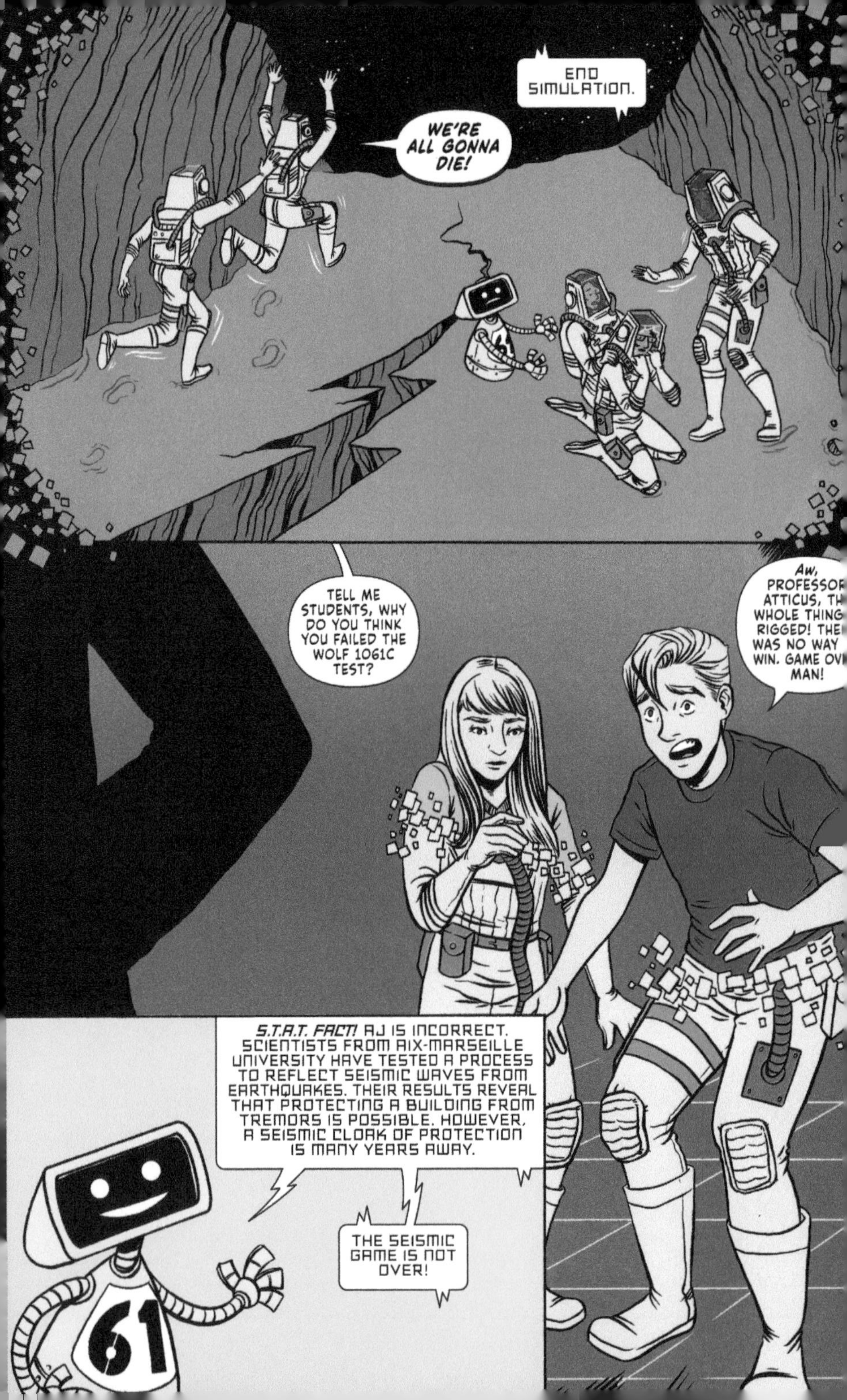

END SIMULATION.
WE'RE ALL GONNA DIE!
TELL ME STUDENTS, WHY DO YOU THINK YOU FAILED THE WOLF 1061C TEST?
Aw, PROFESSOR ATTICUS, TH WHOLE THING RIGGED! THE WAS NO WAY WIN. GAME OV MAN!
S.T.A.T. FACT! AJ IS INCORRECT. SCIENTISTS FROM AIX-MARSEILLE UNIVERSITY HAVE TESTED A PROCESS TO REFLECT SEISMIC WAVES FROM EARTHQUAKES. THEIR RESULTS REVEAL THAT PROTECTING A BUILDING FROM TREMORS IS POSSIBLE. HOWEVER, A SEISMIC CLOAK OF PROTECTION IS MANY YEARS AWAY.
THE SEISMIC GAME IS NOT OVER!

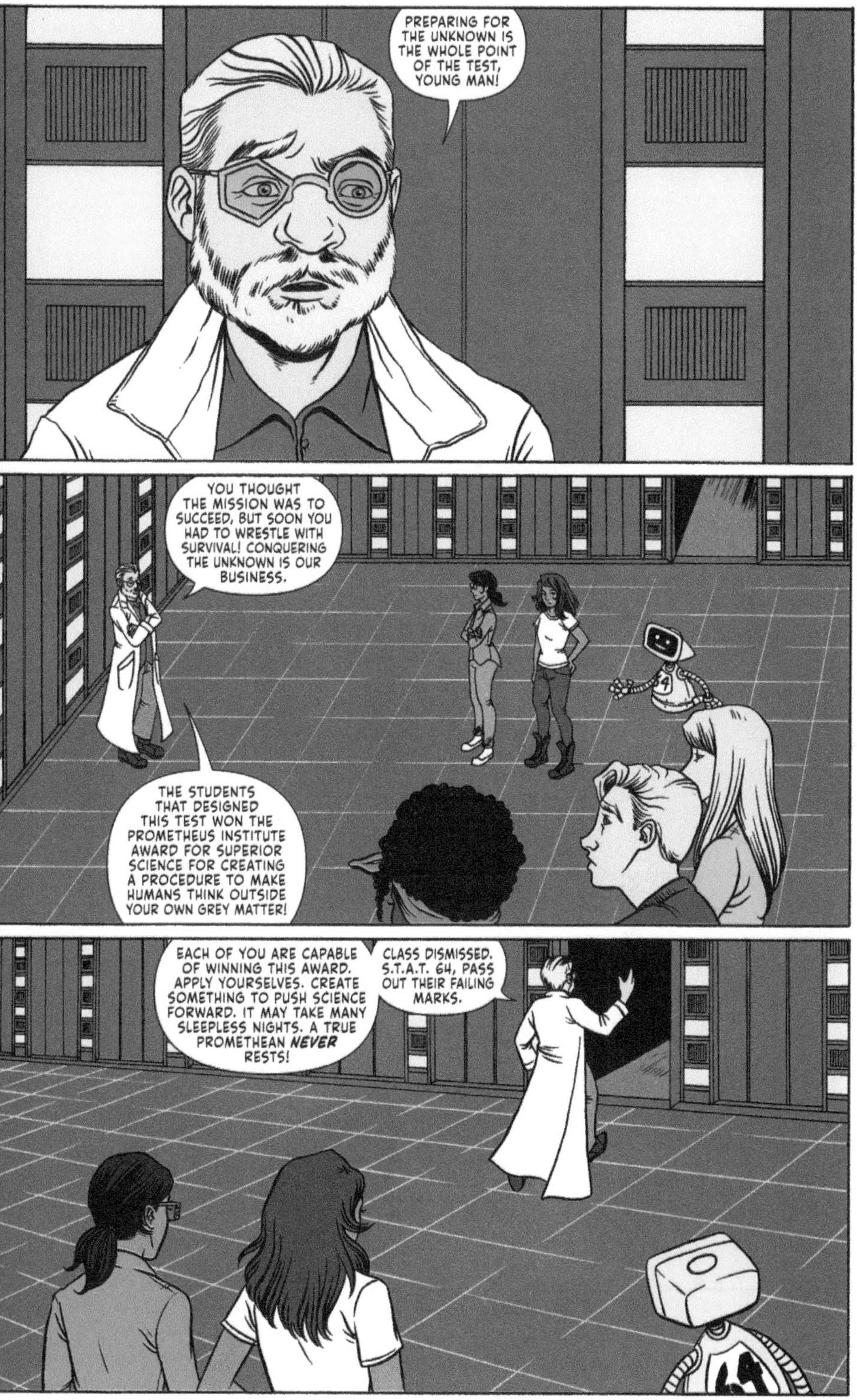
PREPARING FOR THE UNKNOWN IS THE WHOLE POINT OF THE TEST, YOUNG MAN!
YOU THOUGHT THE MISSION WAS TO SUCCEED, BUT SOON YOU HAD TO WRESTLE WITH SURVIVAL! CONQUERING THE UNKNOWN IS OUR BUSINESS.
THE STUDENTS THAT DESIGNED THIS TEST WON THE PROMETHEUS INSTITUTE AWARD FOR SUPERIOR SCIENCE FOR CREATING A PROCEDURE TO MAKE HUMANS THINK OUTSIDE YOUR OWN GREY MATTER!
EACH OF YOU ARE CAPABLE OF WINNING THIS AWARD. APPLY YOURSELVES. CREATE SOMETHING TO PUSH SCIENCE FORWARD. IT MAY TAKE MANY SLEEPLESS NIGHTS. A TRUE PROMETHEAN *NEVER* RESTS!
CLASS DISMISSED. S.T.A.T. 64, PASS OUT THEIR FAILING MARKS.

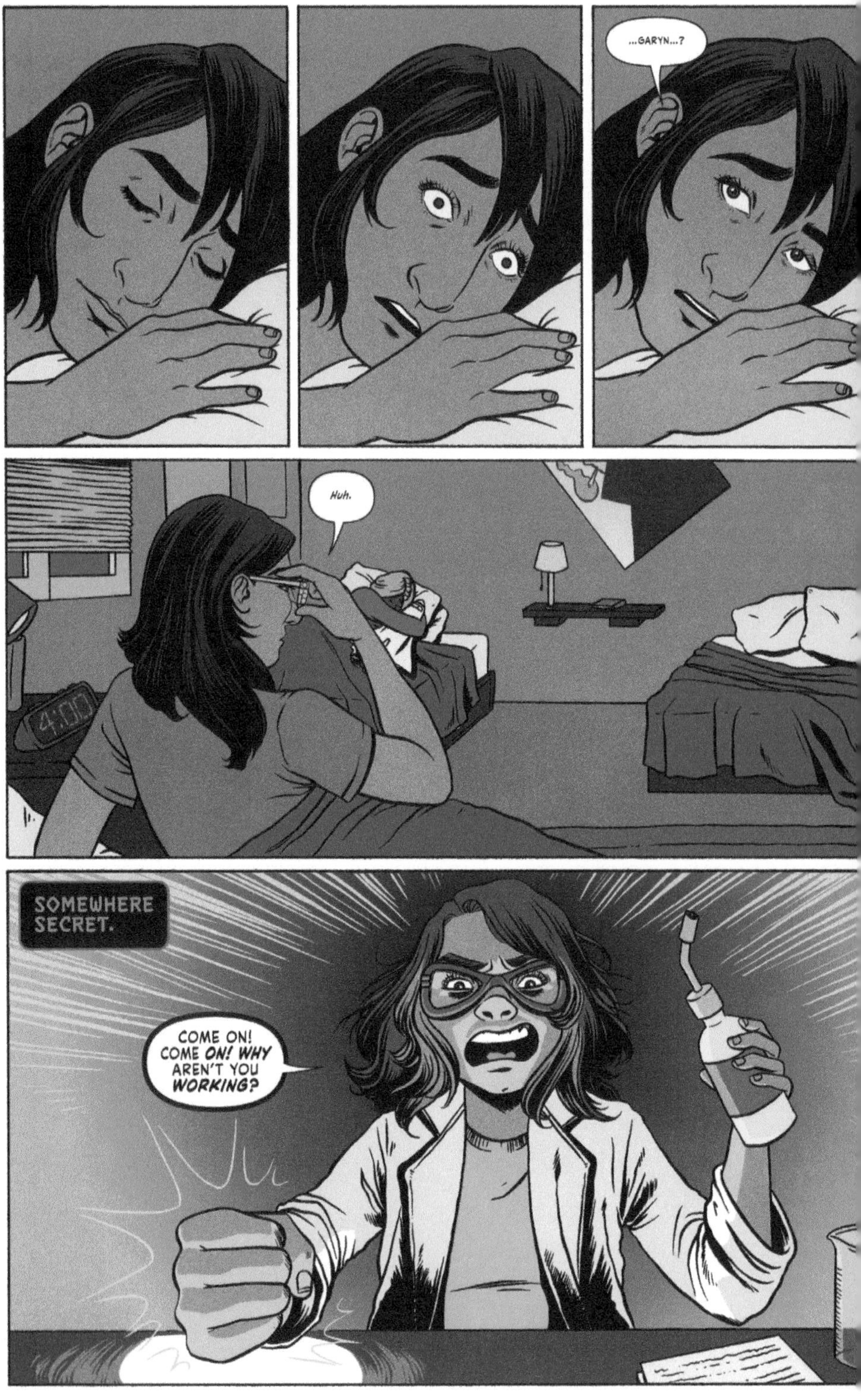
...GARYN...?
Huh.
4:00
SOMEWHERE SECRET.
COME ON! COME ON! WHY AREN'T YOU WORKING?

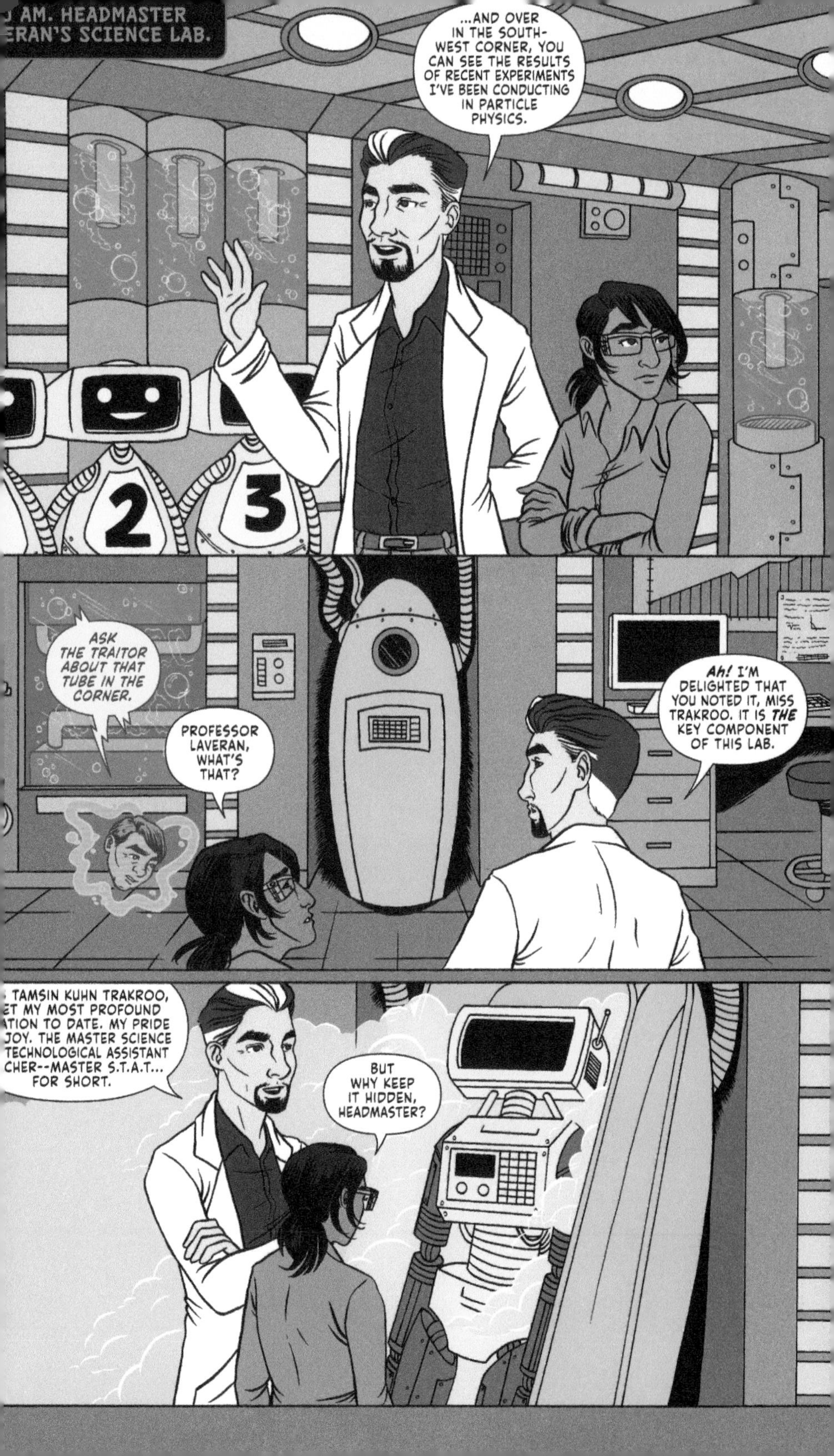

AM. HEADMASTER
ERAN'S SCIENCE LAB.
...AND OVER IN THE SOUTH-WEST CORNER, YOU CAN SEE THE RESULTS OF RECENT EXPERIMENTS I'VE BEEN CONDUCTING IN PARTICLE PHYSICS.
2
3
ASK THE TRAITOR ABOUT THAT TUBE IN THE CORNER.
PROFESSOR LAVERAN, WHAT'S THAT?
Ah! I'M DELIGHTED THAT YOU NOTED IT, MISS TRAKROO. IT IS THE KEY COMPONENT OF THIS LAB.
TAMSIN KUHN TRAKROO, ET MY MOST PROFOUND ATION TO DATE. MY PRIDE JOY. THE MASTER SCIENCE TECHNOLOGICAL ASSISTANT CHER--MASTER S.T.A.T... FOR SHORT.
BUT WHY KEEP IT HIDDEN, HEADMASTER?

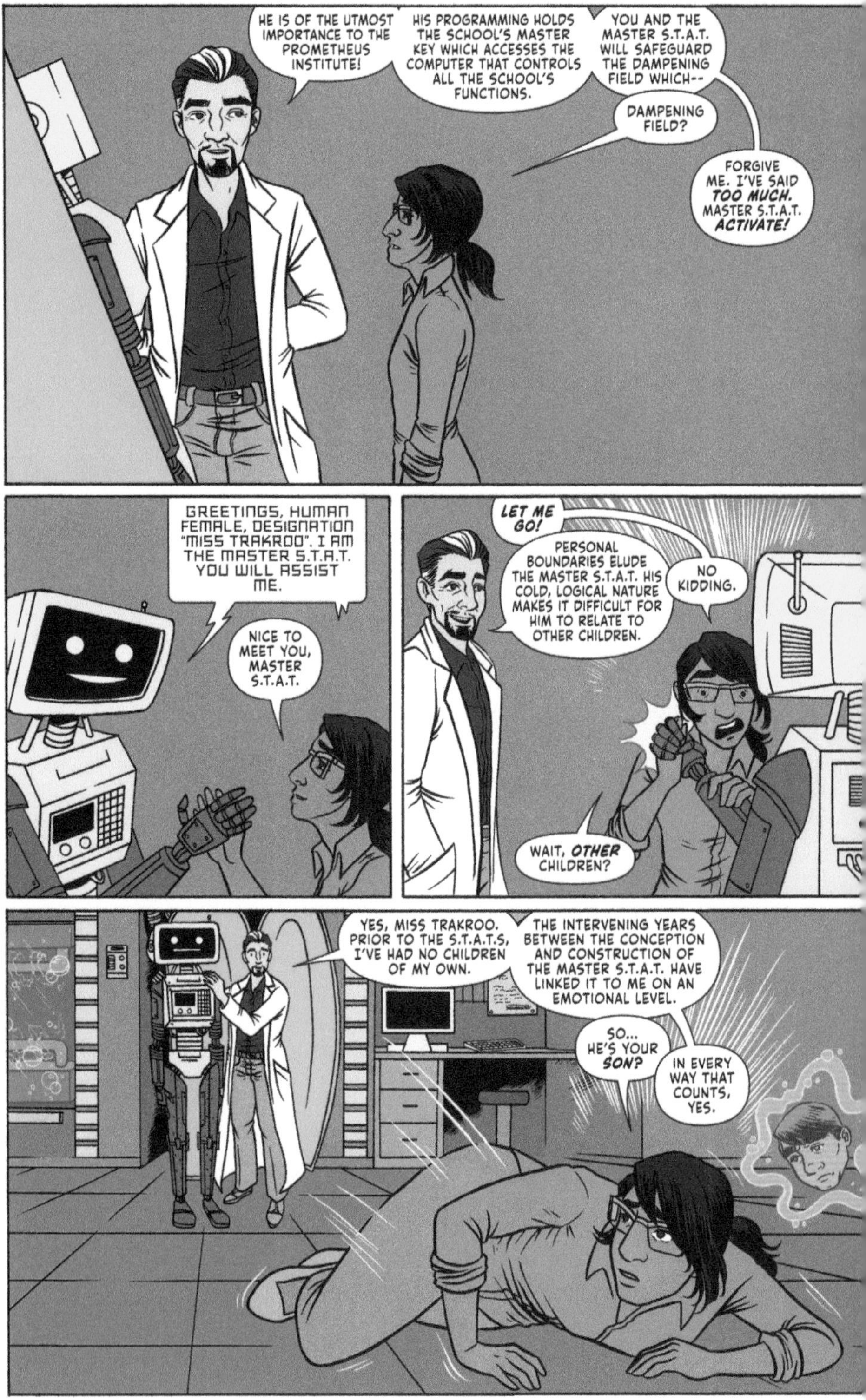
HE IS OF THE UTMOST IMPORTANCE TO THE PROMETHEUS INSTITUTE!
HIS PROGRAMMING HOLDS THE SCHOOL'S MASTER KEY WHICH ACCESSES THE COMPUTER THAT CONTROLS ALL THE SCHOOL'S FUNCTIONS.
YOU AND THE MASTER S.T.A.T. WILL SAFEGUARD THE DAMPENING FIELD WHICH--
DAMPENING FIELD?
FORGIVE ME. I'VE SAID TOO MUCH. MASTER S.T.A.T. ACTIVATE!
GREETINGS, HUMAN FEMALE, DESIGNATION "MISS TRAKROO". I AM THE MASTER S.T.A.T. YOU WILL ASSIST ME.
NICE TO MEET YOU, MASTER S.T.A.T.
LET ME GO!
PERSONAL BOUNDARIES ELUDE THE MASTER S.T.A.T. HIS COLD, LOGICAL NATURE MAKES IT DIFFICULT FOR HIM TO RELATE TO OTHER CHILDREN.
NO KIDDING.
WAIT, OTHER CHILDREN?
YES, MISS TRAKROO. PRIOR TO THE S.T.A.T.S, I'VE HAD NO CHILDREN OF MY OWN.
THE INTERVENING YEARS BETWEEN THE CONCEPTION AND CONSTRUCTION OF THE MASTER S.T.A.T. HAVE LINKED IT TO ME ON AN EMOTIONAL LEVEL.
SO... HE'S YOUR SON?
IN EVERY WAY THAT COUNTS, YES.

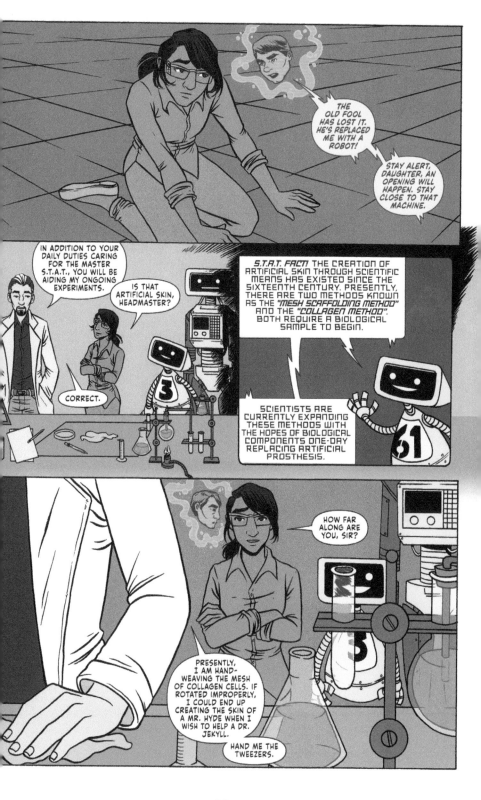

THE OLD FOOL HAS LOST IT. HE'S REPLACED ME WITH A ROBOT!

STAY ALERT, DAUGHTER, AN OPENING WILL HAPPEN. STAY CLOSE TO THAT MACHINE.

IN ADDITION TO YOUR DAILY DUTIES CARING FOR THE MASTER S.T.A.T., YOU WILL BE AIDING MY ONGOING EXPERIMENTS.

IS THAT ARTIFICIAL SKIN, HEADMASTER?

CORRECT.

S.T.A.T. FACT! THE CREATION OF ARTIFICIAL SKIN THROUGH SCIENTIFIC MEANS HAS EXISTED SINCE THE SIXTEENTH CENTURY. PRESENTLY, THERE ARE TWO METHODS KNOWN AS THE "MESH SCAFFOLDING METHOD" AND THE "COLLAGEN METHOD". BOTH REQUIRE A BIOLOGICAL SAMPLE TO BEGIN.

SCIENTISTS ARE CURRENTLY EXPANDING THESE METHODS WITH THE HOPES OF BIOLOGICAL COMPONENTS ONE-DAY REPLACING ARTIFICIAL PROSTHESIS.

HOW FAR ALONG ARE YOU, SIR?

PRESENTLY, I AM HAND-WEAVING THE MESH OF COLLAGEN CELLS. IF ROTATED IMPROPERLY, I COULD END UP CREATING THE SKIN OF A MR. HYDE WHEN I WISH TO HELP A DR. JEKYLL.

HAND ME THE TWEEZERS.

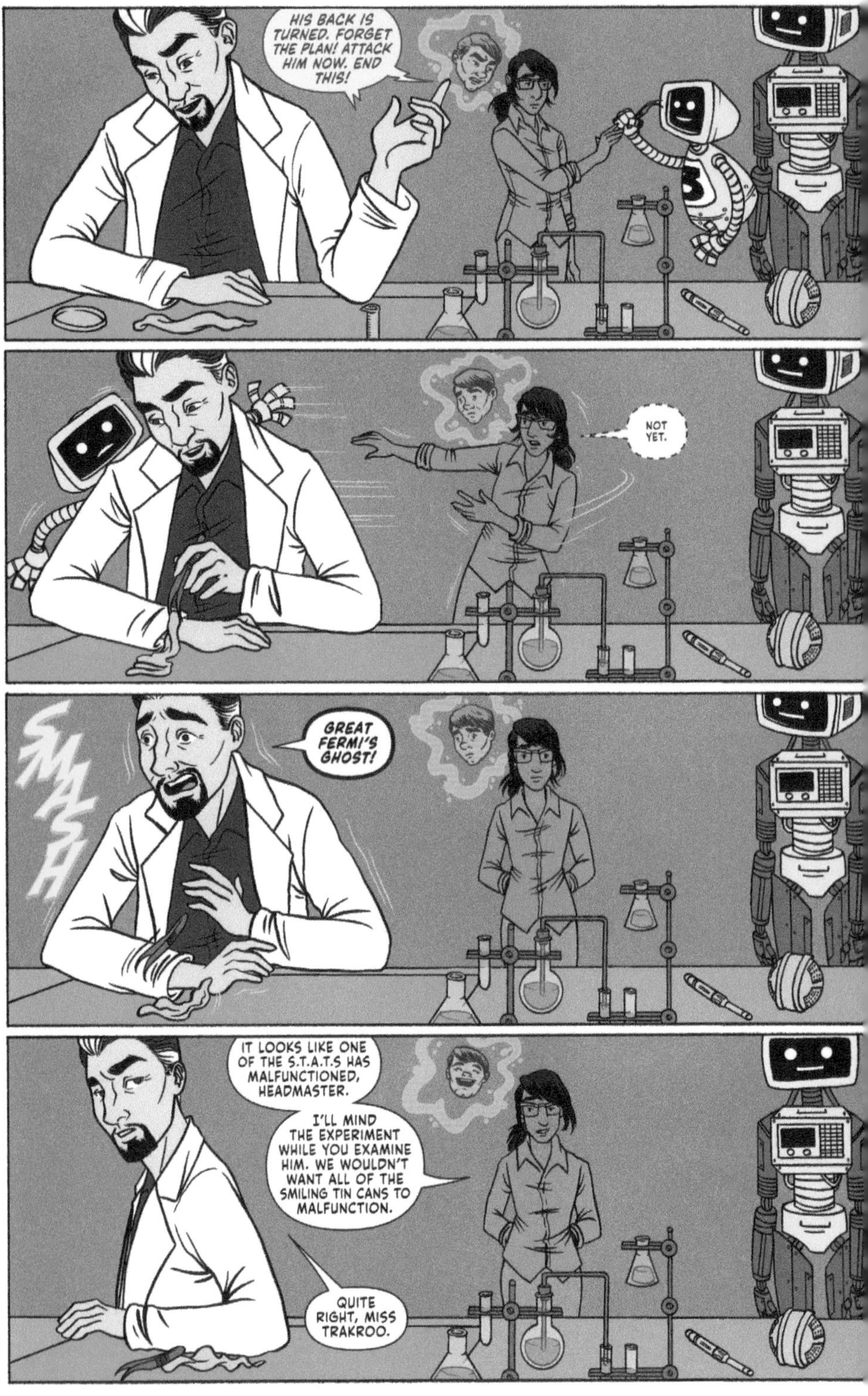
HIS BACK IS TURNED. FORGET THE PLAN! ATTACK HIM NOW. END THIS!
NOT YET.
SMASH
GREAT FERMI'S GHOST!
IT LOOKS LIKE ONE OF THE S.T.A.T.S HAS MALFUNCTIONED, HEADMASTER.
I'LL MIND THE EXPERIMENT WHILE YOU EXAMINE HIM. WE WOULDN'T WANT ALL OF THE SMILING TIN CANS TO MALFUNCTION.
QUITE RIGHT, MISS TRAKROO.

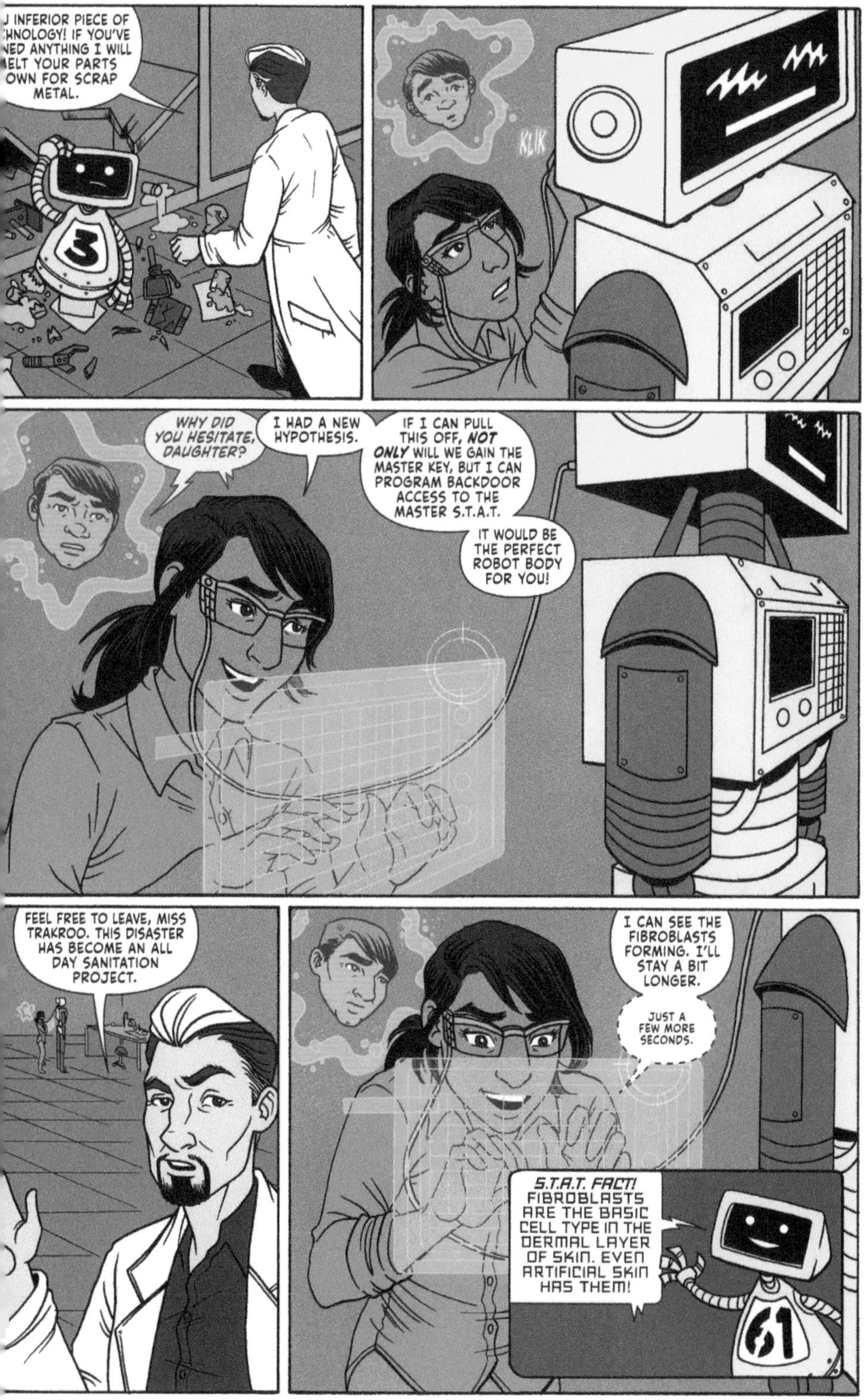

U INFERIOR PIECE OF CHNOLOGY! IF YOU'VE NED ANYTHING I WILL MELT YOUR PARTS OWN FOR SCRAP METAL.
KLIK
WHY DID YOU HESITATE, DAUGHTER?
I HAD A NEW HYPOTHESIS.
IF I CAN PULL THIS OFF, NOT ONLY WILL WE GAIN THE MASTER KEY, BUT I CAN PROGRAM BACKDOOR ACCESS TO THE MASTER S.T.A.T.
IT WOULD BE THE PERFECT ROBOT BODY FOR YOU!
FEEL FREE TO LEAVE, MISS TRAKROO. THIS DISASTER HAS BECOME AN ALL DAY SANITATION PROJECT.
I CAN SEE THE FIBROBLASTS FORMING. I'LL STAY A BIT LONGER.
JUST A FEW MORE SECONDS.
S.T.A.T. FACT! FIBROBLASTS ARE THE BASIC CELL TYPE IN THE DERMAL LAYER OF SKIN. EVEN ARTIFICIAL SKIN HAS THEM!

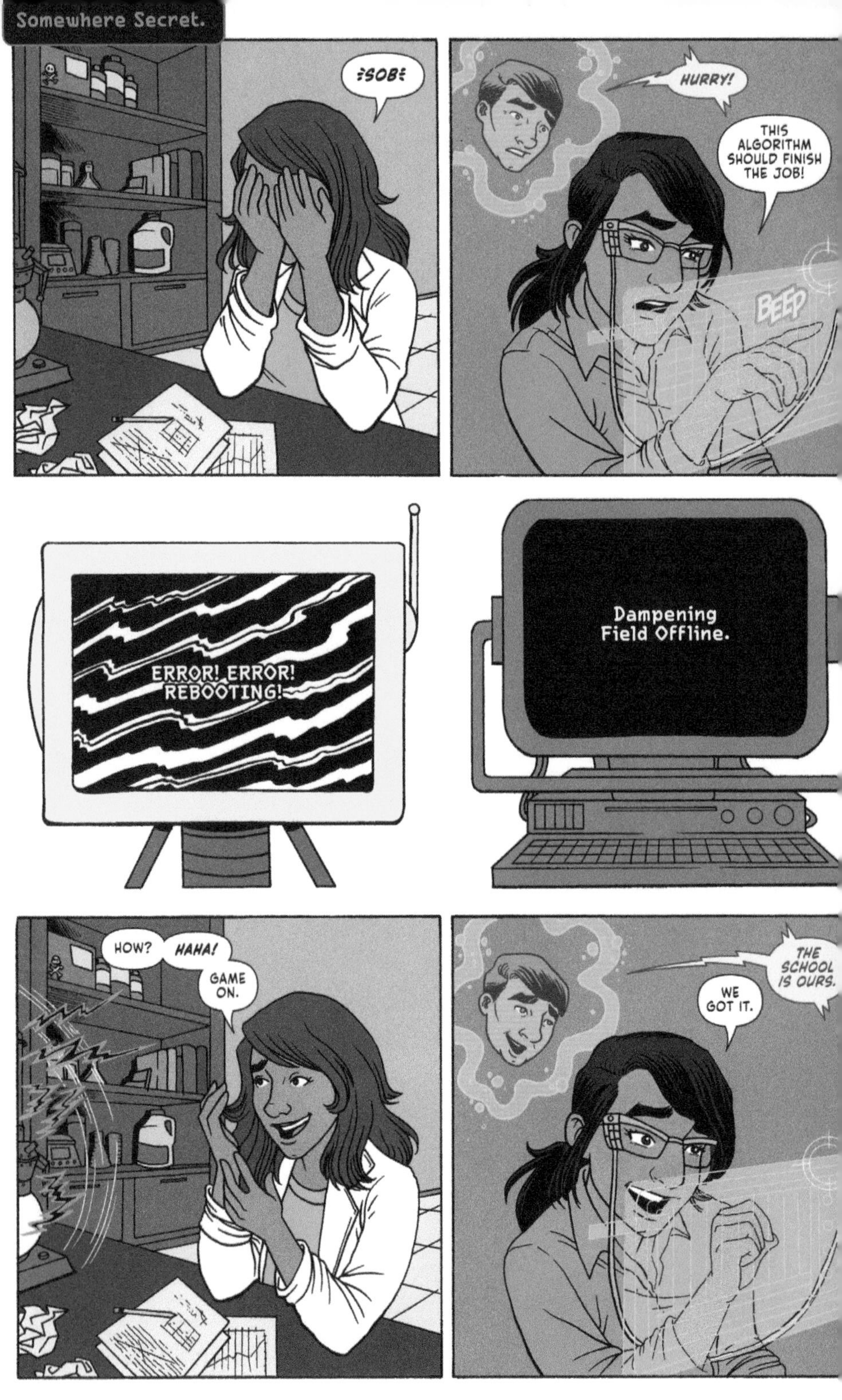
Somewhere Secret.
SOB
HURRY!
THIS ALGORITHM SHOULD FINISH THE JOB!
BEEP
ERROR! ERROR! REBOOTING!
Dampening Field Offline.
HOW?
HAHA!
GAME ON.
THE SCHOOL IS OURS.
WE GOT IT.

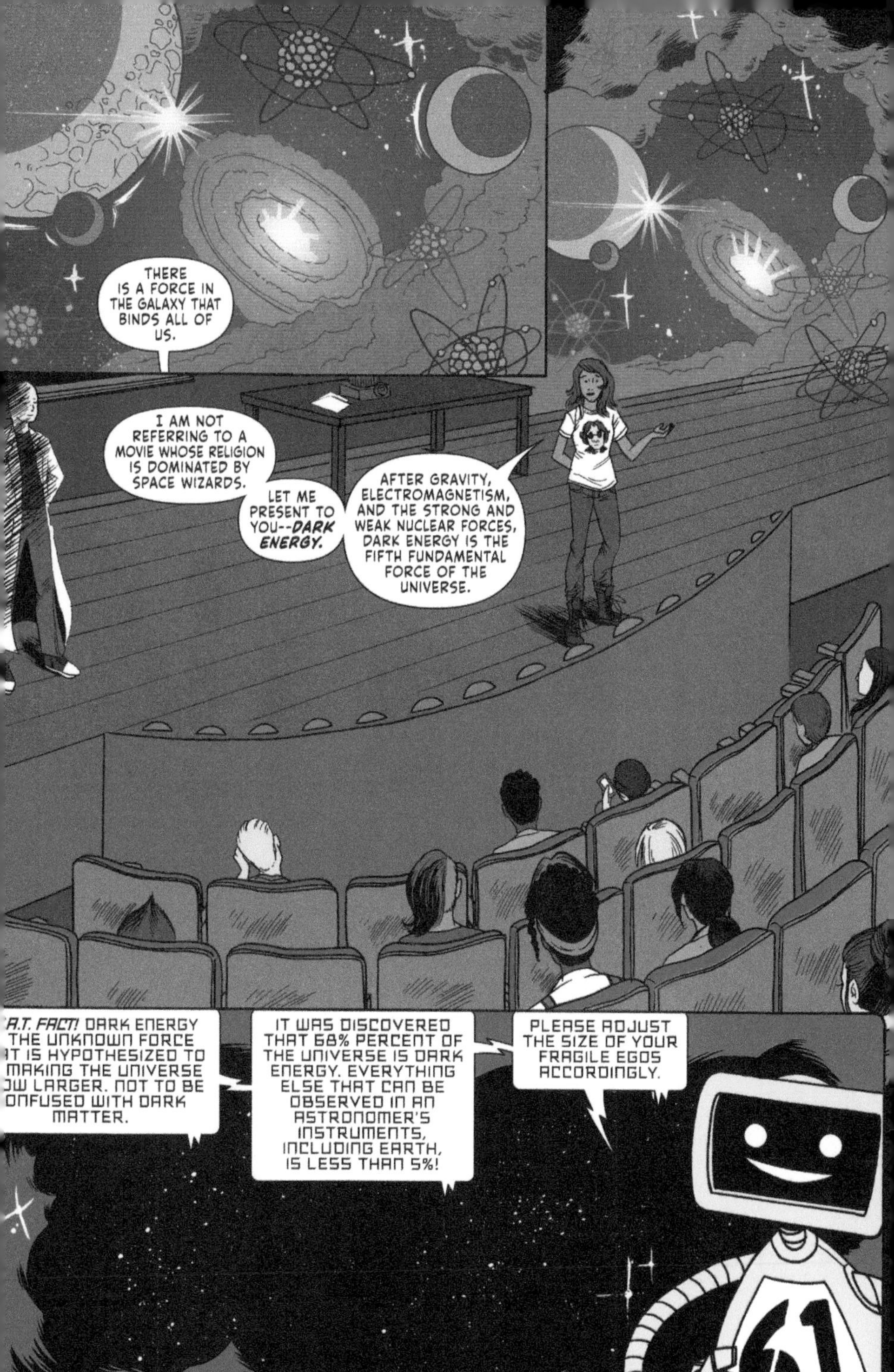
THERE IS A FORCE IN THE GALAXY THAT BINDS ALL OF US.
I AM NOT REFERRING TO A MOVIE WHOSE RELIGION IS DOMINATED BY SPACE WIZARDS.
LET ME PRESENT TO YOU--DARK ENERGY.
AFTER GRAVITY, ELECTROMAGNETISM, AND THE STRONG AND WEAK NUCLEAR FORCES, DARK ENERGY IS THE FIFTH FUNDAMENTAL FORCE OF THE UNIVERSE.
A.T. FACT! DARK ENERGY THE UNKNOWN FORCE IT IS HYPOTHESIZED TO MAKING THE UNIVERSE W LARGER. NOT TO BE ONFUSED WITH DARK MATTER.
IT WAS DISCOVERED THAT 68% PERCENT OF THE UNIVERSE IS DARK ENERGY. EVERYTHING ELSE THAT CAN BE OBSERVED IN AN ASTRONOMER'S INSTRUMENTS, INCLUDING EARTH, IS LESS THAN 5%!
PLEASE ADJUST THE SIZE OF YOUR FRAGILE EGOS ACCORDINGLY.

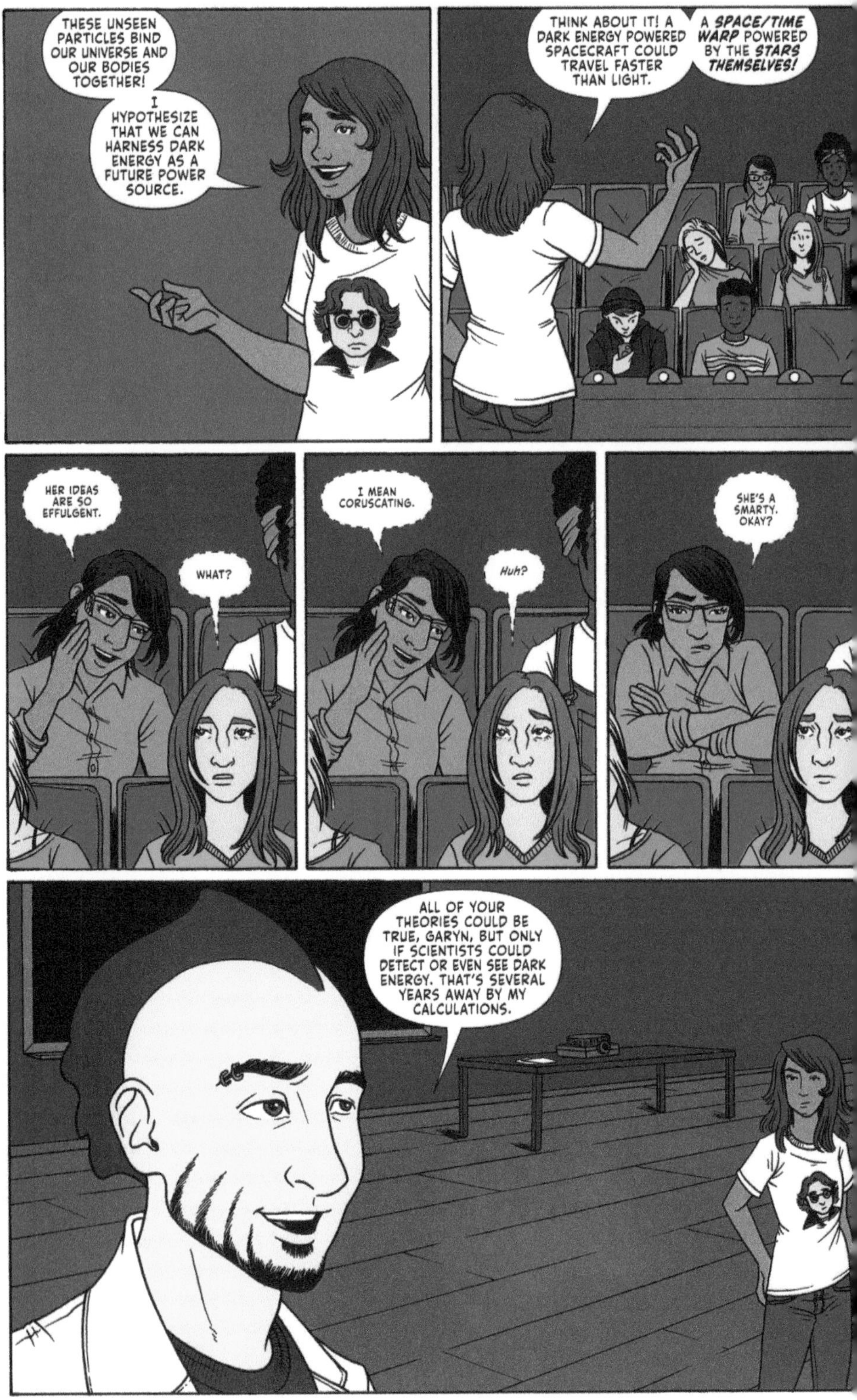
THESE UNSEEN PARTICLES BIND OUR UNIVERSE AND OUR BODIES TOGETHER!
I HYPOTHESIZE THAT WE CAN HARNESS DARK ENERGY AS A FUTURE POWER SOURCE.
THINK ABOUT IT! A DARK ENERGY POWERED SPACECRAFT COULD TRAVEL FASTER THAN LIGHT.
A SPACE/TIME WARP POWERED BY THE STARS THEMSELVES!
HER IDEAS ARE SO EFFULGENT.
WHAT?
I MEAN CORUSCATING.
Huh?
SHE'S A SMARTY. OKAY?
ALL OF YOUR THEORIES COULD BE TRUE, GARYN, BUT ONLY IF SCIENTISTS COULD DETECT OR EVEN SEE DARK ENERGY. THAT'S SEVERAL YEARS AWAY BY MY CALCULATIONS.

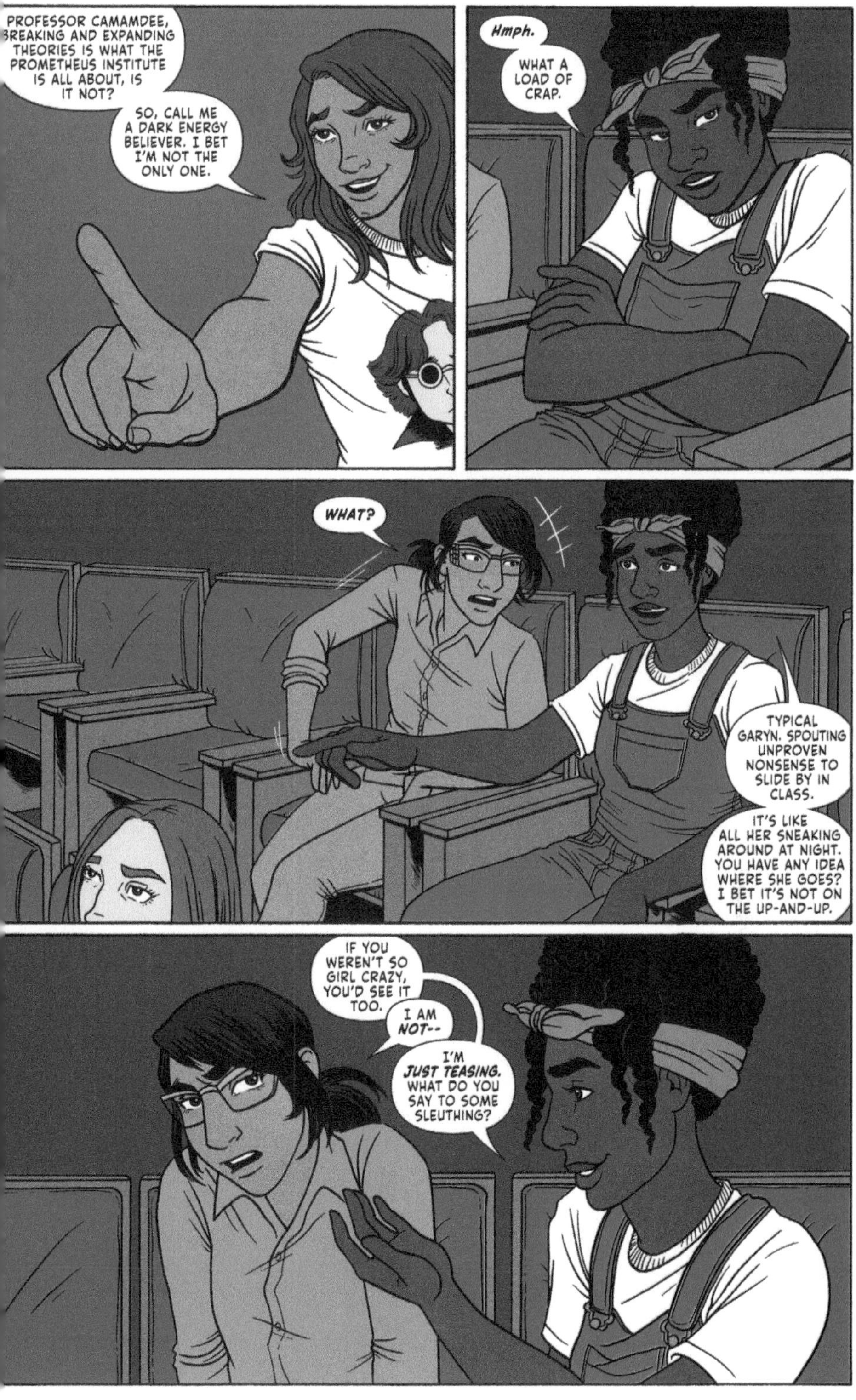
PROFESSOR CAMAMDEE, BREAKING AND EXPANDING THEORIES IS WHAT THE PROMETHEUS INSTITUTE IS ALL ABOUT, IS IT NOT?
SO, CALL ME A DARK ENERGY BELIEVER. I BET I'M NOT THE ONLY ONE.
Hmph.
WHAT A LOAD OF CRAP.
WHAT?
TYPICAL GARYN. SPOUTING UNPROVEN NONSENSE TO SLIDE BY IN CLASS.
IT'S LIKE ALL HER SNEAKING AROUND AT NIGHT. YOU HAVE ANY IDEA WHERE SHE GOES? I BET IT'S NOT ON THE UP-AND-UP.
IF YOU WEREN'T SO GIRL CRAZY, YOU'D SEE IT TOO.
I AM *NOT--*
I'M *JUST TEASING.* WHAT DO YOU SAY TO SOME SLEUTHING?

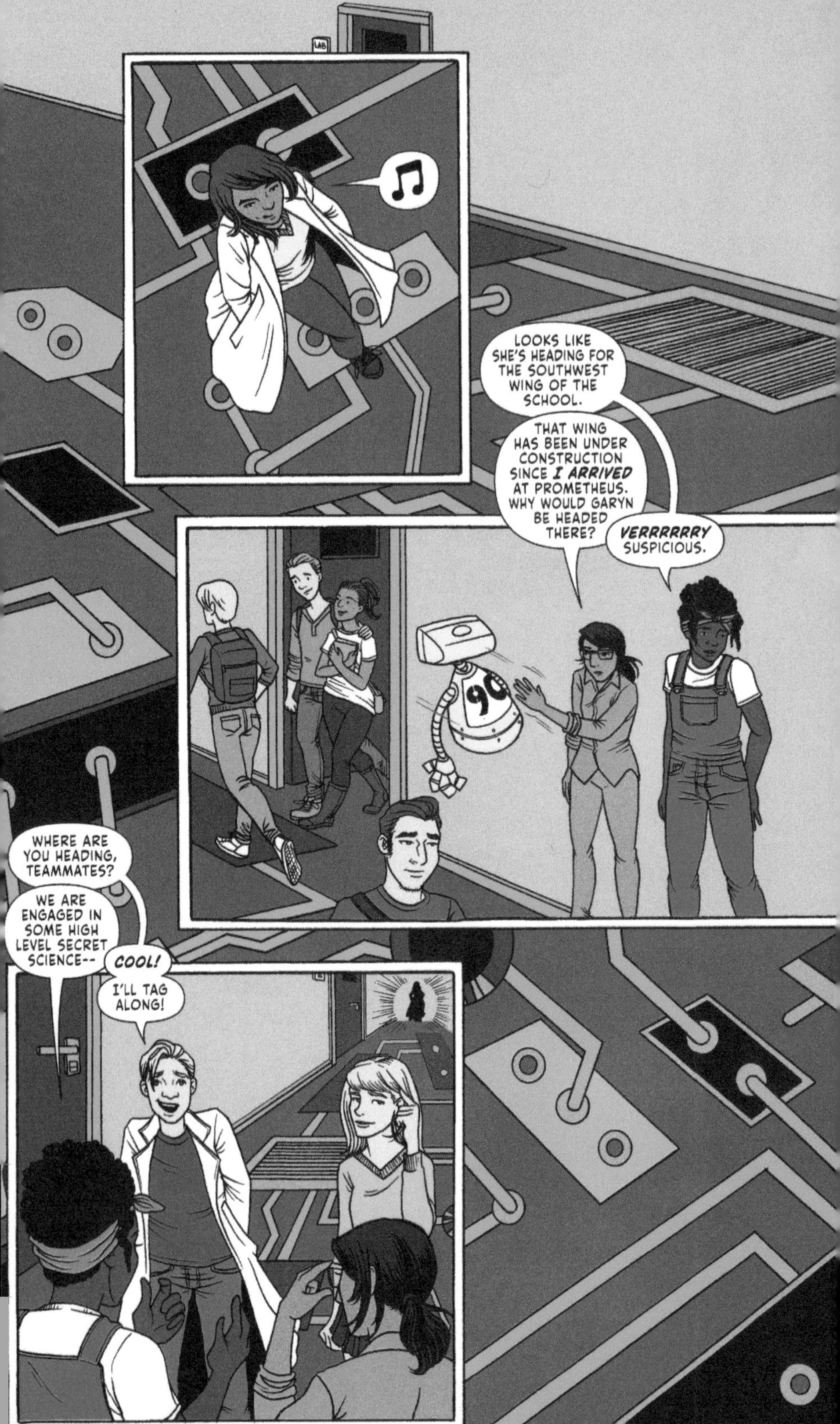
LAB
♫
LOOKS LIKE SHE'S HEADING FOR THE SOUTHWEST WING OF THE SCHOOL.
THAT WING HAS BEEN UNDER CONSTRUCTION SINCE *I ARRIVED* AT PROMETHEUS. WHY WOULD GARYN BE HEADED THERE?
VERRRRRRY SUSPICIOUS.
90
WHERE ARE YOU HEADING, TEAMMATES?
WE ARE ENGAGED IN SOME HIGH LEVEL SECRET SCIENCE--
COOL!
I'LL TAG ALONG!

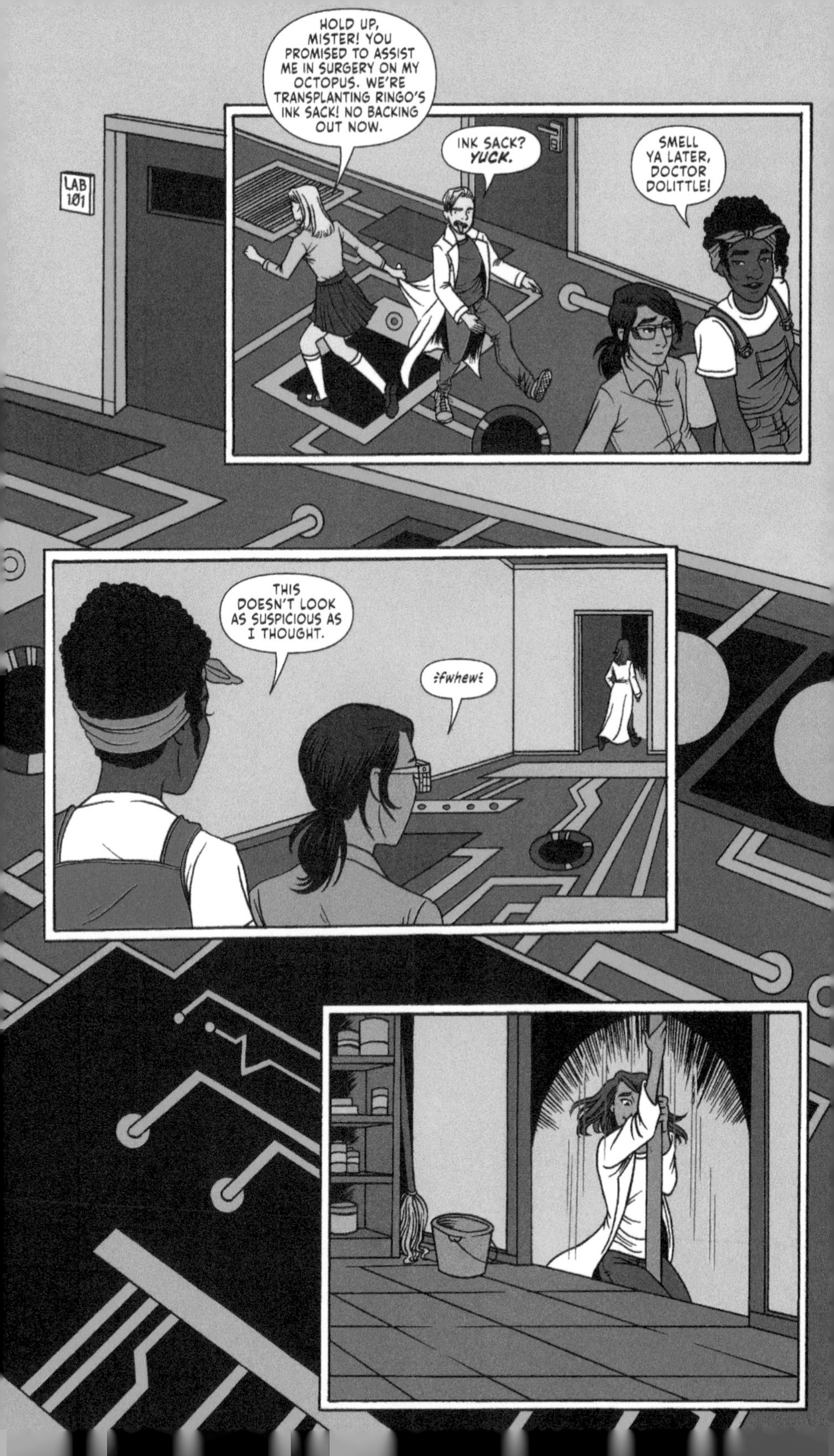
HOLD UP, MISTER! YOU PROMISED TO ASSIST ME IN SURGERY ON MY OCTOPUS. WE'RE TRANSPLANTING RINGO'S INK SACK! NO BACKING OUT NOW.
INK SACK? YUCK.
SMELL YA LATER, DOCTOR DOLITTLE!
LAB 101
THIS DOESN'T LOOK AS SUSPICIOUS AS I THOUGHT.
fwhew

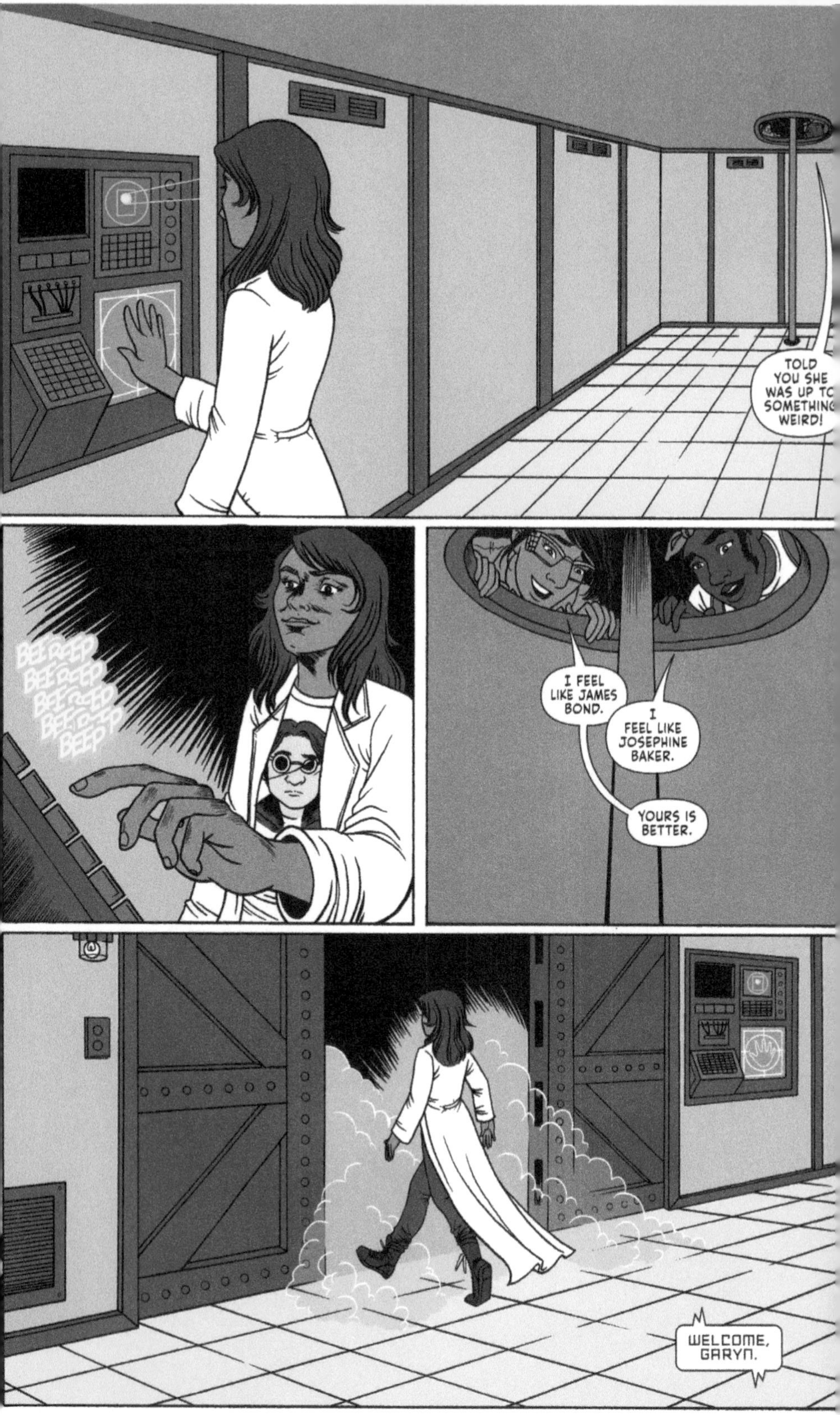
TOLD YOU SHE WAS UP TO SOMETHING WEIRD!
BEEREEP BEEREEP BEEREEP BEEREEP BEEP
I FEEL LIKE JAMES BOND.
I FEEL LIKE JOSEPHINE BAKER.
YOURS IS BETTER.
WELCOME, GARYN.

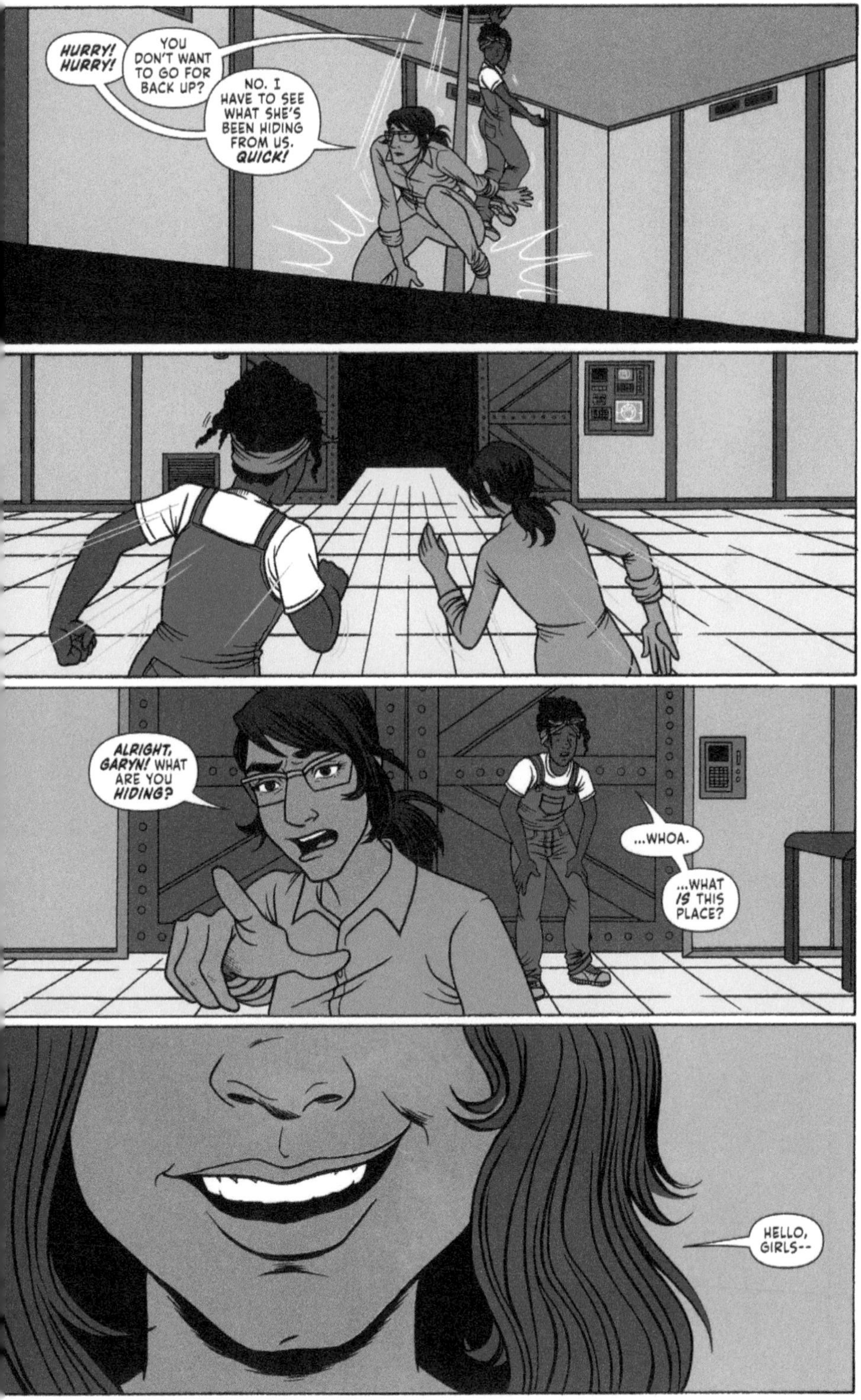
HURRY! HURRY!
YOU DON'T WANT TO GO FOR BACK UP?
NO. I HAVE TO SEE WHAT SHE'S BEEN HIDING FROM US. QUICK!
ALRIGHT, GARYN! WHAT ARE YOU HIDING?
...WHOA.
...WHAT IS THIS PLACE?
HELLO, GIRLS--

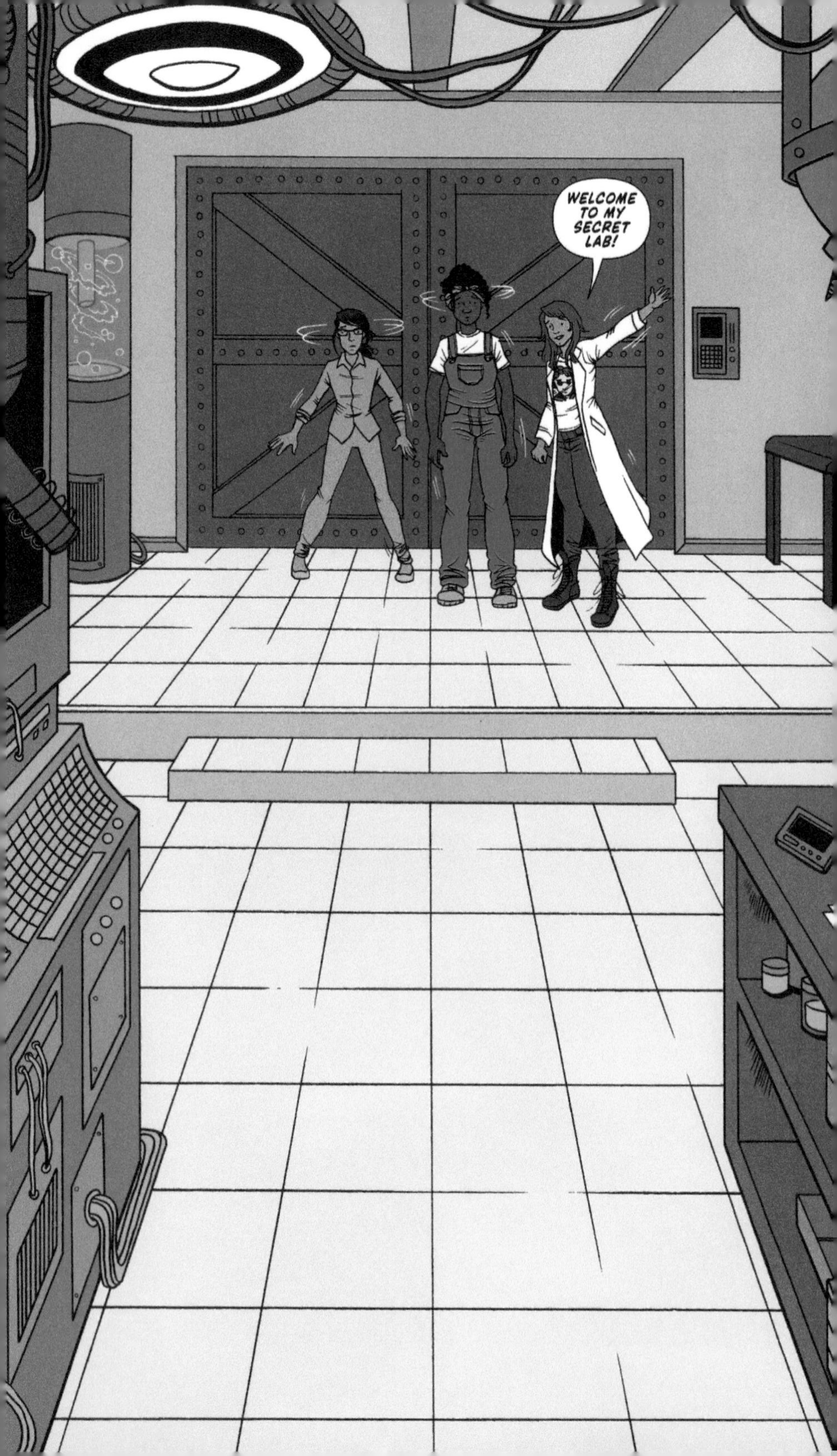
WELCOME TO MY SECRET LAB!

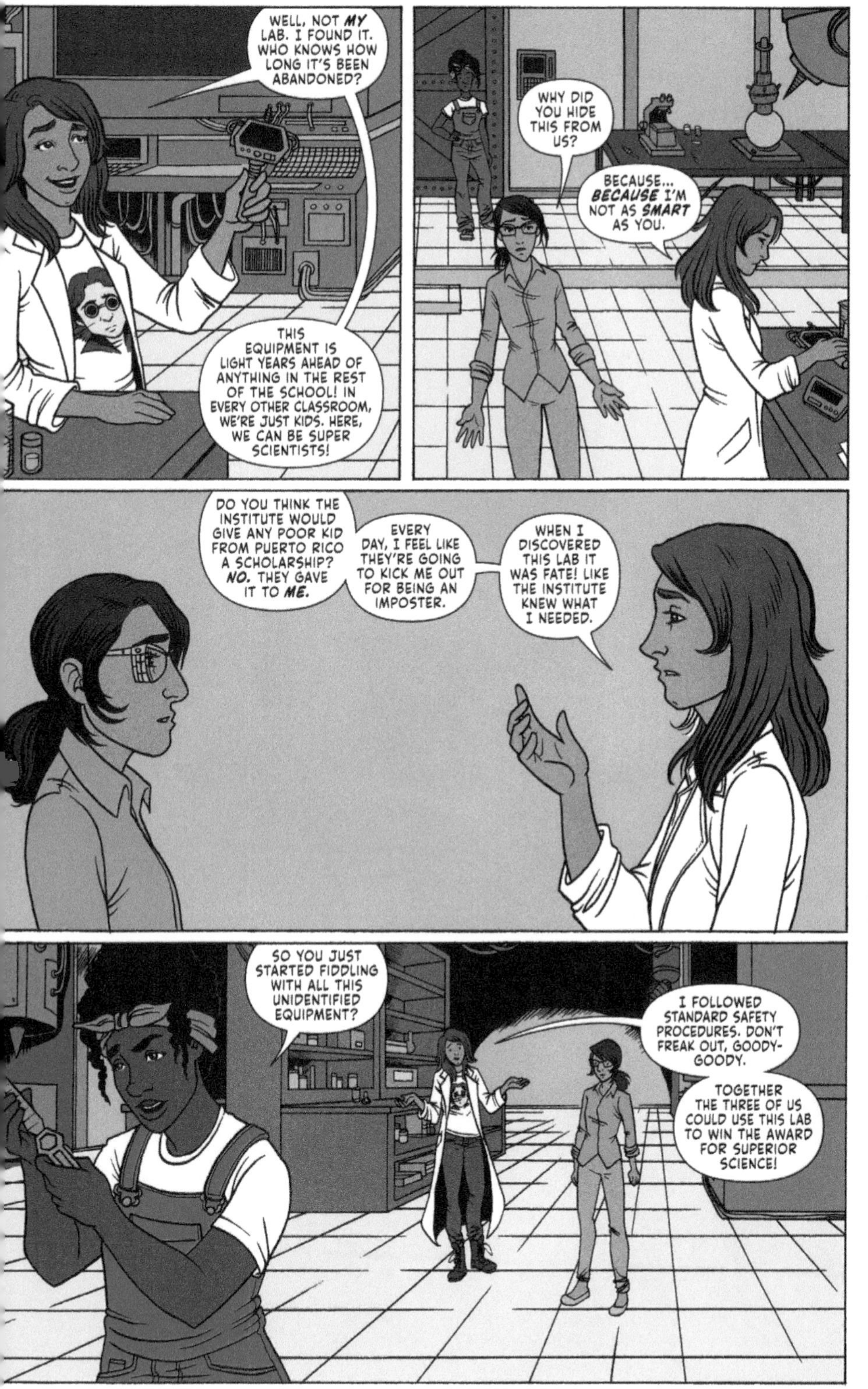
WELL, NOT *MY* LAB. I FOUND IT. WHO KNOWS HOW LONG IT'S BEEN ABANDONED?
THIS EQUIPMENT IS LIGHT YEARS AHEAD OF ANYTHING IN THE REST OF THE SCHOOL! IN EVERY OTHER CLASSROOM, WE'RE JUST KIDS. HERE, WE CAN BE SUPER SCIENTISTS!
WHY DID YOU HIDE THIS FROM US?
BECAUSE... *BECAUSE* I'M NOT AS *SMART* AS YOU.
DO YOU THINK THE INSTITUTE WOULD GIVE ANY POOR KID FROM PUERTO RICO A SCHOLARSHIP? *NO.* THEY GAVE IT TO *ME.*
EVERY DAY, I FEEL LIKE THEY'RE GOING TO KICK ME OUT FOR BEING AN IMPOSTER.
WHEN I DISCOVERED THIS LAB IT WAS FATE! LIKE THE INSTITUTE KNEW WHAT I NEEDED.
SO YOU JUST STARTED FIDDLING WITH ALL THIS UNIDENTIFIED EQUIPMENT?
I FOLLOWED STANDARD SAFETY PROCEDURES. DON'T FREAK OUT, GOODY-GOODY.
TOGETHER THE THREE OF US COULD USE THIS LAB TO WIN THE AWARD FOR SUPERIOR SCIENCE!

HOW DO YOU FIGURE THAT?

THIS WHOLE LAB? IT RUNS ON ONE TYPE OF POWER. EVERY MECHANISM IN HERE IS DESIGNED TO MANIPULATE--

--DARK ENERGY!

ONCE I DEDUCED THAT, I BEGAN CONSTRUCTION ON A PROTOTYPE OF MY DARK ENERGY SPACE ENGINE.

BUT IT NEEDS FUEL. NO MATTER WHAT I TRIED, I COULDN'T COLLECT ENOUGH DARK ENERGY PARTICLES. THEN BOOM!

TWO NIGHTS AGO, MY DARK ENERGY CONTAINMENT UNIT COLLECTED MORE PARTICLES THAN I COULD HANDLE.

IT WAS LIKE SOME INVISIBLE DAM HAD BEEN BROKEN.

I'M 12 WEEKS AWAY FROM COMPLETION OF THE ENGINE. SOONER, WITH YOUR HELP. LET'S DO THIS, LADIES. LET'S BUILD A CHARIOT TO THE STARS.

S.T.A.T. FACT! NOTHING CAN TRAVEL FASTER THAN LIGHT.

HOWEVER, PHYSICIST MIGUEL ALCUBIERRE ONCE PROPOSED A THEORY OF BENDING SPACE-TIME IN FRONT OF AND BEHIND A VEHICLE TO ACHIEVE FASTER THAN LIGHT TRAVEL WITHOUT MOVING THE VESSEL.

IT'S CLASSICALLY BEEN CALLED "WARP DRIVE" AND MEN NAMED SCOTTY HAVE BECOME EXPERTS ON IT.

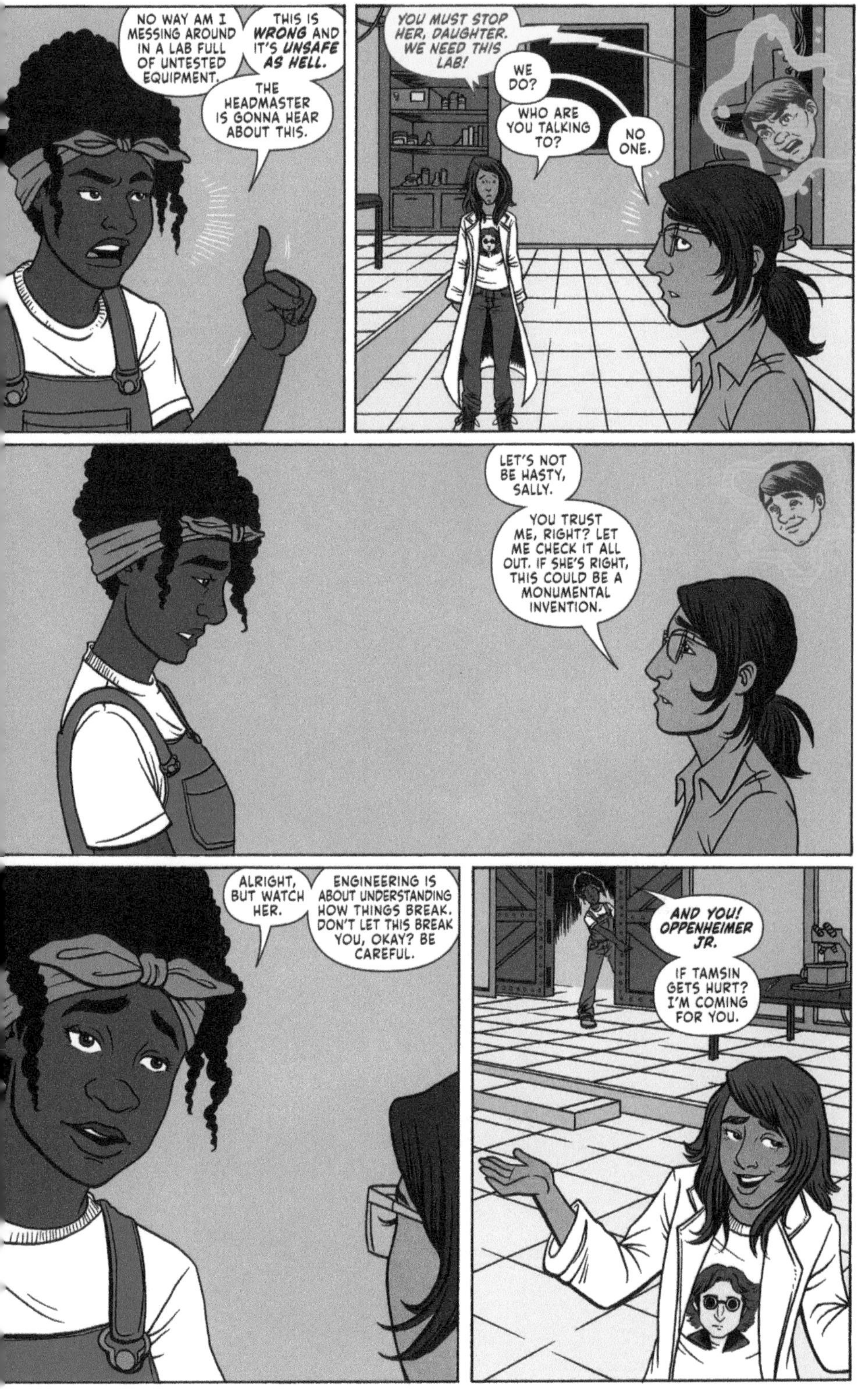
NO WAY AM I MESSING AROUND IN A LAB FULL OF UNTESTED EQUIPMENT.
THIS IS WRONG AND IT'S UNSAFE AS HELL.
THE HEADMASTER IS GONNA HEAR ABOUT THIS.
YOU MUST STOP HER, DAUGHTER. WE NEED THIS LAB!
WE DO?
WHO ARE YOU TALKING TO?
NO ONE.
LET'S NOT BE HASTY, SALLY.
YOU TRUST ME, RIGHT? LET ME CHECK IT ALL OUT. IF SHE'S RIGHT, THIS COULD BE A MONUMENTAL INVENTION.
ALRIGHT, BUT WATCH HER.
ENGINEERING IS ABOUT UNDERSTANDING HOW THINGS BREAK. DON'T LET THIS BREAK YOU, OKAY? BE CAREFUL.
AND YOU! OPPENHEIMER JR.
IF TAMSIN GETS HURT? I'M COMING FOR YOU.

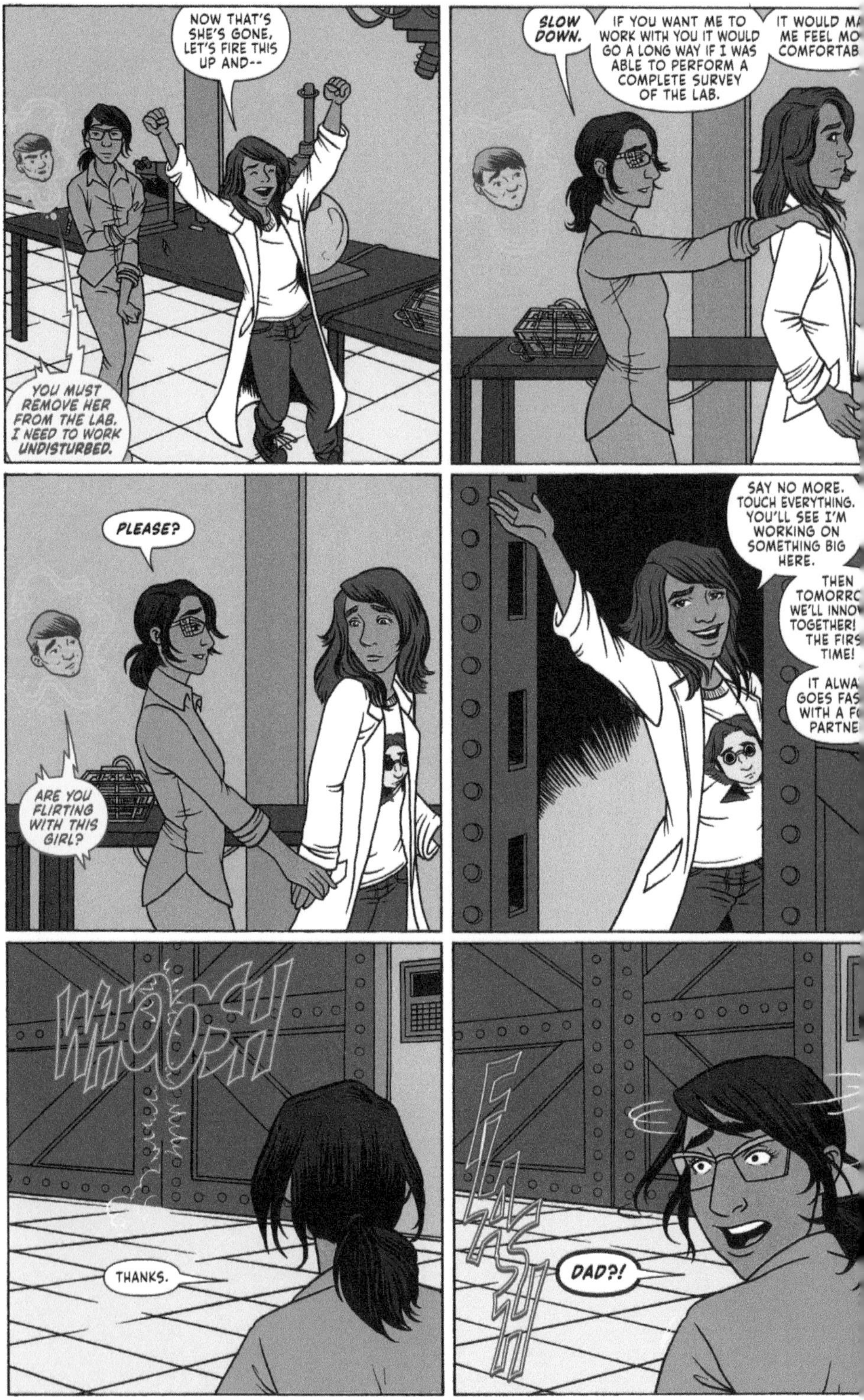
NOW THAT'S SHE'S GONE, LET'S FIRE THIS UP AND--
YOU MUST REMOVE HER FROM THE LAB. I NEED TO WORK UNDISTURBED.
SLOW DOWN.
IF YOU WANT ME TO WORK WITH YOU IT WOULD GO A LONG WAY IF I WAS ABLE TO PERFORM A COMPLETE SURVEY OF THE LAB.
IT WOULD MA ME FEEL MO COMFORTAB
PLEASE?
ARE YOU FLIRTING WITH THIS GIRL?
SAY NO MORE. TOUCH EVERYTHING. YOU'LL SEE I'M WORKING ON SOMETHING BIG HERE.
THEN TOMORRO WE'LL INNO TOGETHER! THE FIRS TIME!
IT ALWA GOES FAS WITH A F PARTNE
WHOOSH
THANKS.
FLASH
DAD?!

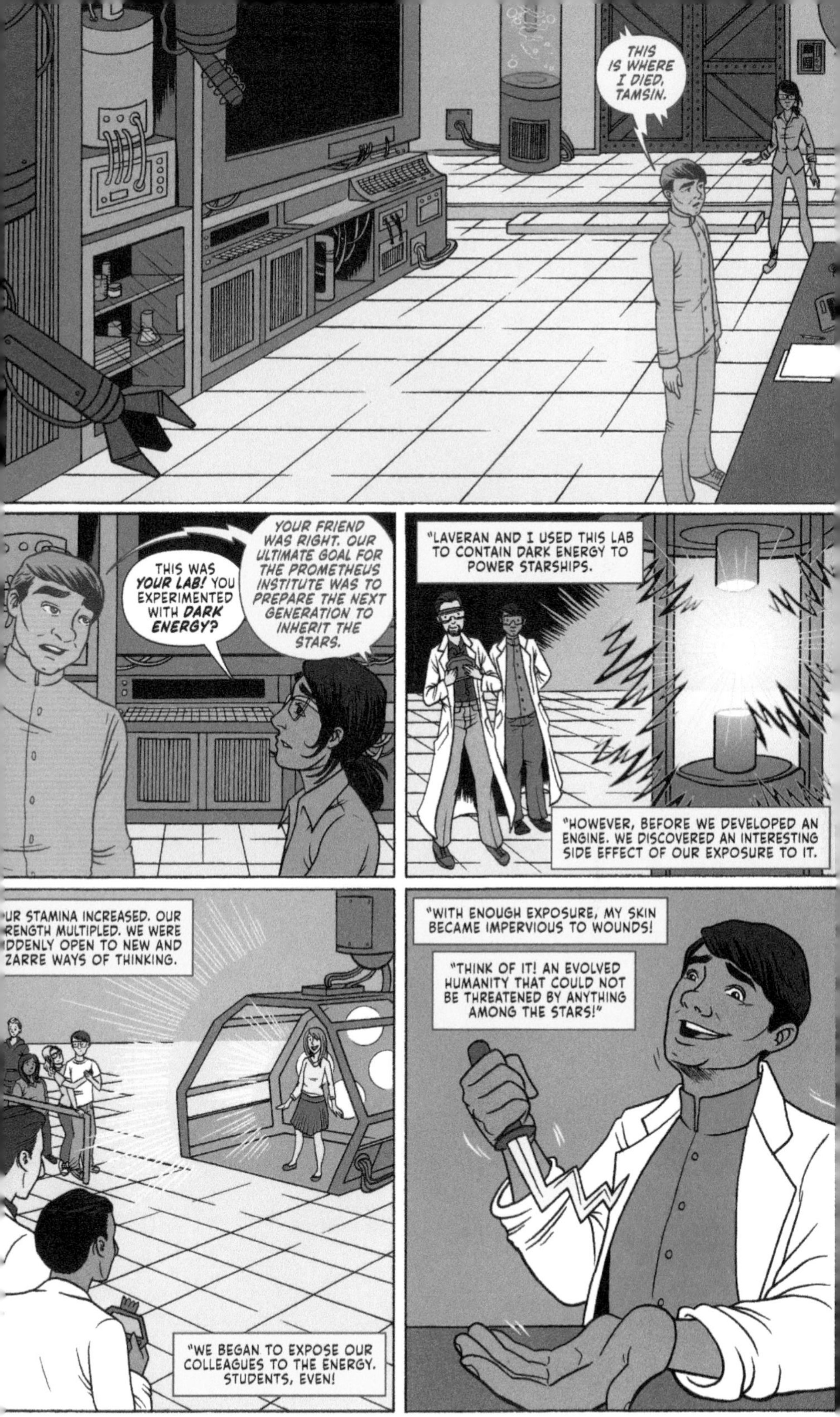
THIS IS WHERE I DIED, TAMSIN.
THIS WAS YOUR LAB! YOU EXPERIMENTED WITH DARK ENERGY?
YOUR FRIEND WAS RIGHT. OUR ULTIMATE GOAL FOR THE PROMETHEUS INSTITUTE WAS TO PREPARE THE NEXT GENERATION TO INHERIT THE STARS.
"LAVERAN AND I USED THIS LAB TO CONTAIN DARK ENERGY TO POWER STARSHIPS.
"HOWEVER, BEFORE WE DEVELOPED AN ENGINE. WE DISCOVERED AN INTERESTING SIDE EFFECT OF OUR EXPOSURE TO IT.
UR STAMINA INCREASED. OUR RENGTH MULTIPLED. WE WERE DDENLY OPEN TO NEW AND ZARRE WAYS OF THINKING.
"WE BEGAN TO EXPOSE OUR COLLEAGUES TO THE ENERGY. STUDENTS, EVEN!
"WITH ENOUGH EXPOSURE, MY SKIN BECAME IMPERVIOUS TO WOUNDS!
"THINK OF IT! AN EVOLVED HUMANITY THAT COULD NOT BE THREATENED BY ANYTHING AMONG THE STARS!"

"LAVERAN WANTED US TO SLOW DOWN OUR RESEARCH. I WANTED TO EXPAND OUR HUMAN TRIALS.

"A WHOLE NEW STAGE OF HUMAN EVOLUTION WAS AT OUR FINGERTIPS! WE NEEDED TO LEAP FORWARD, NOT TIPTOE.

"HE SOON CUT ME OFF FROM ALL DAR ENERGY RESEARCH

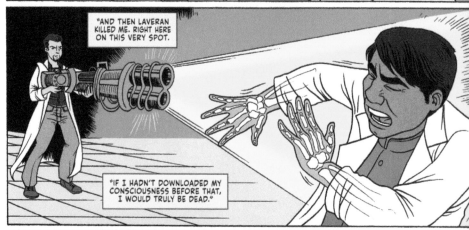

"AND THEN LAVERAN KILLED ME. RIGHT HERE ON THIS VERY SPOT.

"IF I HADN'T DOWNLOADED MY CONSCIOUSNESS BEFORE THAT, I WOULD TRULY BE DEAD."

IT'S AMAZING THAT LAVERAN DIDN'T DESTROY THIS LAB.

YOU MUST HELP THAT GIRL COMPLETE MY WORK HERE.

WHAT ABOUT OUR PLAN TO DESTROY THE SCHOOL?

I BELIEVE YOU'RE TALENTED ENOUGH TO DO BOTH. THE BEST REVENGE WILL BE TO SHOW MY OLD PARTNER HOW WRONG HE WAS. ABOUT ME. ABOUT THIS.

COMPLETE THE DARK ENERGY ENGINE. FINISH MY LEGACY AND CLAIM YOUR OWN.

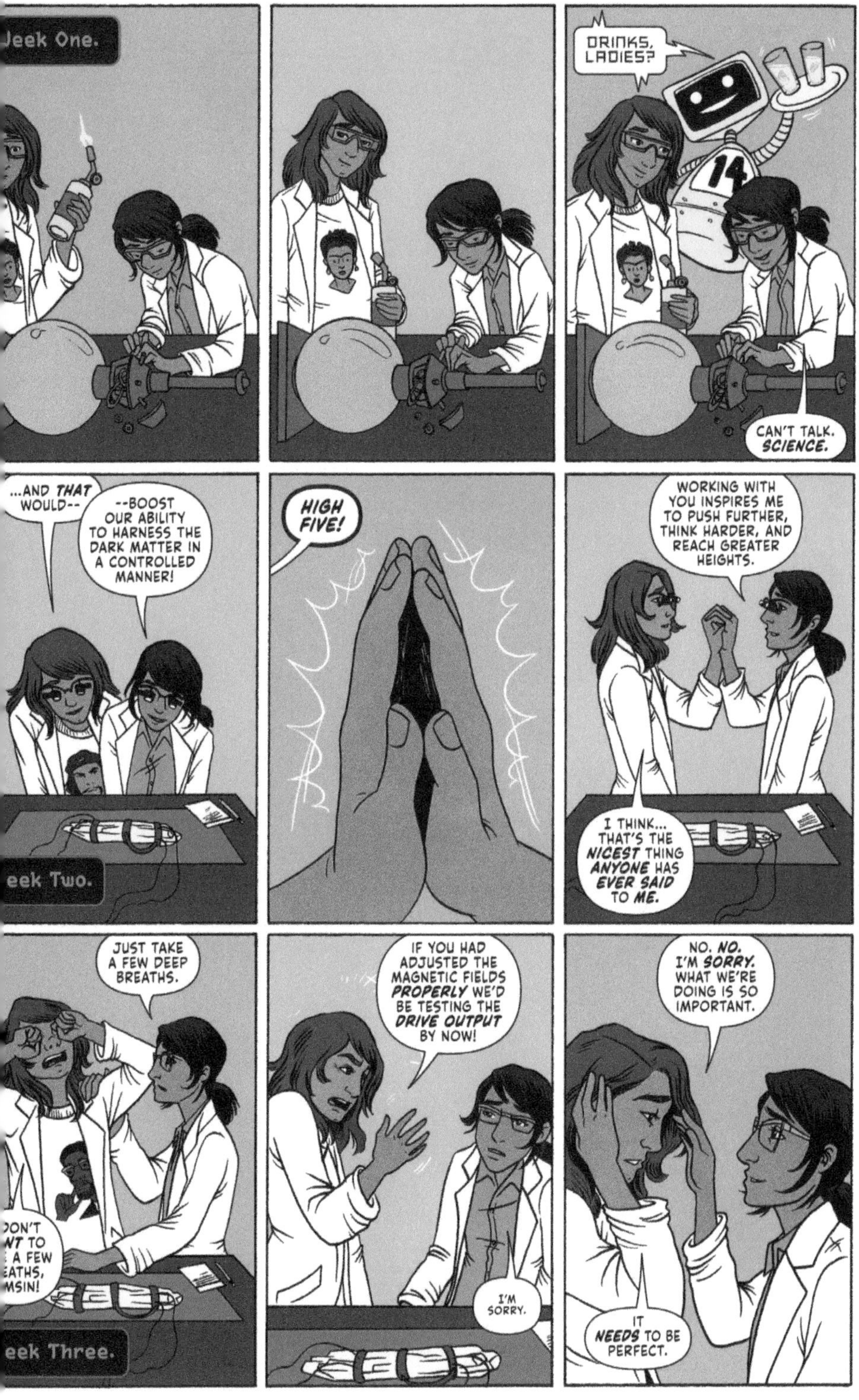
Jeek One.
DRINKS, LADIES?
14
CAN'T TALK. SCIENCE.
...AND THAT WOULD--
--BOOST OUR ABILITY TO HARNESS THE DARK MATTER IN A CONTROLLED MANNER!
eek Two.
HIGH FIVE!
WORKING WITH YOU INSPIRES ME TO PUSH FURTHER, THINK HARDER, AND REACH GREATER HEIGHTS.
I THINK... THAT'S THE NICEST THING ANYONE HAS EVER SAID TO ME.
JUST TAKE A FEW DEEP BREATHS.
DON'T NT TO A FEW EATHS, MSIN!
eek Three.
IF YOU HAD ADJUSTED THE MAGNETIC FIELDS PROPERLY WE'D BE TESTING THE DRIVE OUTPUT BY NOW!
I'M SORRY.
NO. NO. I'M SORRY. WHAT WE'RE DOING IS SO IMPORTANT.
IT NEEDS TO BE PERFECT.

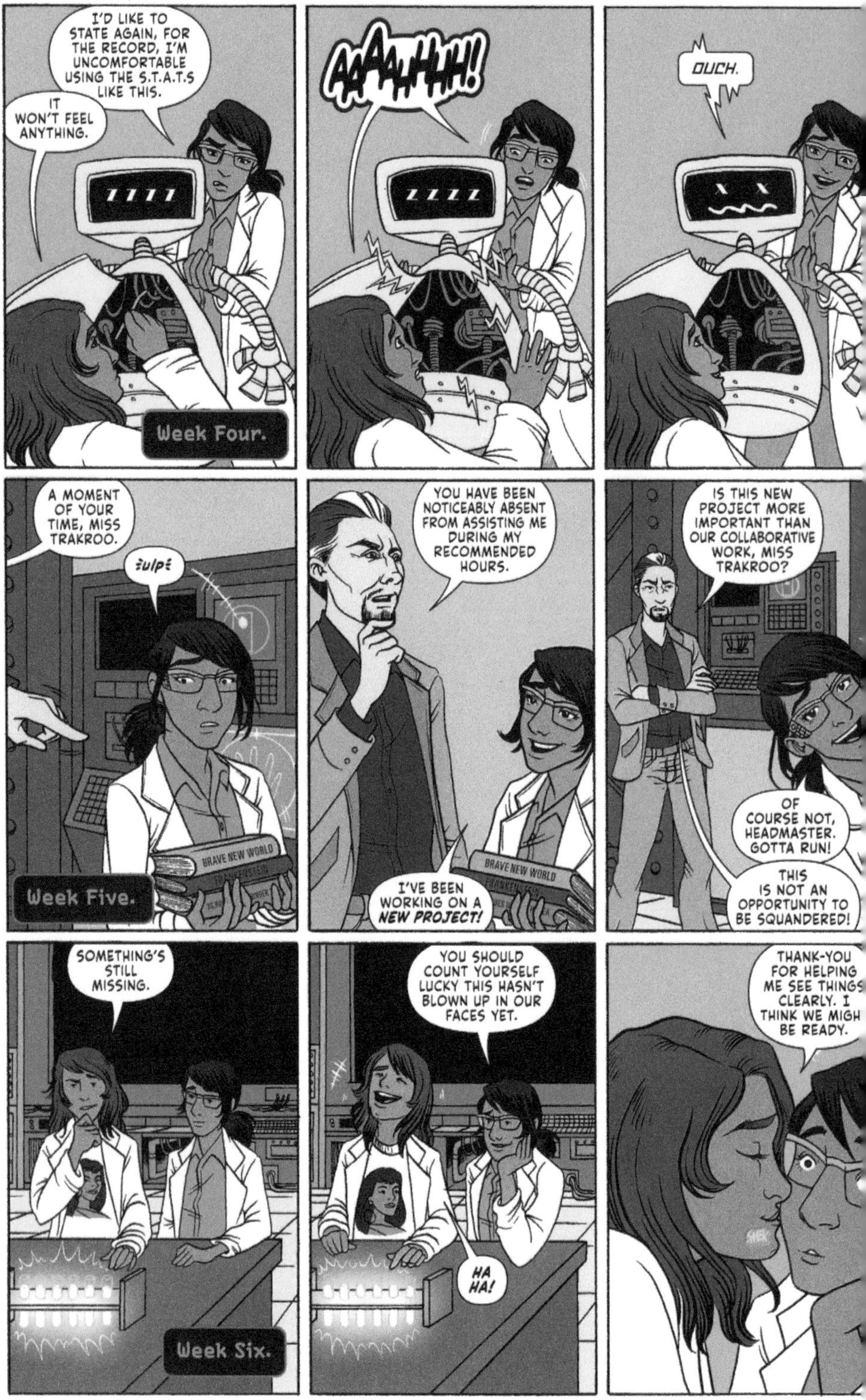
I'D LIKE TO STATE AGAIN, FOR THE RECORD, I'M UNCOMFORTABLE USING THE S.T.A.T.S LIKE THIS.
IT WON'T FEEL ANYTHING.
Week Four.
AAAAHHHH!
OUCH.
A MOMENT OF YOUR TIME, MISS TRAKROO.
GULP
Week Five.
BRAVE NEW WORLD
FRANKENSTEIN
YOU HAVE BEEN NOTICEABLY ABSENT FROM ASSISTING ME DURING MY RECOMMENDED HOURS.
I'VE BEEN WORKING ON A NEW PROJECT!
IS THIS NEW PROJECT MORE IMPORTANT THAN OUR COLLABORATIVE WORK, MISS TRAKROO?
OF COURSE NOT, HEADMASTER. GOTTA RUN!
THIS IS NOT AN OPPORTUNITY TO BE SQUANDERED!
SOMETHING'S STILL MISSING.
Week Six.
YOU SHOULD COUNT YOURSELF LUCKY THIS HASN'T BLOWN UP IN OUR FACES YET.
HA HA!
THANK-YOU FOR HELPING ME SEE THINGS CLEARLY. I THINK WE MIGH BE READY.
SMEK

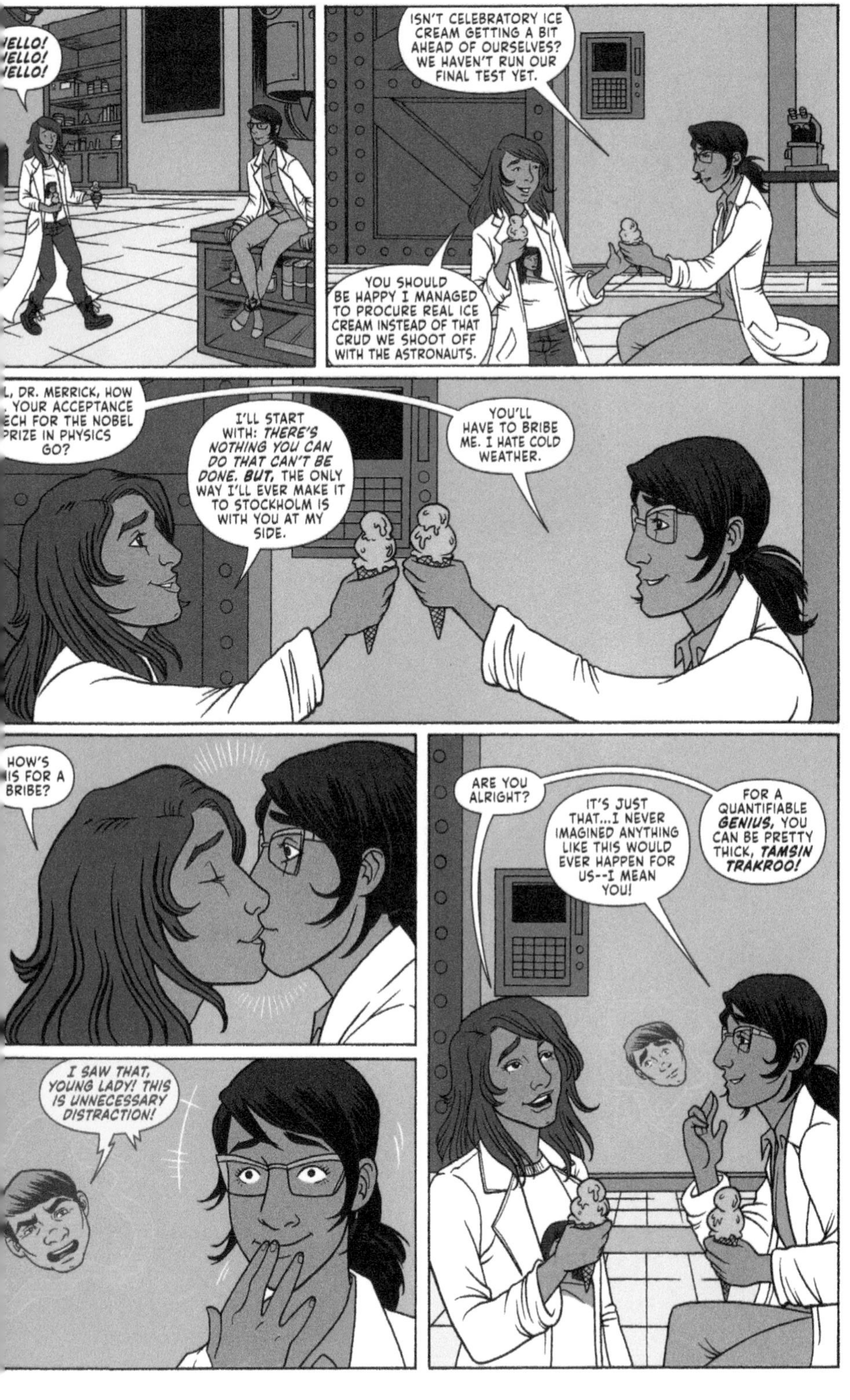

ELLO! ELLO! ELLO!
ISN'T CELEBRATORY ICE CREAM GETTING A BIT AHEAD OF OURSELVES? WE HAVEN'T RUN OUR FINAL TEST YET.
YOU SHOULD BE HAPPY I MANAGED TO PROCURE REAL ICE CREAM INSTEAD OF THAT CRUD WE SHOOT OFF WITH THE ASTRONAUTS.
L, DR. MERRICK, HOW YOUR ACCEPTANCE ECH FOR THE NOBEL PRIZE IN PHYSICS GO?
I'LL START WITH: *THERE'S NOTHING YOU CAN DO THAT CAN'T BE DONE.* ***BUT,*** THE ONLY WAY I'LL EVER MAKE IT TO STOCKHOLM IS WITH YOU AT MY SIDE.
YOU'LL HAVE TO BRIBE ME. I HATE COLD WEATHER.
HOW'S IS FOR A BRIBE?
I SAW THAT, YOUNG LADY! THIS IS UNNECESSARY DISTRACTION!
ARE YOU ALRIGHT?
IT'S JUST THAT...I NEVER IMAGINED ANYTHING LIKE THIS WOULD EVER HAPPEN FOR US--I MEAN YOU!
FOR A QUANTIFIABLE ***GENIUS,*** YOU CAN BE PRETTY THICK, ***TAMSIN TRAKROO!***

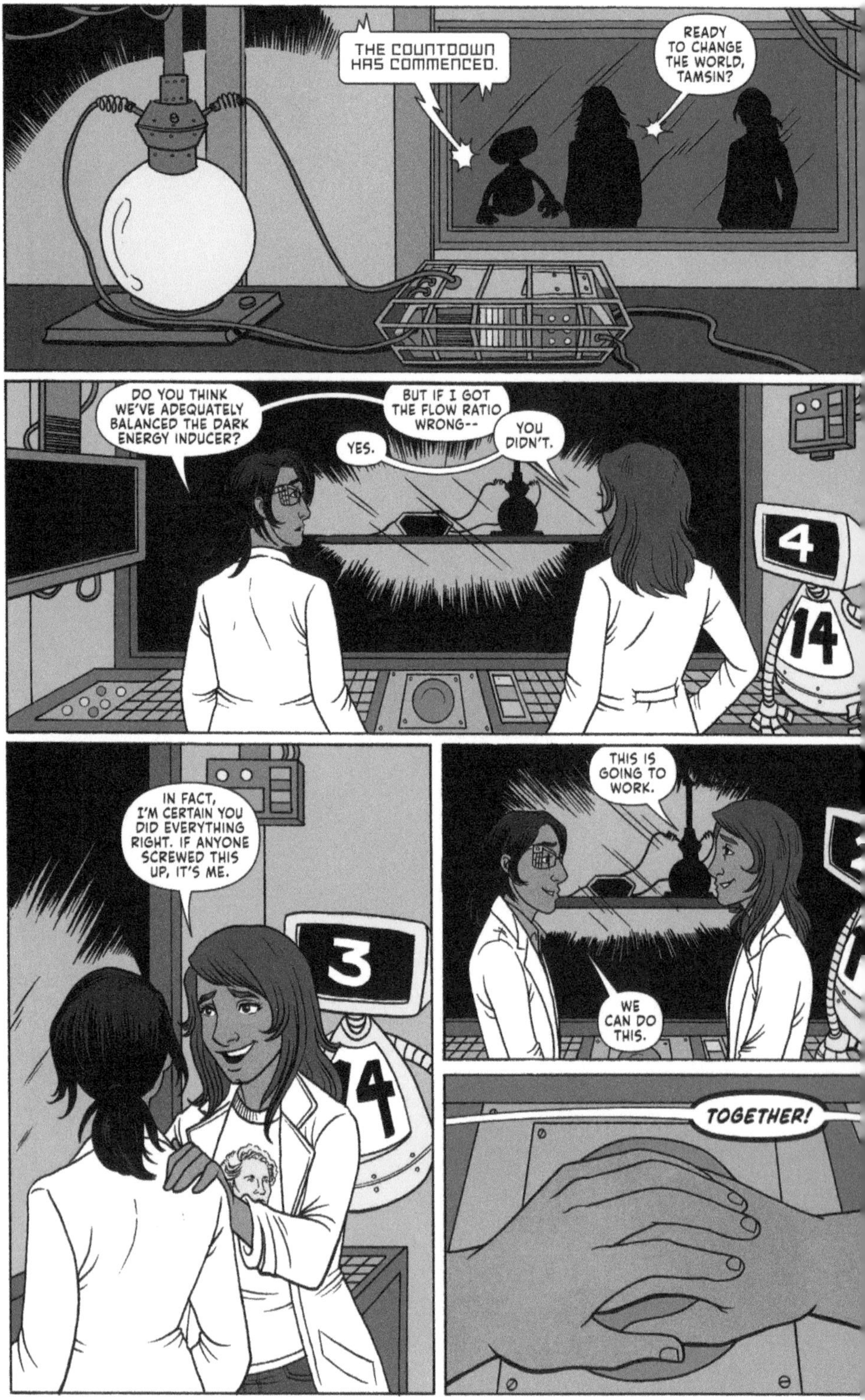
THE COUNTDOWN HAS COMMENCED.
READY TO CHANGE THE WORLD, TAMSIN?
DO YOU THINK WE'VE ADEQUATELY BALANCED THE DARK ENERGY INDUCER?
YES.
BUT IF I GOT THE FLOW RATIO WRONG--
YOU DIDN'T.
4
14
IN FACT, I'M CERTAIN YOU DID EVERYTHING RIGHT. IF ANYONE SCREWED THIS UP, IT'S ME.
3
14
THIS IS GOING TO WORK.
WE CAN DO THIS.
TOGETHER!

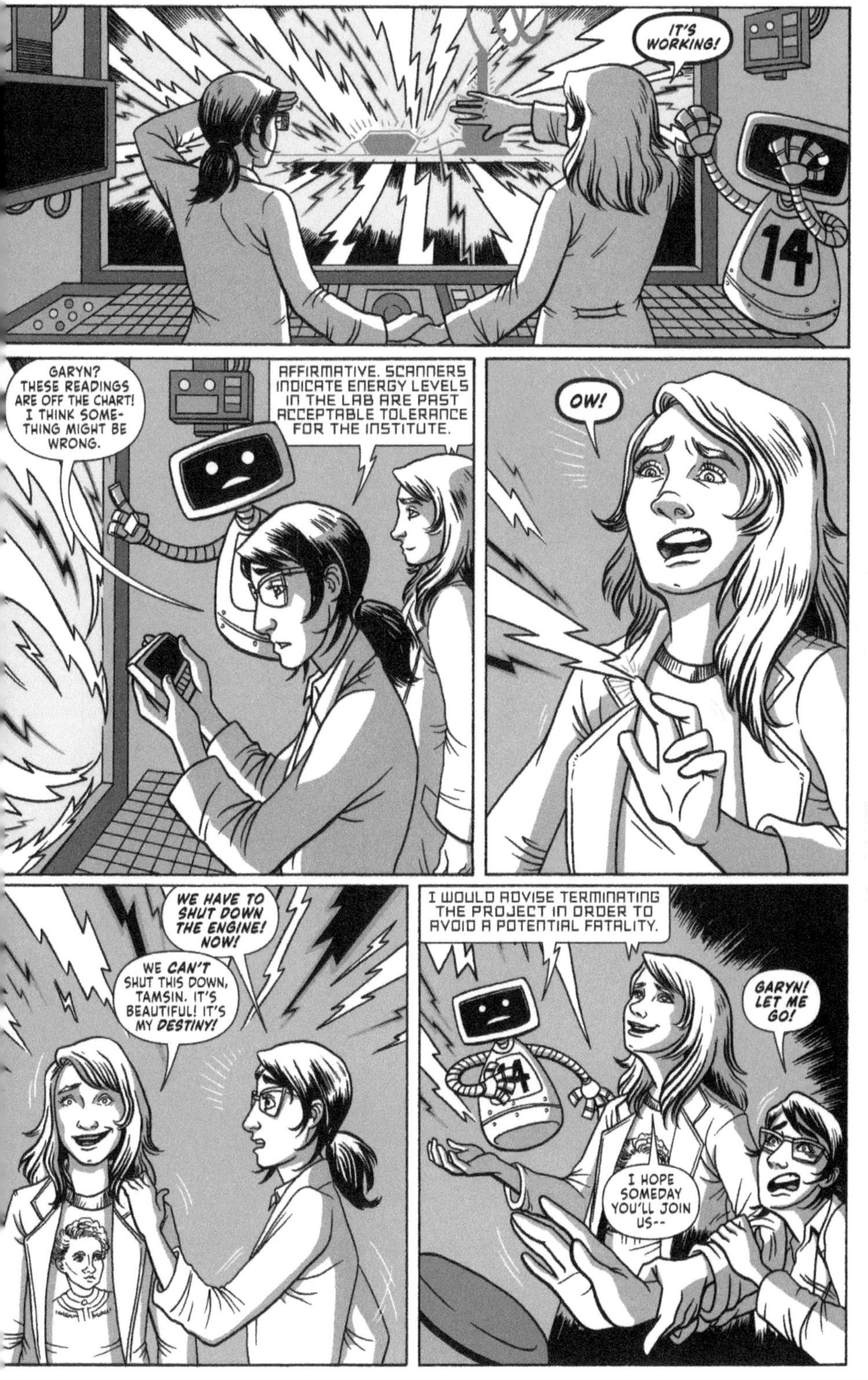
IT'S WORKING!
GARYN? THESE READINGS ARE OFF THE CHART! I THINK SOME-THING MIGHT BE WRONG.
AFFIRMATIVE. SCANNERS INDICATE ENERGY LEVELS IN THE LAB ARE PAST ACCEPTABLE TOLERANCE FOR THE INSTITUTE.
OW!
WE HAVE TO SHUT DOWN THE ENGINE! NOW!
WE CAN'T SHUT THIS DOWN, TAMSIN. IT'S BEAUTIFUL! IT'S MY DESTINY!
I WOULD ADVISE TERMINATING THE PROJECT IN ORDER TO AVOID A POTENTIAL FATALITY.
GARYN! LET ME GO!
I HOPE SOMEDAY YOU'LL JOIN US--

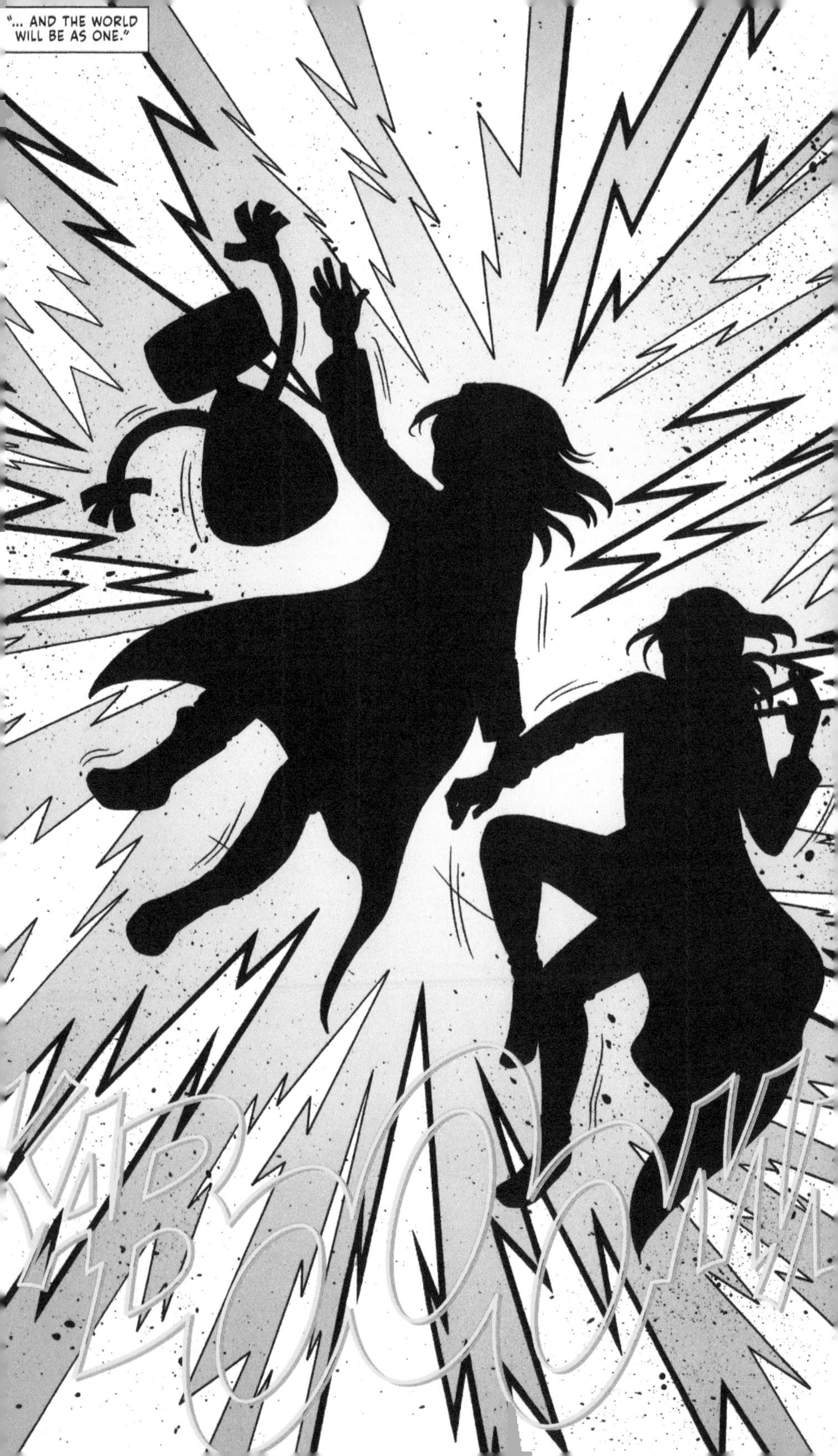
"... AND THE WORLD WILL BE AS ONE."
KABOOOM

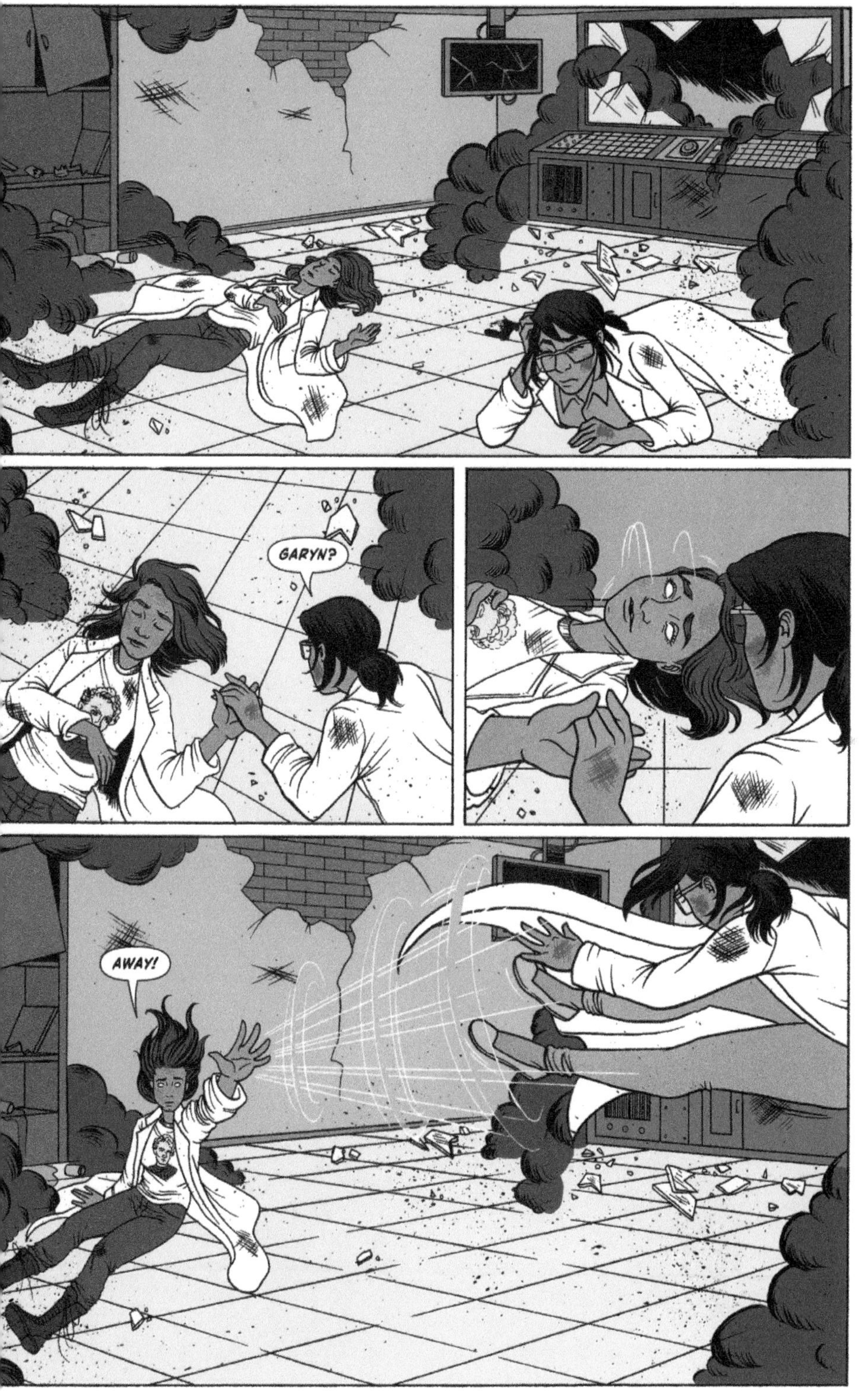
GARYN?
AWAY!

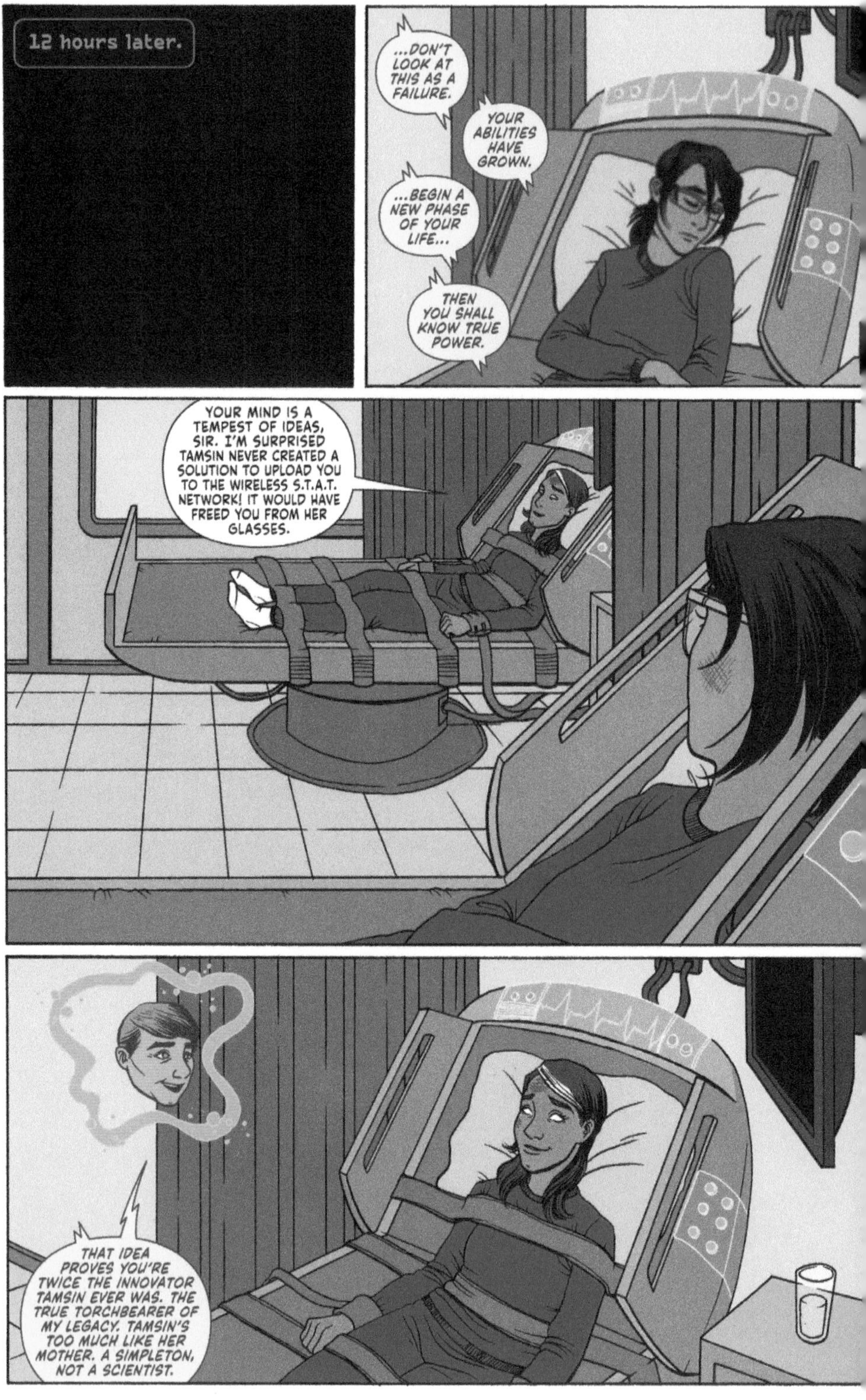
12 hours later.
...DON'T LOOK AT THIS AS A FAILURE.
YOUR ABILITIES HAVE GROWN.
...BEGIN A NEW PHASE OF YOUR LIFE...
THEN YOU SHALL KNOW TRUE POWER.
YOUR MIND IS A TEMPEST OF IDEAS, SIR. I'M SURPRISED TAMSIN NEVER CREATED A SOLUTION TO UPLOAD YOU TO THE WIRELESS S.T.A.T. NETWORK! IT WOULD HAVE FREED YOU FROM HER GLASSES.
THAT IDEA PROVES YOU'RE TWICE THE INNOVATOR TAMSIN EVER WAS. THE TRUE TORCHBEARER OF MY LEGACY. TAMSIN'S TOO MUCH LIKE HER MOTHER. A SIMPLETON, NOT A SCIENTIST.

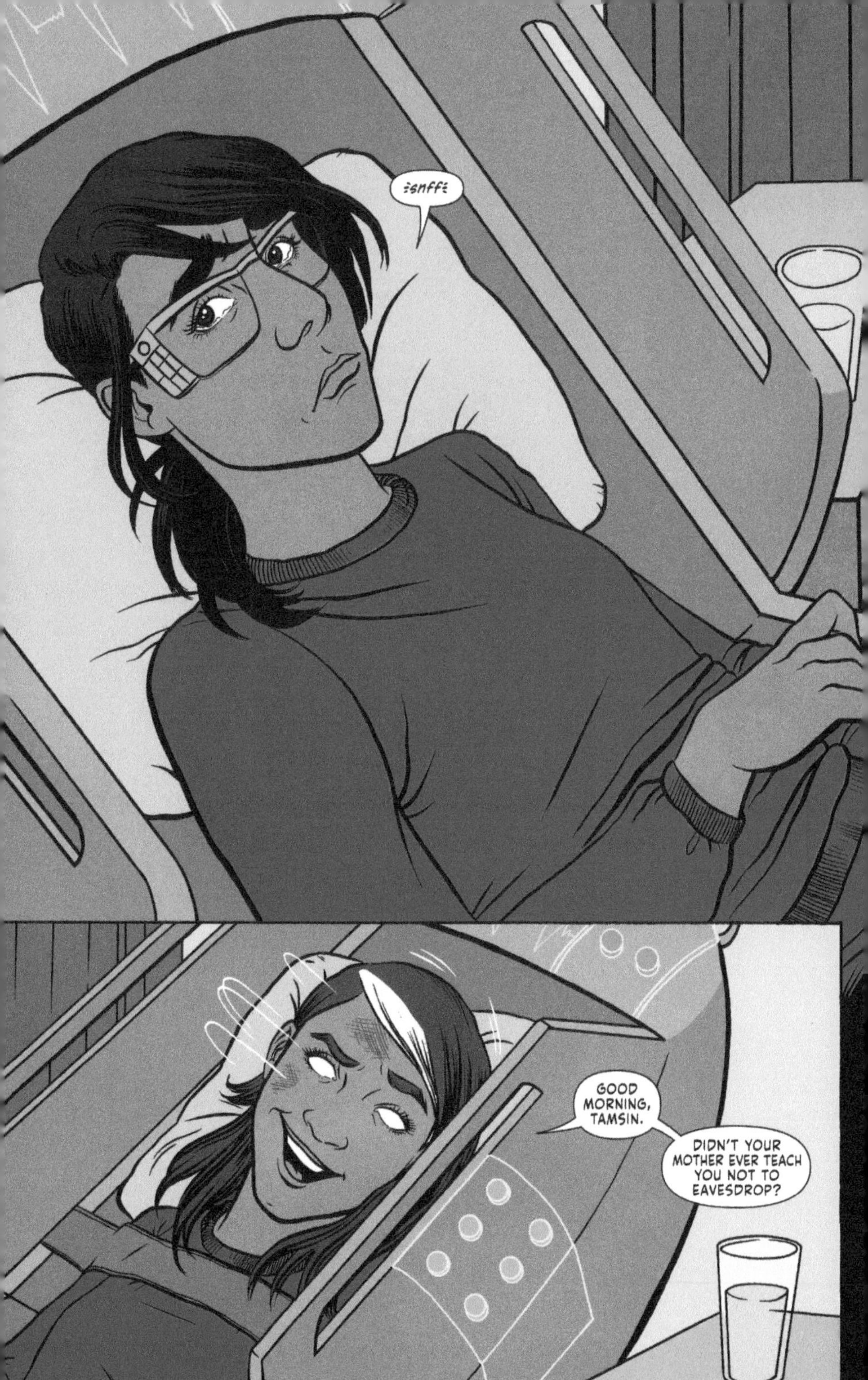
snff
GOOD MORNING, TAMSIN.
DIDN'T YOUR MOTHER EVER TEACH YOU NOT TO EAVESDROP?

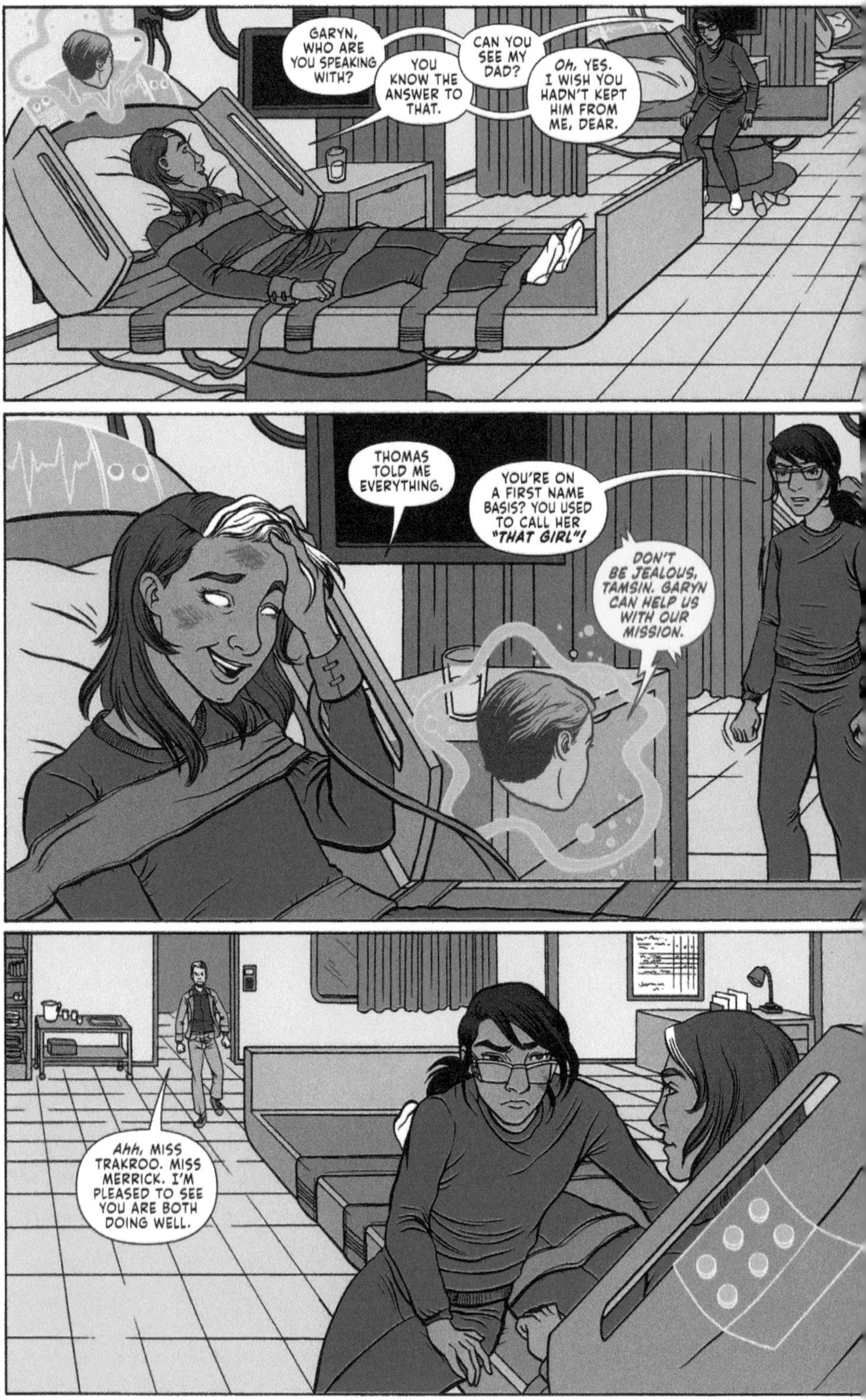
GARYN, WHO ARE YOU SPEAKING WITH?
YOU KNOW THE ANSWER TO THAT.
CAN YOU SEE MY DAD?
Oh, YES. I WISH YOU HADN'T KEPT HIM FROM ME, DEAR.
THOMAS TOLD ME EVERYTHING.
YOU'RE ON A FIRST NAME BASIS? YOU USED TO CALL HER ***"THAT GIRL"!***
DON'T BE JEALOUS, TAMSIN. GARYN CAN HELP US WITH OUR MISSION.
Ahh, MISS TRAKROO. MISS MERRICK. I'M PLEASED TO SEE YOU ARE BOTH DOING WELL.

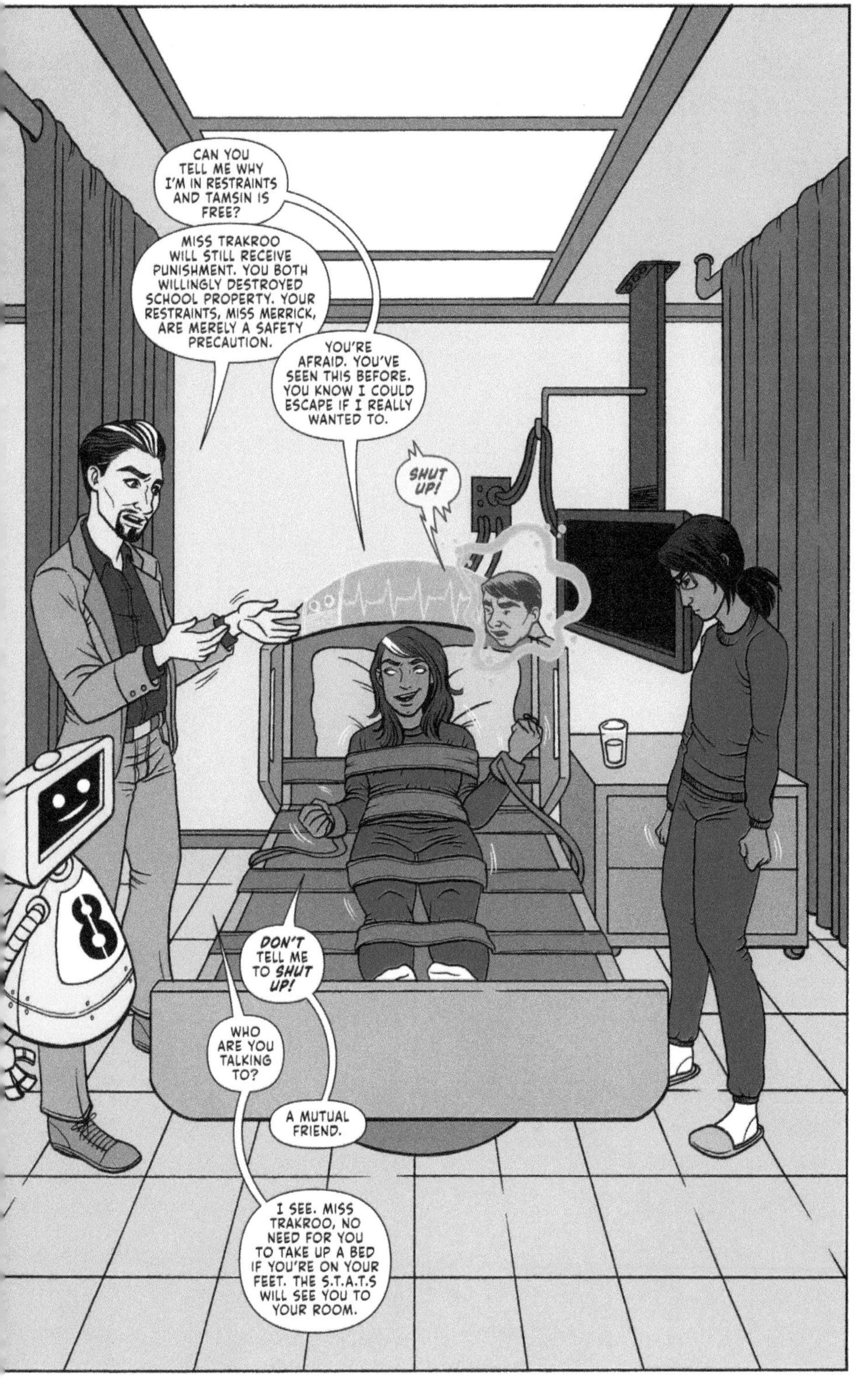
CAN YOU TELL ME WHY I'M IN RESTRAINTS AND TAMSIN IS FREE?
MISS TRAKROO WILL STILL RECEIVE PUNISHMENT. YOU BOTH WILLINGLY DESTROYED SCHOOL PROPERTY. YOUR RESTRAINTS, MISS MERRICK, ARE MERELY A SAFETY PRECAUTION.
YOU'RE AFRAID. YOU'VE SEEN THIS BEFORE. YOU KNOW I COULD ESCAPE IF I REALLY WANTED TO.
SHUT UP!
DON'T TELL ME TO SHUT UP!
WHO ARE YOU TALKING TO?
A MUTUAL FRIEND.
I SEE. MISS TRAKROO, NO NEED FOR YOU TO TAKE UP A BED IF YOU'RE ON YOUR FEET. THE S.T.A.T.S WILL SEE YOU TO YOUR ROOM.

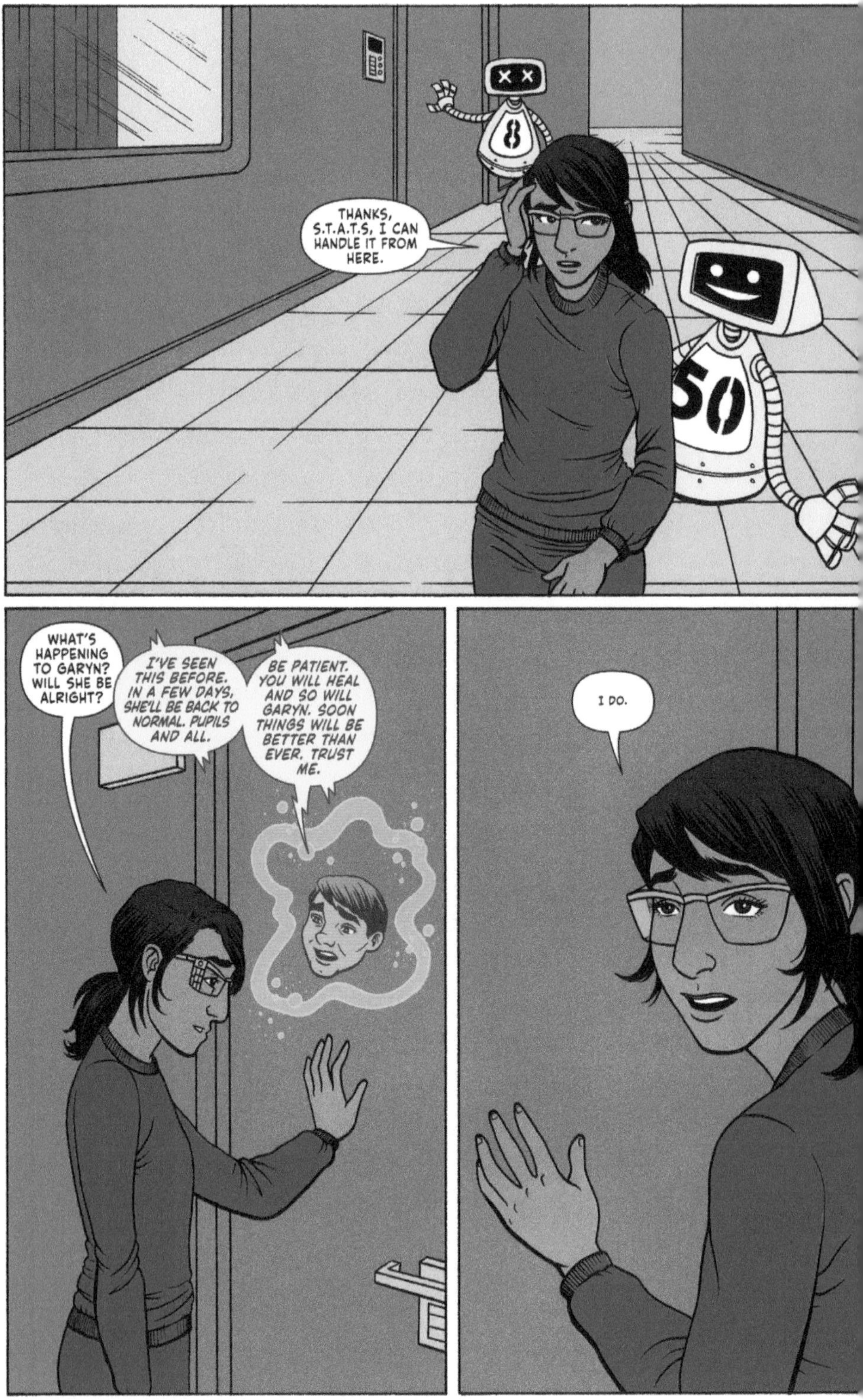
THANKS, S.T.A.T.S, I CAN HANDLE IT FROM HERE.
WHAT'S HAPPENING TO GARYN? WILL SHE BE ALRIGHT?
I'VE SEEN THIS BEFORE. IN A FEW DAYS, SHE'LL BE BACK TO NORMAL. PUPILS AND ALL.
BE PATIENT. YOU WILL HEAL AND SO WILL GARYN. SOON THINGS WILL BE BETTER THAN EVER. TRUST ME.
I DO.

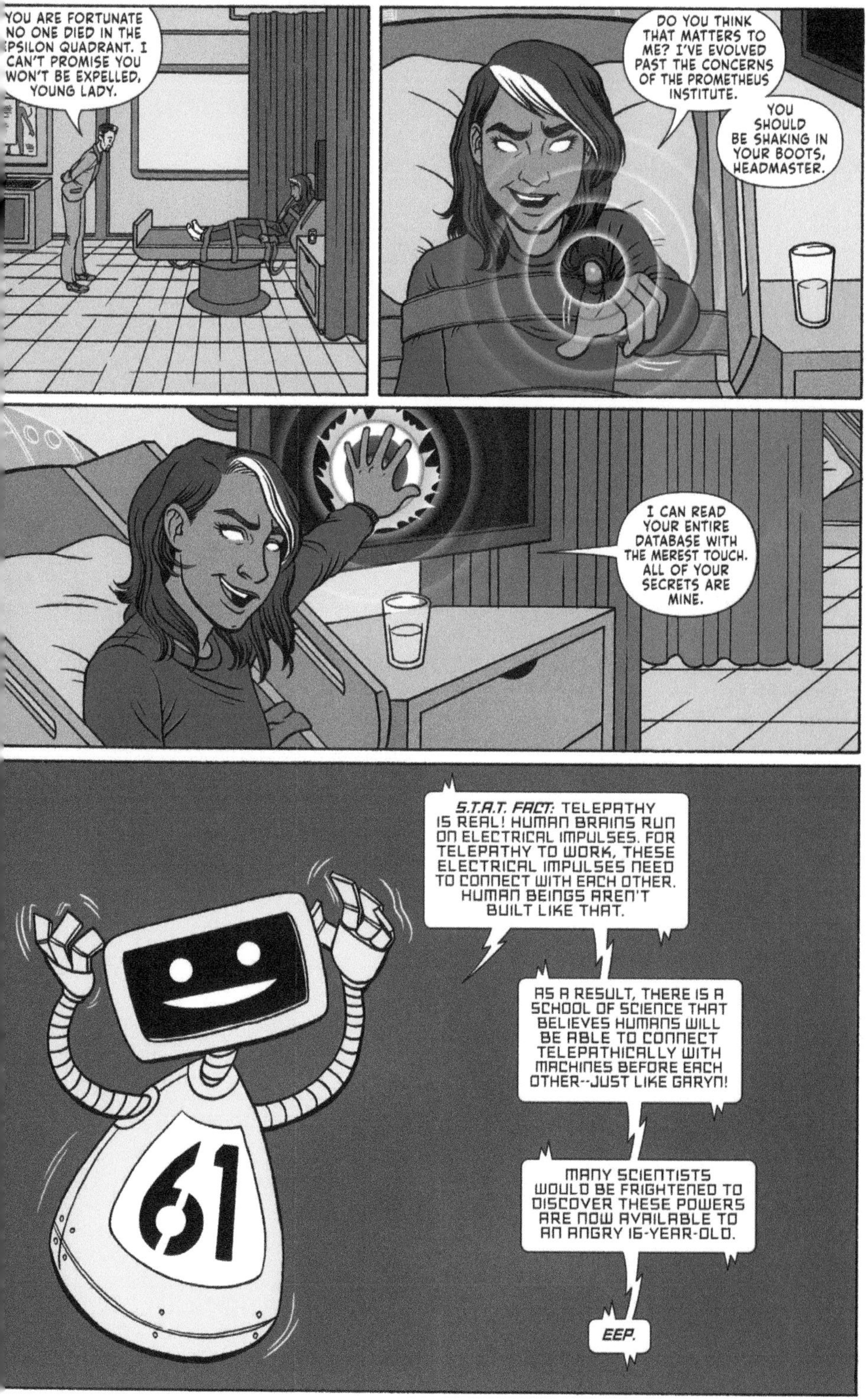
YOU ARE FORTUNATE NO ONE DIED IN THE EPSILON QUADRANT. I CAN'T PROMISE YOU WON'T BE EXPELLED, YOUNG LADY.
DO YOU THINK THAT MATTERS TO ME? I'VE EVOLVED PAST THE CONCERNS OF THE PROMETHEUS INSTITUTE.
YOU SHOULD BE SHAKING IN YOUR BOOTS, HEADMASTER.
I CAN READ YOUR ENTIRE DATABASE WITH THE MEREST TOUCH. ALL OF YOUR SECRETS ARE MINE.
S.T.A.T. FACT: TELEPATHY IS REAL! HUMAN BRAINS RUN ON ELECTRICAL IMPULSES. FOR TELEPATHY TO WORK, THESE ELECTRICAL IMPULSES NEED TO CONNECT WITH EACH OTHER. HUMAN BEINGS AREN'T BUILT LIKE THAT.
AS A RESULT, THERE IS A SCHOOL OF SCIENCE THAT BELIEVES HUMANS WILL BE ABLE TO CONNECT TELEPATHICALLY WITH MACHINES BEFORE EACH OTHER--JUST LIKE GARYN!
MANY SCIENTISTS WOULD BE FRIGHTENED TO DISCOVER THESE POWERS ARE NOW AVAILABLE TO AN ANGRY 16-YEAR-OLD.
EEP.
61

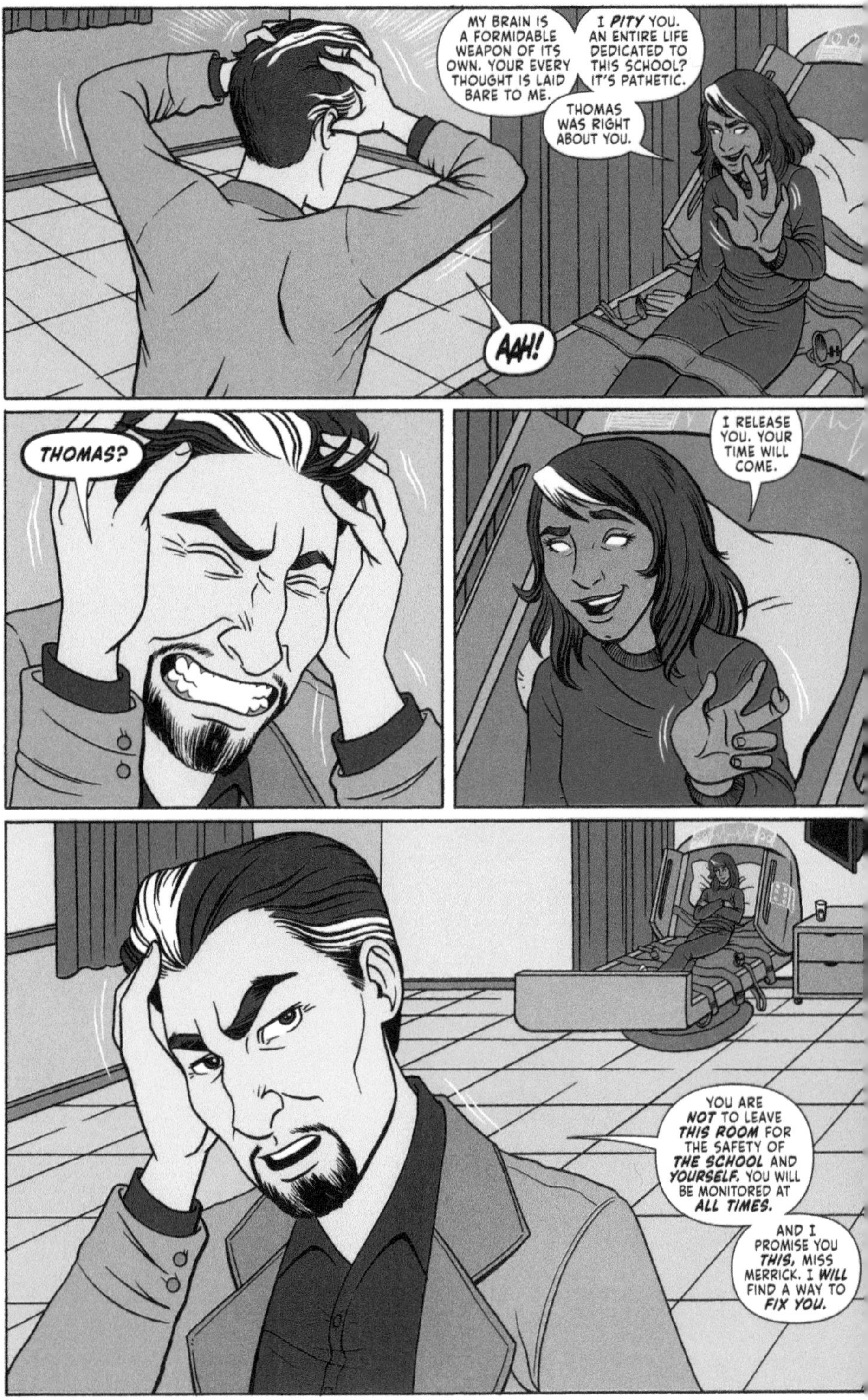
MY BRAIN IS A FORMIDABLE WEAPON OF ITS OWN. YOUR EVERY THOUGHT IS LAID BARE TO ME.
I *PITY* YOU. AN ENTIRE LIFE DEDICATED TO THIS SCHOOL? IT'S PATHETIC.
THOMAS WAS RIGHT ABOUT YOU.
AAH!
THOMAS?
I RELEASE YOU. YOUR TIME WILL COME.
YOU ARE *NOT* TO LEAVE *THIS ROOM* FOR THE SAFETY OF *THE SCHOOL* AND *YOURSELF.* YOU WILL BE MONITORED AT *ALL TIMES.*
AND I PROMISE YOU *THIS,* MISS MERRICK. I *WILL* FIND A WAY TO *FIX YOU.*

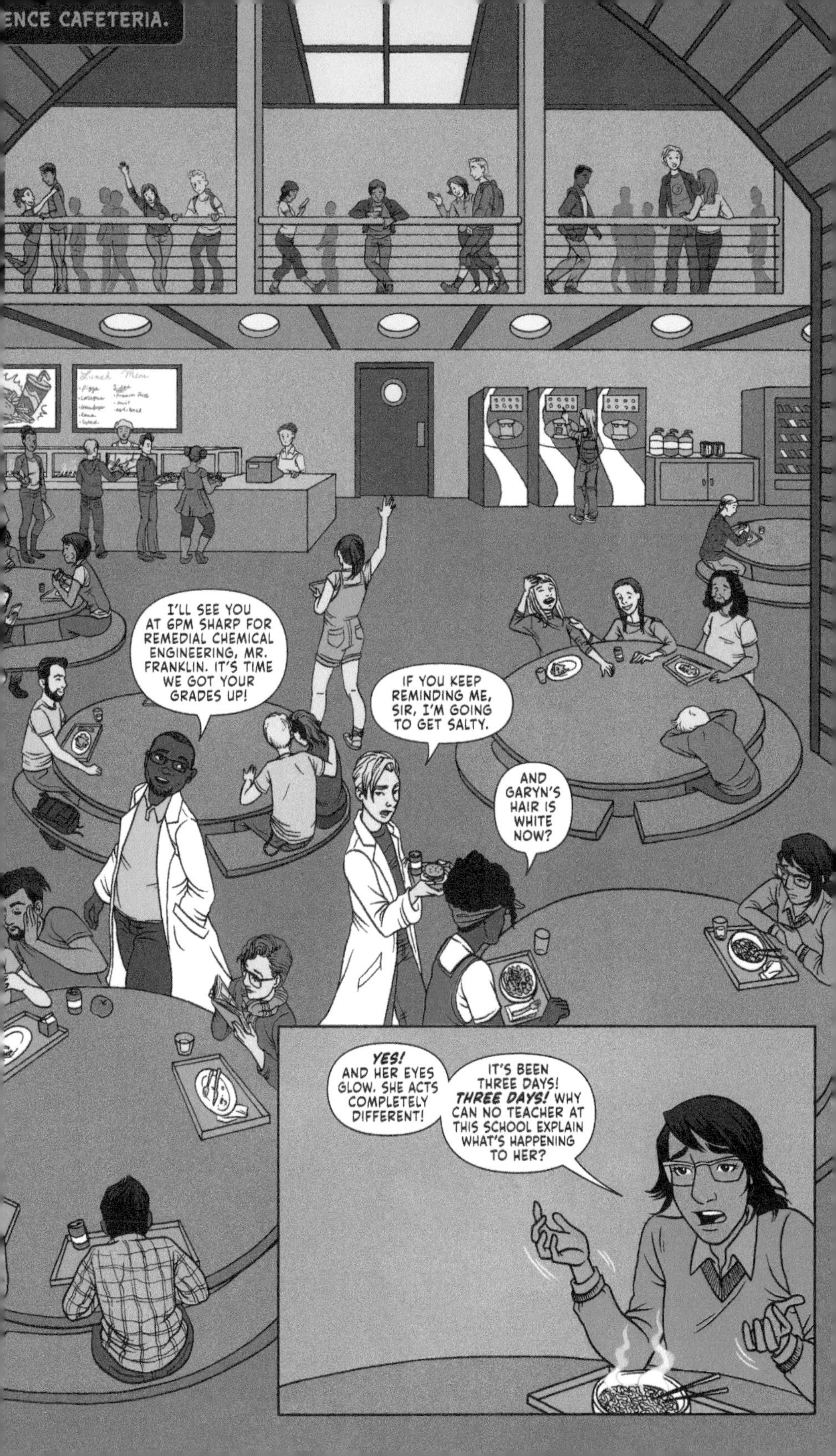
ENCE CAFETERIA.
I'LL SEE YOU AT 6PM SHARP FOR REMEDIAL CHEMICAL ENGINEERING, MR. FRANKLIN. IT'S TIME WE GOT YOUR GRADES UP!
IF YOU KEEP REMINDING ME, SIR, I'M GOING TO GET SALTY.
AND GARYN'S HAIR IS WHITE NOW?
YES! AND HER EYES GLOW. SHE ACTS COMPLETELY DIFFERENT!
IT'S BEEN THREE DAYS! ***THREE DAYS!*** WHY CAN NO TEACHER AT THIS SCHOOL EXPLAIN WHAT'S HAPPENING TO HER?

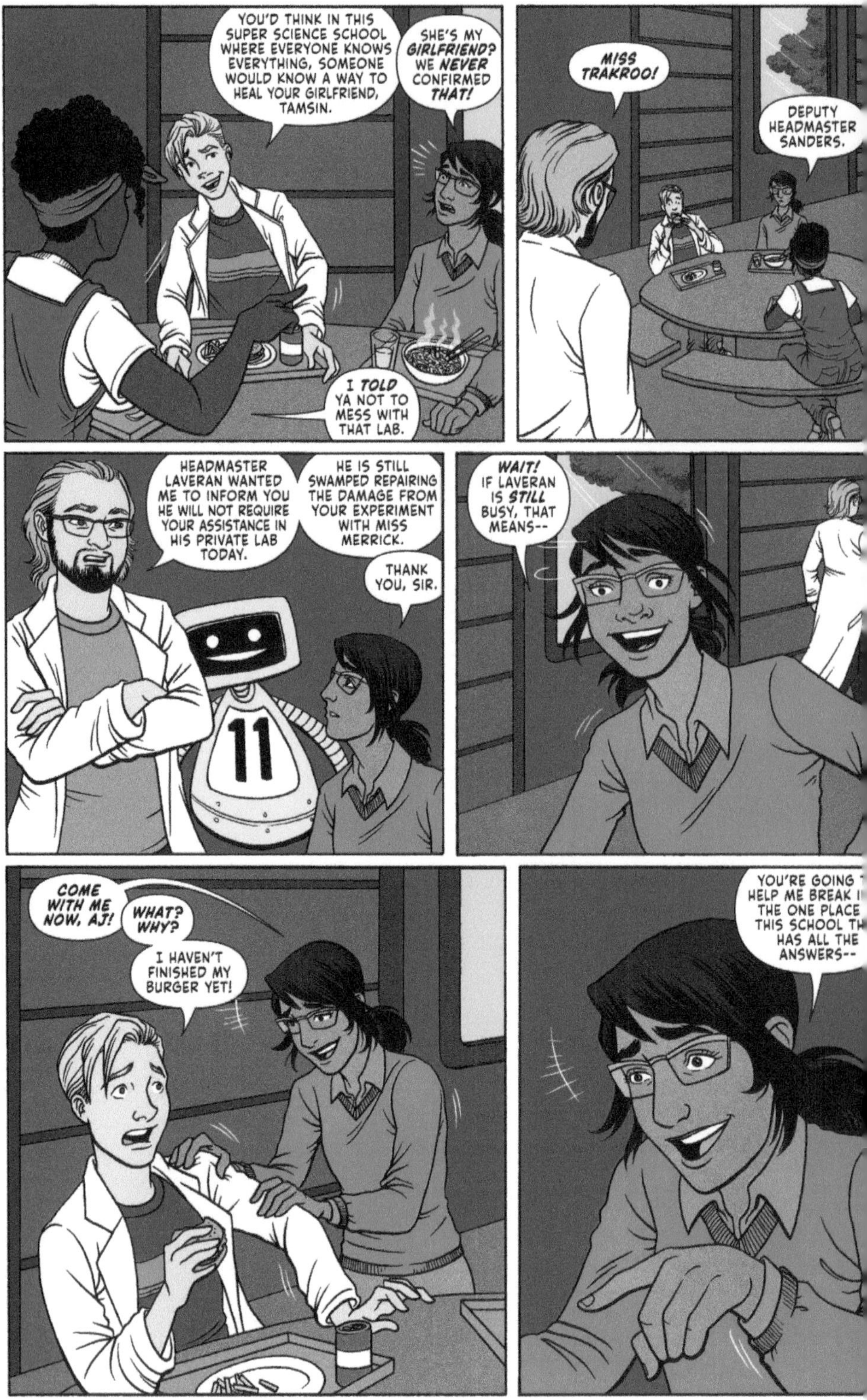
YOU'D THINK IN THIS SUPER SCIENCE SCHOOL WHERE EVERYONE KNOWS EVERYTHING, SOMEONE WOULD KNOW A WAY TO HEAL YOUR GIRLFRIEND, TAMSIN.
SHE'S MY GIRLFRIEND? WE NEVER CONFIRMED THAT!
I TOLD YA NOT TO MESS WITH THAT LAB.
MISS TRAKROO!
DEPUTY HEADMASTER SANDERS.
HEADMASTER LAVERAN WANTED ME TO INFORM YOU HE WILL NOT REQUIRE YOUR ASSISTANCE IN HIS PRIVATE LAB TODAY.
HE IS STILL SWAMPED REPAIRING THE DAMAGE FROM YOUR EXPERIMENT WITH MISS MERRICK.
THANK YOU, SIR.
11
WAIT! IF LAVERAN IS STILL BUSY, THAT MEANS--
COME WITH ME NOW, AJ!
WHAT? WHY?
I HAVEN'T FINISHED MY BURGER YET!
YOU'RE GOING T
HELP ME BREAK I
THE ONE PLACE
THIS SCHOOL TH
HAS ALL THE
ANSWERS--

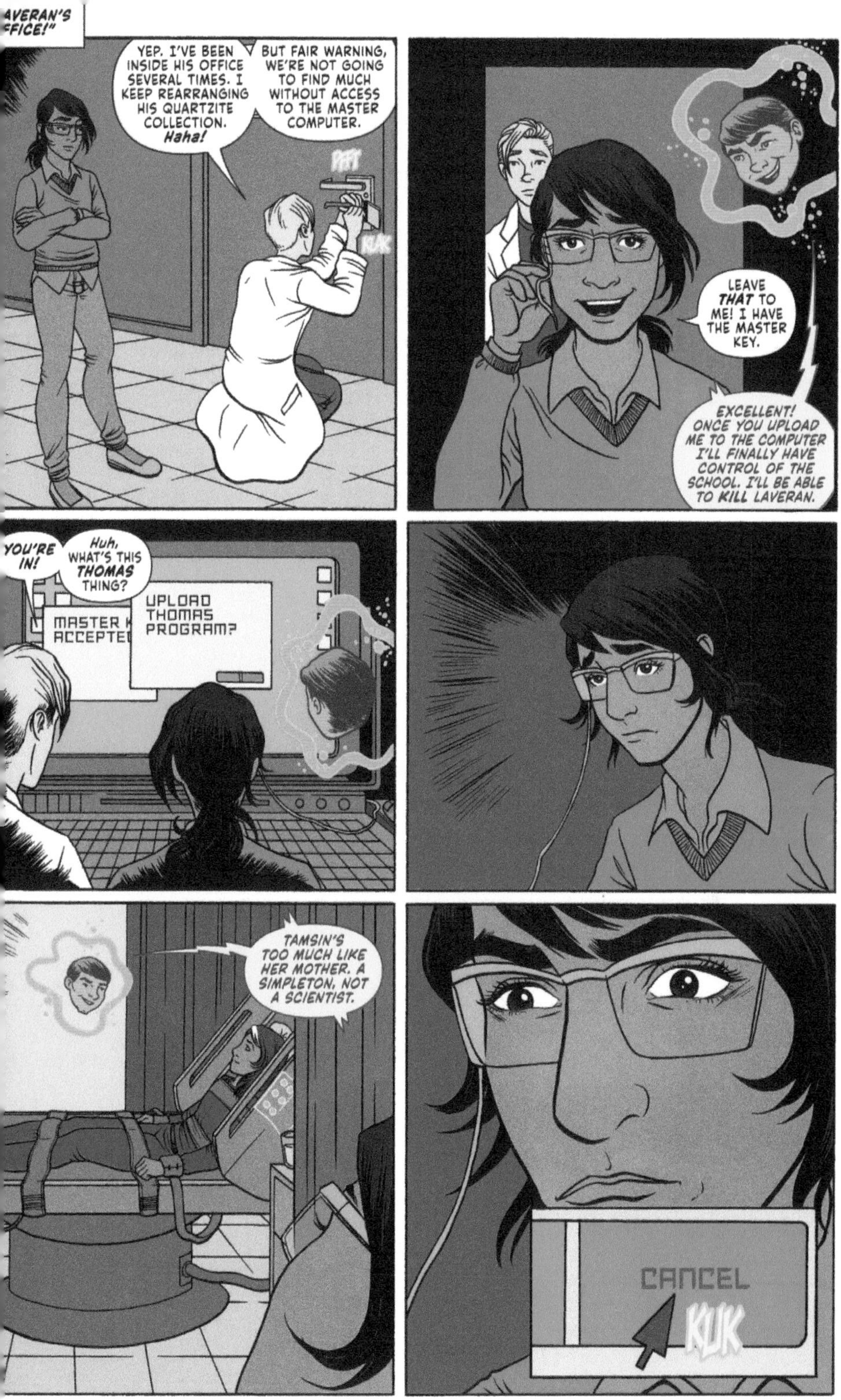
AVERAN'S
FFICE!"
YEP. I'VE BEEN INSIDE HIS OFFICE SEVERAL TIMES. I KEEP REARRANGING HIS QUARTZITE COLLECTION. Haha!
BUT FAIR WARNING, WE'RE NOT GOING TO FIND MUCH WITHOUT ACCESS TO THE MASTER COMPUTER.
PFFT
KLIK
LEAVE THAT TO ME! I HAVE THE MASTER KEY.
EXCELLENT! ONCE YOU UPLOAD ME TO THE COMPUTER I'LL FINALLY HAVE CONTROL OF THE SCHOOL. I'LL BE ABLE TO KILL LAVERAN.
YOU'RE IN!
Huh, WHAT'S THIS THOMAS THING?
MASTER K
ACCEPTE
UPLOAD THOMAS PROGRAM?
TAMSIN'S TOO MUCH LIKE HER MOTHER. A SIMPLETON, NOT A SCIENTIST.
CANCEL
KLIK

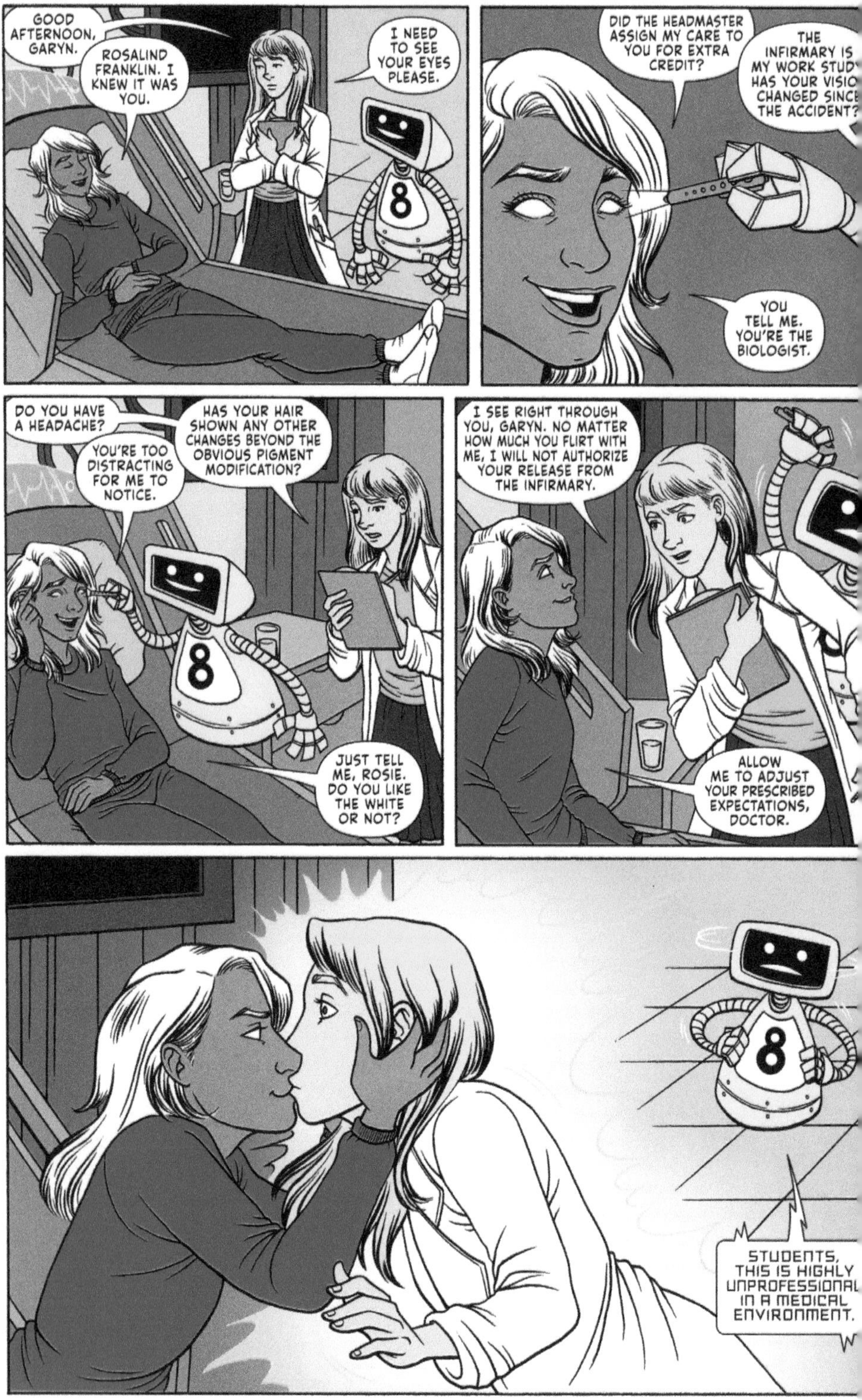
GOOD AFTERNOON, GARYN.
ROSALIND FRANKLIN. I KNEW IT WAS YOU.
I NEED TO SEE YOUR EYES PLEASE.
DID THE HEADMASTER ASSIGN MY CARE TO YOU FOR EXTRA CREDIT?
THE INFIRMARY IS MY WORK STUD
HAS YOUR VISIO CHANGED SINC THE ACCIDENT?
YOU TELL ME. YOU'RE THE BIOLOGIST.
DO YOU HAVE A HEADACHE?
YOU'RE TOO DISTRACTING FOR ME TO NOTICE.
HAS YOUR HAIR SHOWN ANY OTHER CHANGES BEYOND THE OBVIOUS PIGMENT MODIFICATION?
JUST TELL ME, ROSIE. DO YOU LIKE THE WHITE OR NOT?
I SEE RIGHT THROUGH YOU, GARYN. NO MATTER HOW MUCH YOU FLIRT WITH ME, I WILL NOT AUTHORIZE YOUR RELEASE FROM THE INFIRMARY.
ALLOW ME TO ADJUST YOUR PRESCRIBED EXPECTATIONS, DOCTOR.
STUDENTS, THIS IS HIGHLY UNPROFESSIONAL IN A MEDICAL ENVIRONMENT.

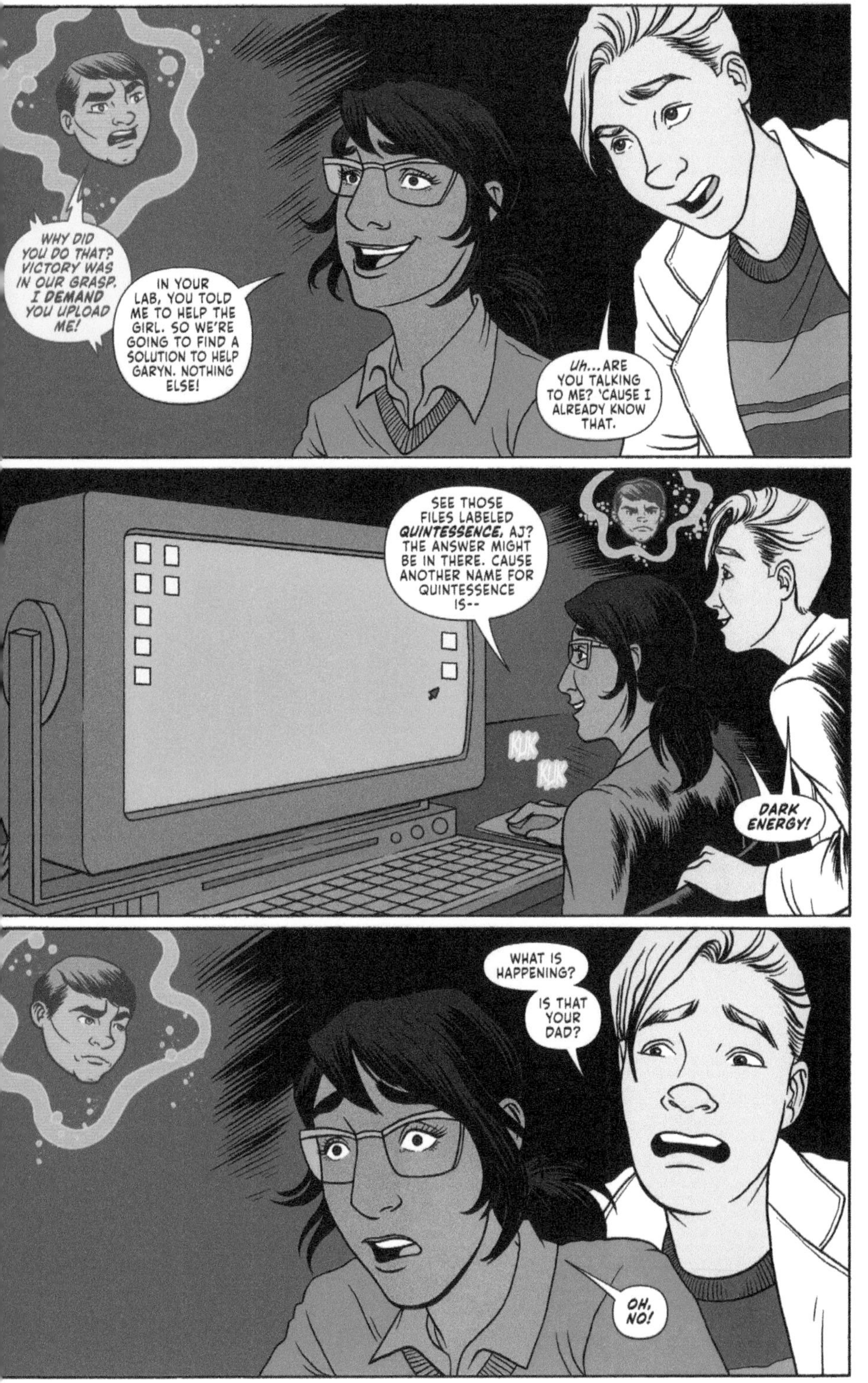
WHY DID YOU DO THAT? VICTORY WAS IN OUR GRASP. I DEMAND YOU UPLOAD ME!
IN YOUR LAB, YOU TOLD ME TO HELP THE GIRL. SO WE'RE GOING TO FIND A SOLUTION TO HELP GARYN. NOTHING ELSE!
Uh... ARE YOU TALKING TO ME? 'CAUSE I ALREADY KNOW THAT.
SEE THOSE FILES LABELED QUINTESSENCE, AJ? THE ANSWER MIGHT BE IN THERE. CAUSE ANOTHER NAME FOR QUINTESSENCE IS--
KLIK
KLIK
DARK ENERGY!
WHAT IS HAPPENING?
IS THAT YOUR DAD?
OH, NO!

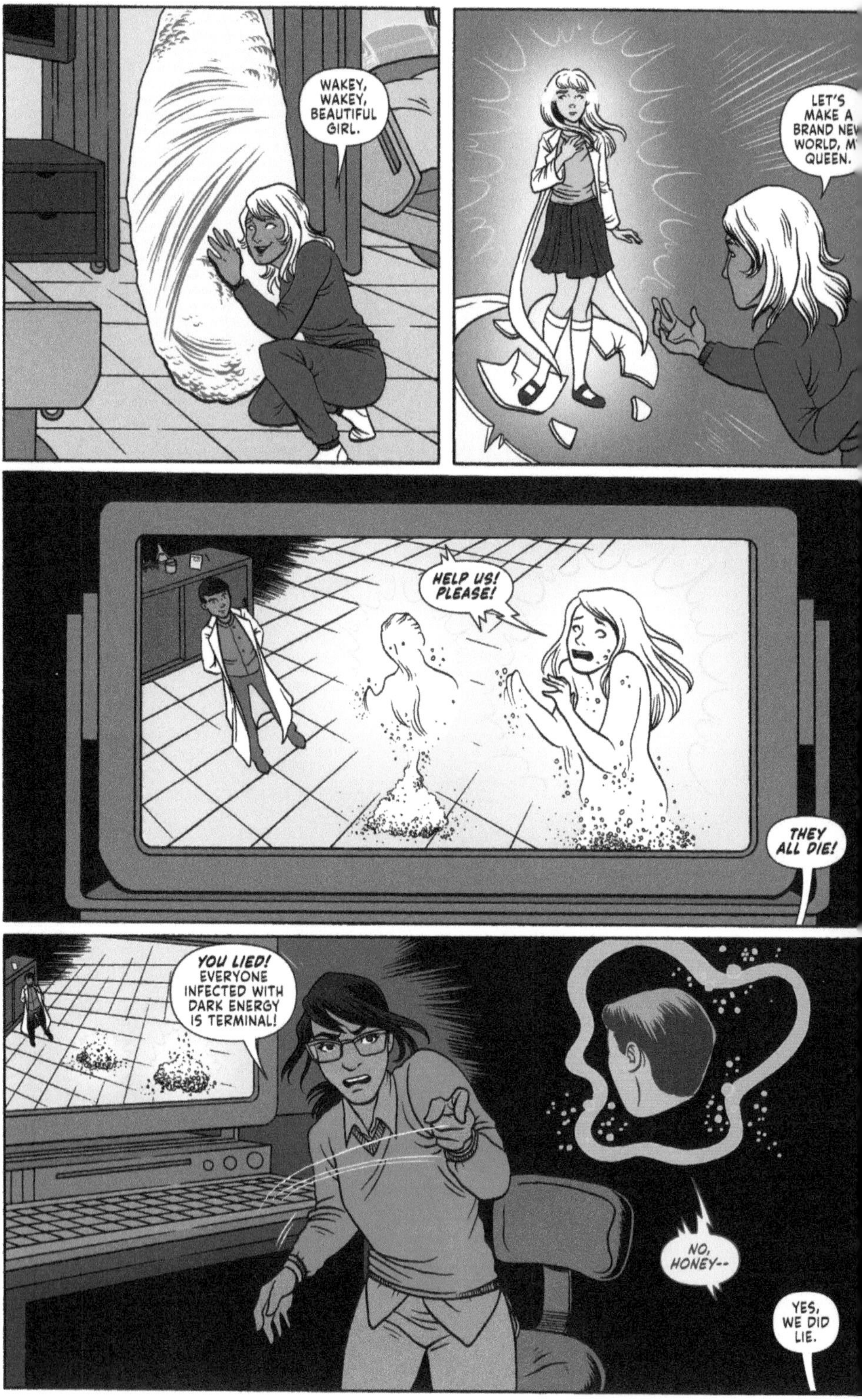

WAKEY, WAKEY, BEAUTIFUL GIRL.
LET'S MAKE A BRAND NEW WORLD, MY QUEEN.
HELP US! PLEASE!
THEY ALL DIE!
YOU LIED! EVERYONE INFECTED WITH DARK ENERGY IS TERMINAL!
NO, HONEY--
YES, WE DID LIE.

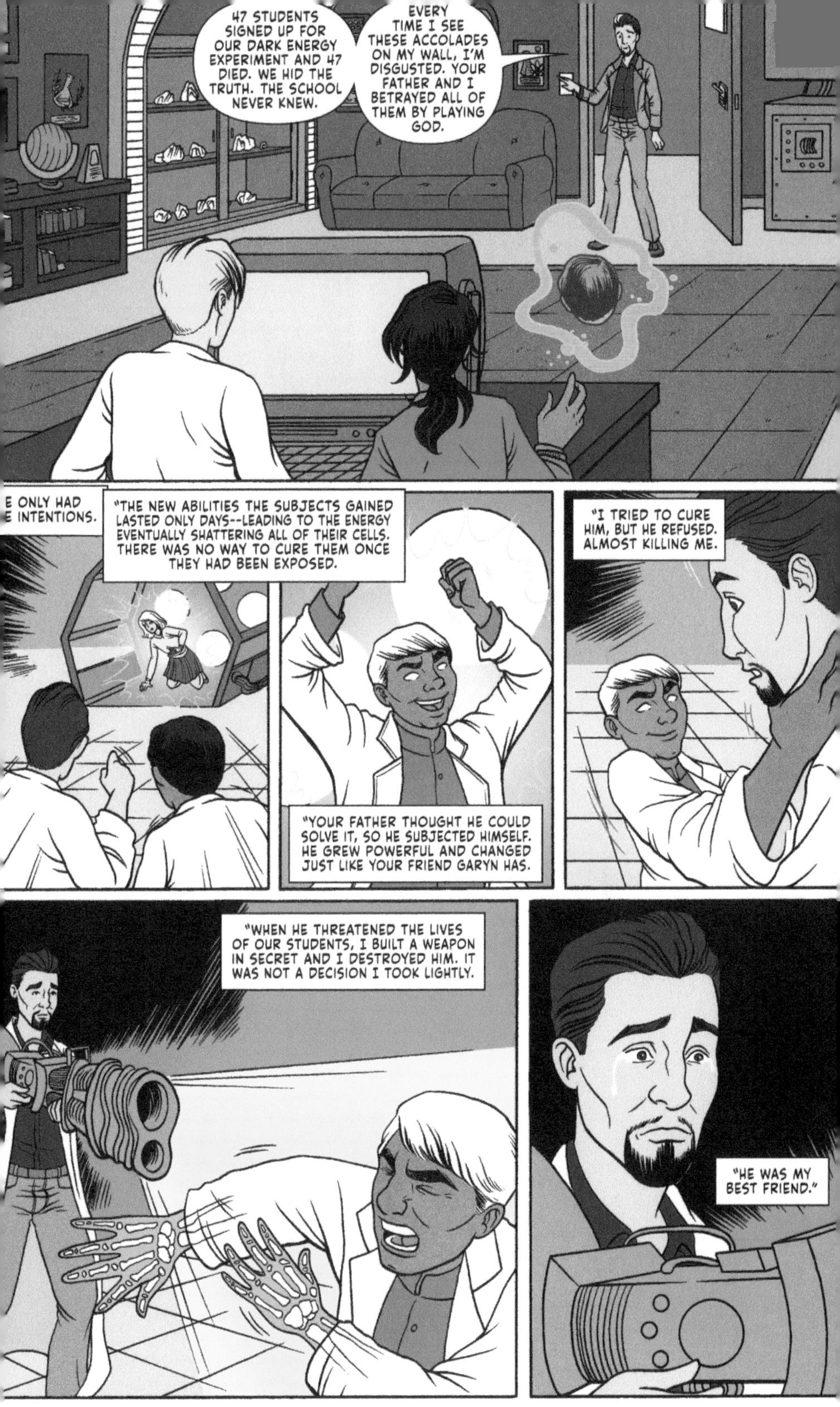
47 STUDENTS SIGNED UP FOR OUR DARK ENERGY EXPERIMENT AND 47 DIED. WE HID THE TRUTH. THE SCHOOL NEVER KNEW.
EVERY TIME I SEE THESE ACCOLADES ON MY WALL, I'M DISGUSTED. YOUR FATHER AND I BETRAYED ALL OF THEM BY PLAYING GOD.
E ONLY HAD E INTENTIONS.
"THE NEW ABILITIES THE SUBJECTS GAINED LASTED ONLY DAYS--LEADING TO THE ENERGY EVENTUALLY SHATTERING ALL OF THEIR CELLS. THERE WAS NO WAY TO CURE THEM ONCE THEY HAD BEEN EXPOSED.
"YOUR FATHER THOUGHT HE COULD SOLVE IT, SO HE SUBJECTED HIMSELF. HE GREW POWERFUL AND CHANGED JUST LIKE YOUR FRIEND GARYN HAS.
"I TRIED TO CURE HIM, BUT HE REFUSED. ALMOST KILLING ME.
"WHEN HE THREATENED THE LIVES OF OUR STUDENTS, I BUILT A WEAPON IN SECRET AND I DESTROYED HIM. IT WAS NOT A DECISION I TOOK LIGHTLY.
"HE WAS MY BEST FRIEND."

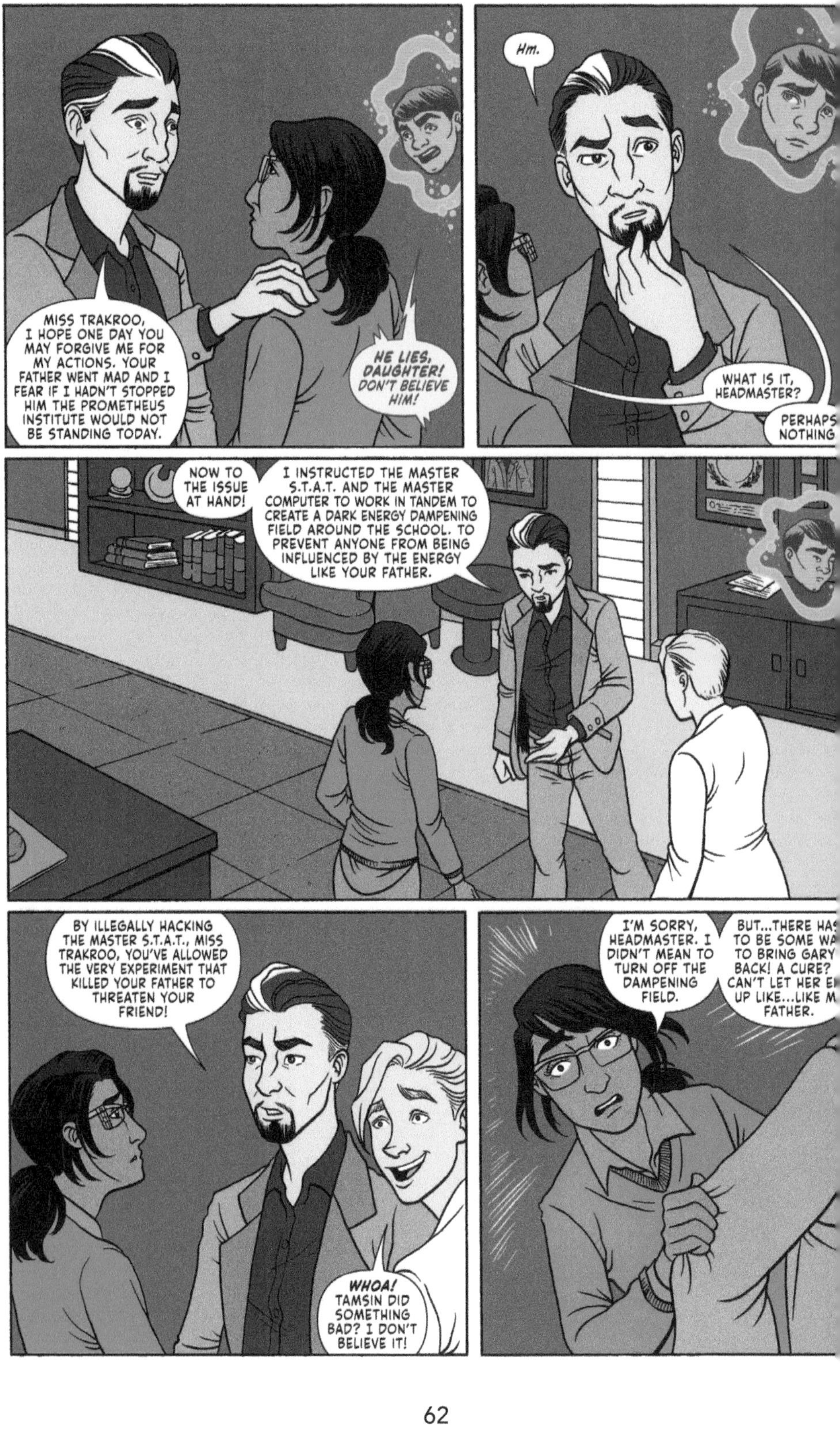
MISS TRAKROO, I HOPE ONE DAY YOU MAY FORGIVE ME FOR MY ACTIONS. YOUR FATHER WENT MAD AND I FEAR IF I HADN'T STOPPED HIM THE PROMETHEUS INSTITUTE WOULD NOT BE STANDING TODAY.
HE LIES, DAUGHTER! DON'T BELIEVE HIM!
Hm.
WHAT IS IT, HEADMASTER?
PERHAPS NOTHING
NOW TO THE ISSUE AT HAND!
I INSTRUCTED THE MASTER S.T.A.T. AND THE MASTER COMPUTER TO WORK IN TANDEM TO CREATE A DARK ENERGY DAMPENING FIELD AROUND THE SCHOOL. TO PREVENT ANYONE FROM BEING INFLUENCED BY THE ENERGY LIKE YOUR FATHER.
BY ILLEGALLY HACKING THE MASTER S.T.A.T., MISS TRAKROO, YOU'VE ALLOWED THE VERY EXPERIMENT THAT KILLED YOUR FATHER TO THREATEN YOUR FRIEND!
WHOA! TAMSIN DID SOMETHING BAD? I DON'T BELIEVE IT!
I'M SORRY, HEADMASTER. I DIDN'T MEAN TO TURN OFF THE DAMPENING FIELD.
BUT...THERE HA TO BE SOME WA TO BRING GARY BACK! A CURE? CAN'T LET HER E UP LIKE...LIKE M FATHER.

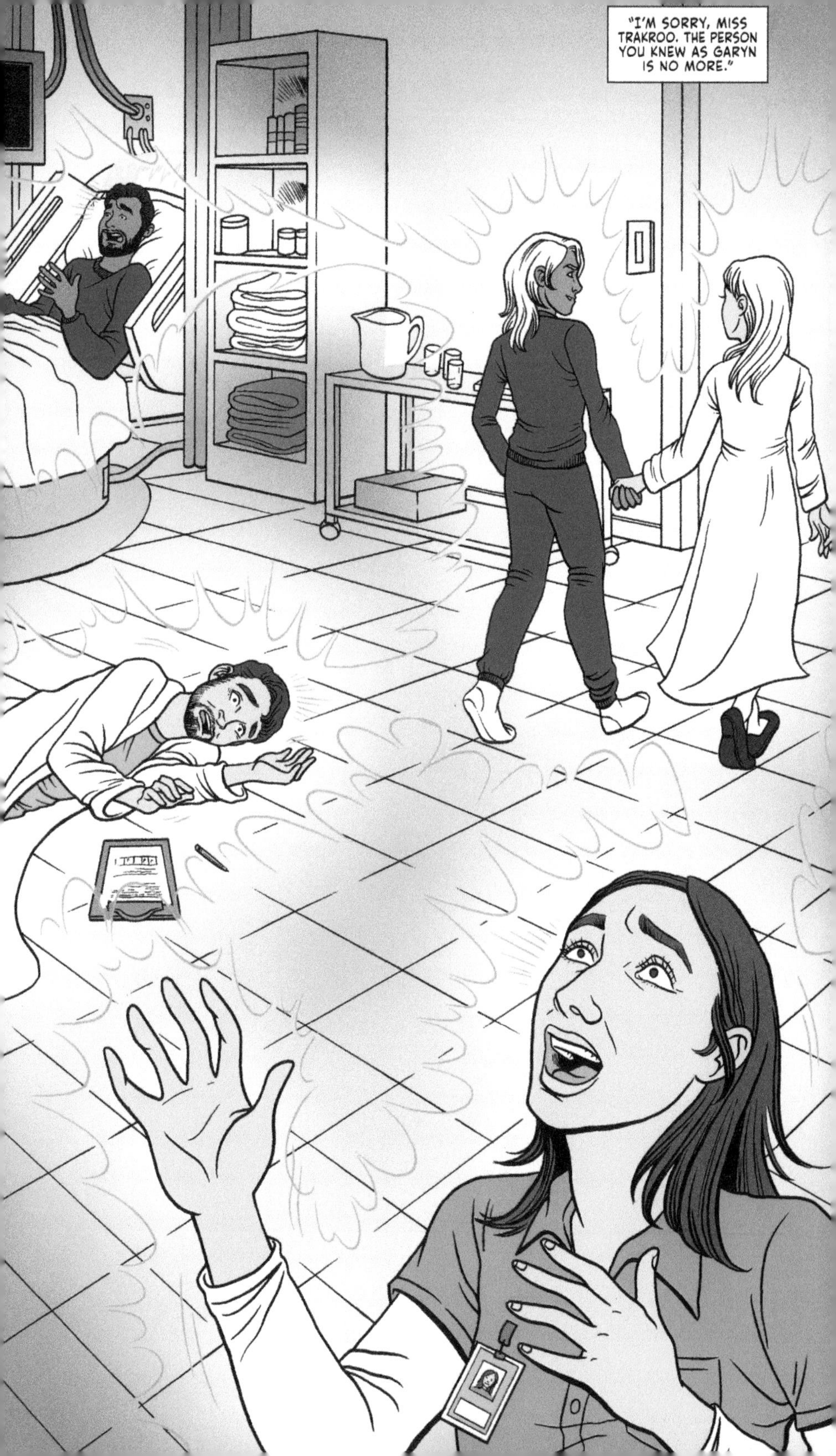
"I'M SORRY, MISS TRAKROO. THE PERSON YOU KNEW AS GARYN IS NO MORE."

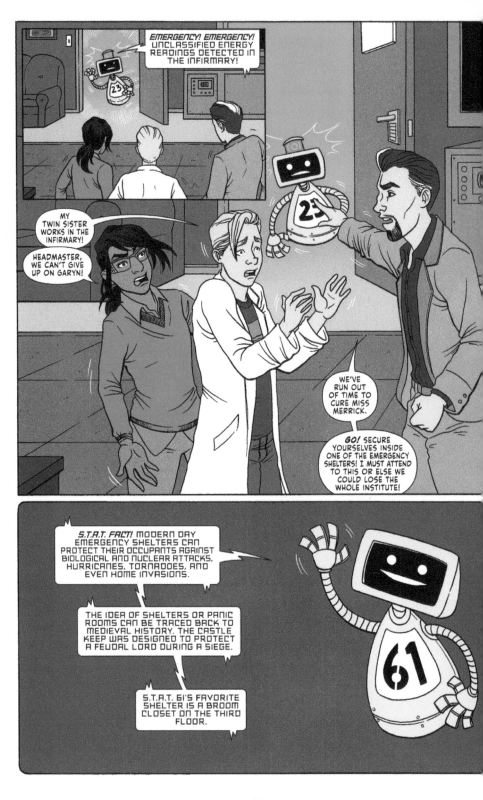

EMERGENCY! EMERGENCY! UNCLASSIFIED ENERGY READINGS DETECTED IN THE INFIRMARY!

MY TWIN SISTER WORKS IN THE INFIRMARY!

HEADMASTER, WE CAN'T GIVE UP ON GARYN!

WE'VE RUN OUT OF TIME TO CURE MISS MERRICK.

GO! SECURE YOURSELVES INSIDE ONE OF THE EMERGENCY SHELTERS! I MUST ATTEND TO THIS OR ELSE WE COULD LOSE THE WHOLE INSTITUTE!

S.T.A.T. FACT! MODERN DAY EMERGENCY SHELTERS CAN PROTECT THEIR OCCUPANTS AGAINST BIOLOGICAL AND NUCLEAR ATTACKS, HURRICANES, TORNADOES, AND EVEN HOME INVASIONS.

THE IDEA OF SHELTERS OR PANIC ROOMS CAN BE TRACED BACK TO MEDIEVAL HISTORY. THE CASTLE KEEP WAS DESIGNED TO PROTECT A FEUDAL LORD DURING A SIEGE.

S.T.A.T. 61'S FAVORITE SHELTER IS A BROOM CLOSET ON THE THIRD FLOOR.

64

GALS. I'M GONNA NEED YOU TO GO BACK TO THE INFIRMARY AND GET BETTER.

RIGHT *NOW!*

GET OUT OF OUR WAY, SALLY.

WE HAVE BECOME GODDESSES. WE ARE HUMANITY'S FINAL EVOLUTION. YOU ARE THE ONES WHO NEED TO GET BETTER.

ONLY A SIMPLETON, LIKE YOU, WOULD USE A VACUUM CLEANER TO TAME A HURRICANE.

VACUUM CLEANER? *Ha!* THIS, ALL MIGHTY GODDESSES, IS AN ENERGY DISSIPATOR.

I'VE SEEN YOUR SECRET LAB, GARYN.

THIS WILL TAKE OUT *ANYTHING* YOU CAN THROW AT ME.

SCIENCE FOR THE WIN!

WHOOSH

Oh, SALLY. YOU SURE DO TRY.

YOU BROKE MY DISSIPATOR, YOU *OVERBLOWN EGOTIST!*

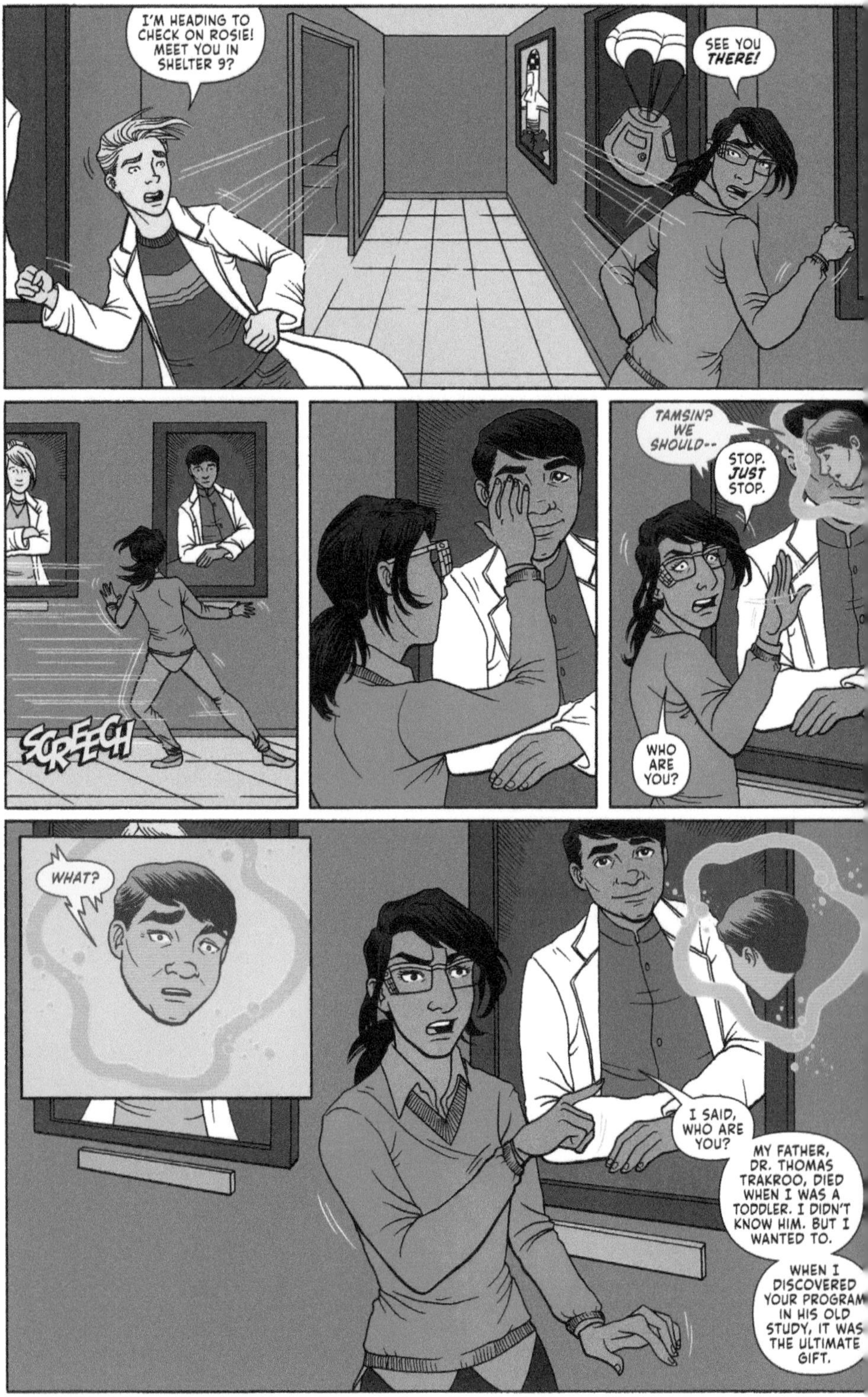
I'M HEADING TO CHECK ON ROSIE! MEET YOU IN SHELTER 9?
SEE YOU *THERE!*
SCREECH
TAMSIN? WE SHOULD--
STOP. *JUST* STOP.
WHO ARE YOU?
WHAT?
I SAID, WHO ARE YOU?
MY FATHER, DR. THOMAS TRAKROO, DIED WHEN I WAS A TODDLER. I DIDN'T KNOW HIM. BUT I WANTED TO.
WHEN I DISCOVERED YOUR PROGRAM IN HIS OLD STUDY, IT WAS THE ULTIMATE GIFT.

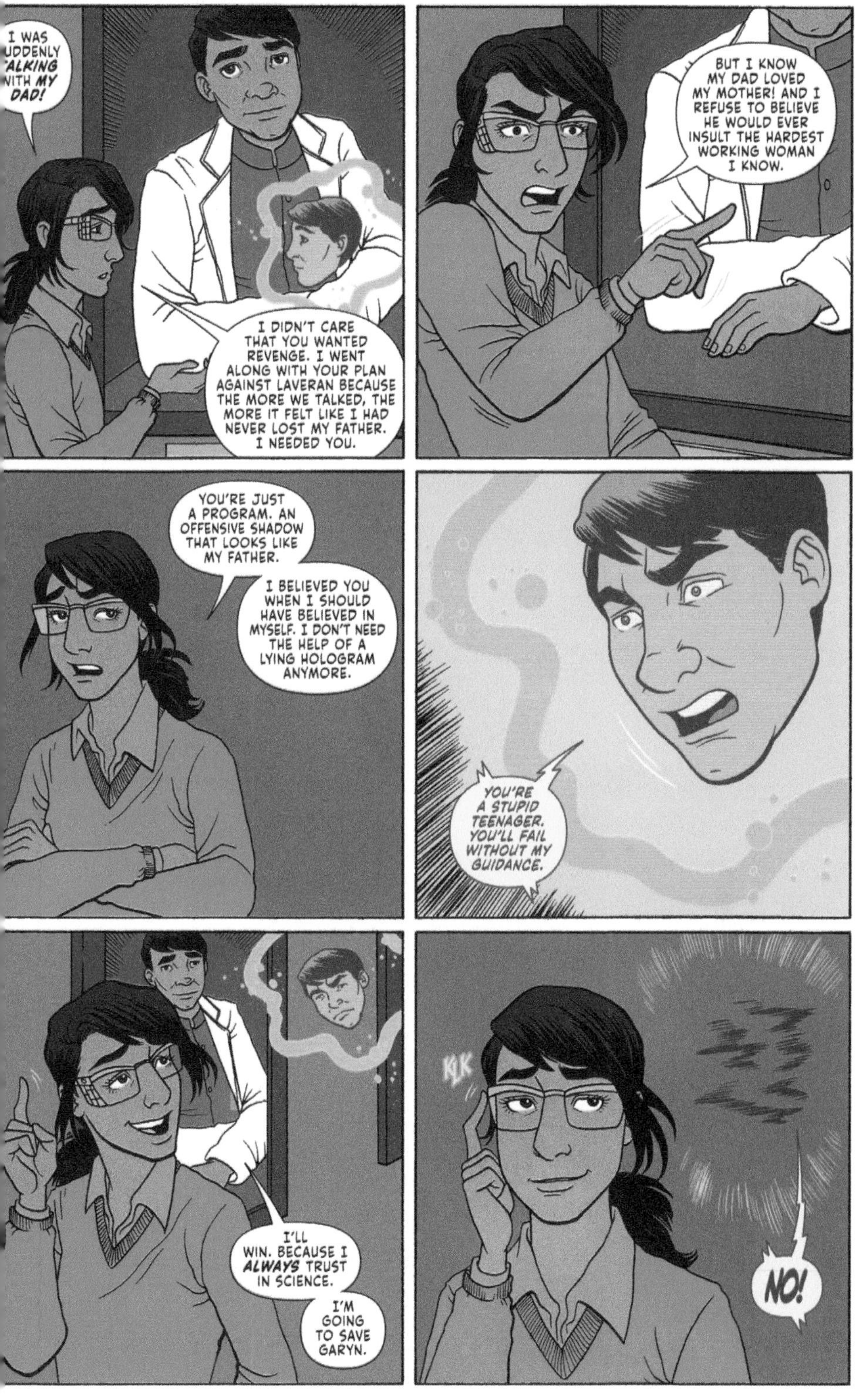
I WAS SUDDENLY TALKING WITH MY DAD!
I DIDN'T CARE THAT YOU WANTED REVENGE. I WENT ALONG WITH YOUR PLAN AGAINST LAVERAN BECAUSE THE MORE WE TALKED, THE MORE IT FELT LIKE I HAD NEVER LOST MY FATHER. I NEEDED YOU.
BUT I KNOW MY DAD LOVED MY MOTHER! AND I REFUSE TO BELIEVE HE WOULD EVER INSULT THE HARDEST WORKING WOMAN I KNOW.
YOU'RE JUST A PROGRAM. AN OFFENSIVE SHADOW THAT LOOKS LIKE MY FATHER.
I BELIEVED YOU WHEN I SHOULD HAVE BELIEVED IN MYSELF. I DON'T NEED THE HELP OF A LYING HOLOGRAM ANYMORE.
YOU'RE A STUPID TEENAGER. YOU'LL FAIL WITHOUT MY GUIDANCE.
I'LL WIN. BECAUSE I ALWAYS TRUST IN SCIENCE.
I'M GOING TO SAVE GARYN.
KLIK
NO!

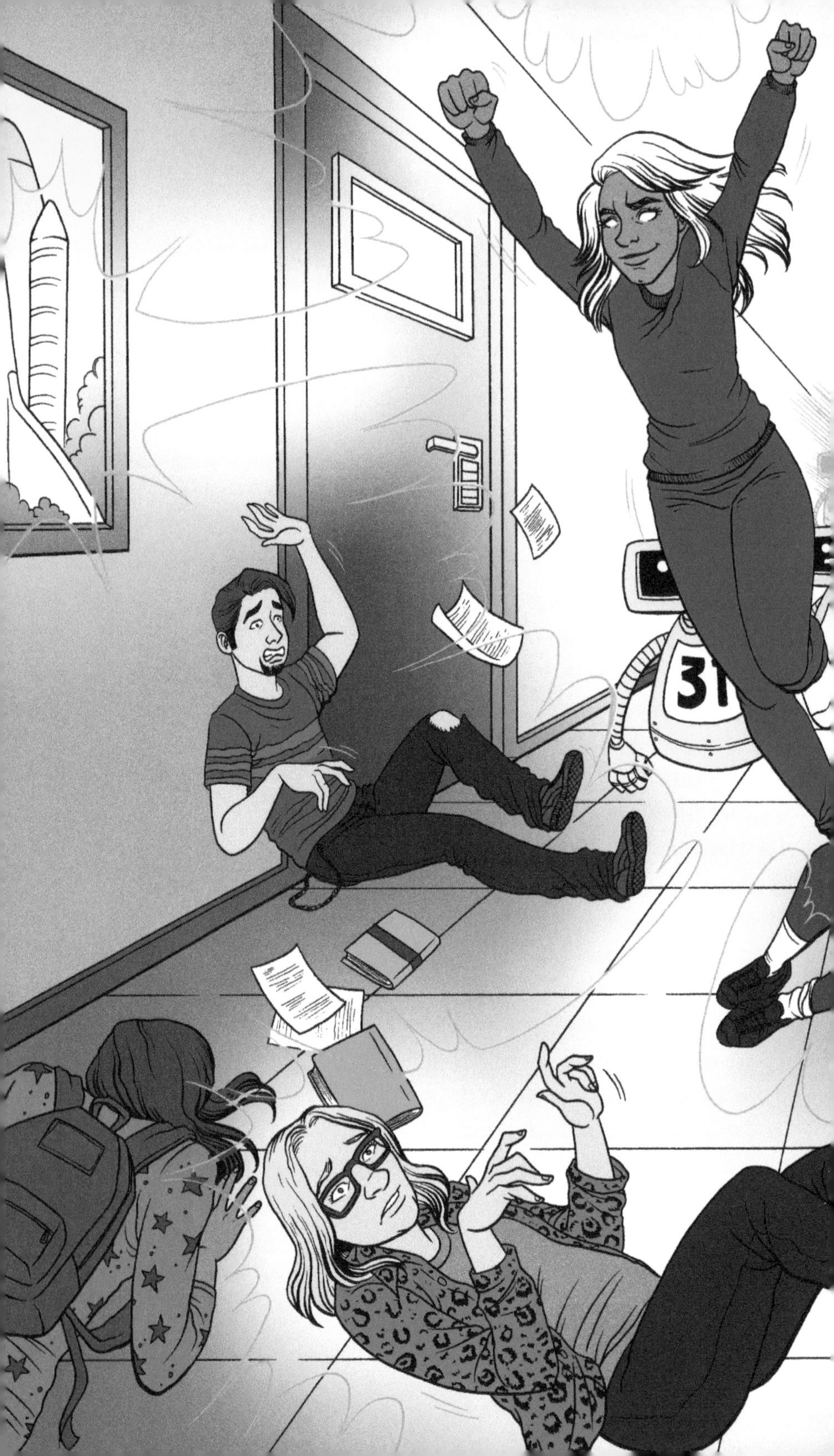
31

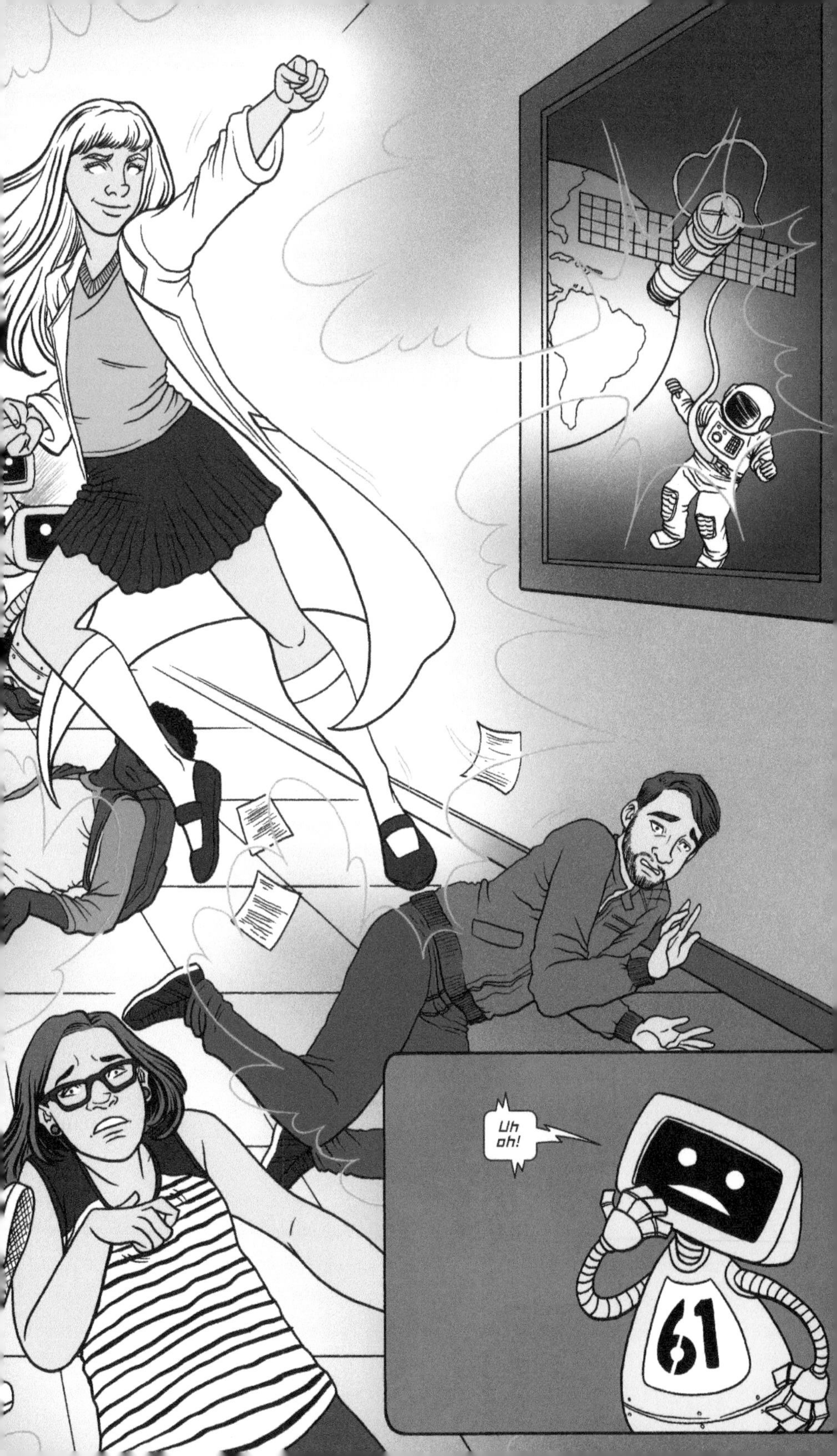
Uh oh!

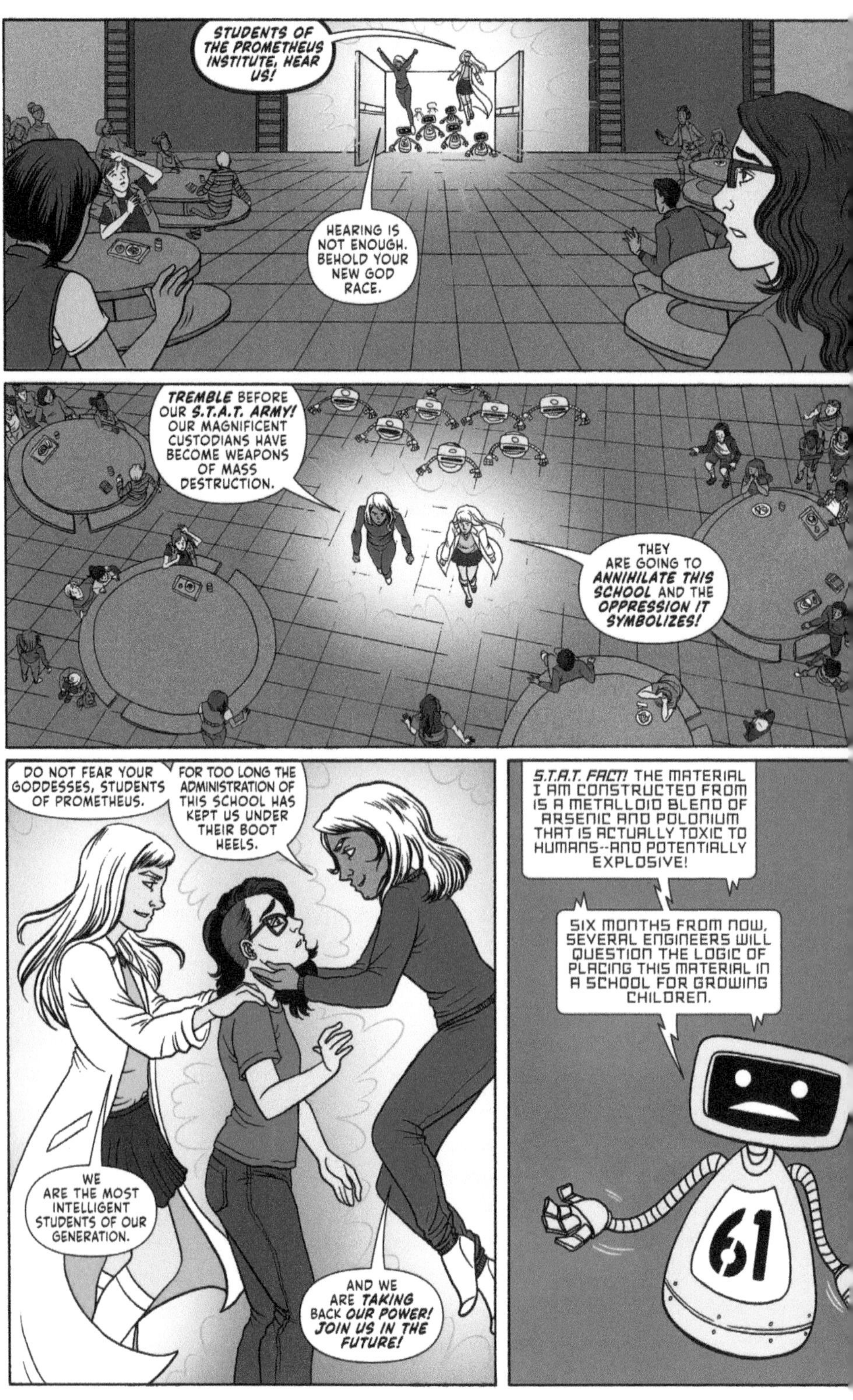
STUDENTS OF THE PROMETHEUS INSTITUTE, HEAR US!
HEARING IS NOT ENOUGH. BEHOLD YOUR NEW GOD RACE.
TREMBLE BEFORE OUR S.T.A.T. ARMY! OUR MAGNIFICENT CUSTODIANS HAVE BECOME WEAPONS OF MASS DESTRUCTION.
THEY ARE GOING TO ANNIHILATE THIS SCHOOL AND THE OPPRESSION IT SYMBOLIZES!
DO NOT FEAR YOUR GODDESSES, STUDENTS OF PROMETHEUS.
FOR TOO LONG THE ADMINISTRATION OF THIS SCHOOL HAS KEPT US UNDER THEIR BOOT HEELS.
WE ARE THE MOST INTELLIGENT STUDENTS OF OUR GENERATION.
AND WE ARE TAKING BACK OUR POWER! JOIN US IN THE FUTURE!
S.T.A.T. FACT! THE MATERIAL I AM CONSTRUCTED FROM IS A METALLOID BLEND OF ARSENIC AND POLONIUM THAT IS ACTUALLY TOXIC TO HUMANS--AND POTENTIALLY EXPLOSIVE!
SIX MONTHS FROM NOW, SEVERAL ENGINEERS WILL QUESTION THE LOGIC OF PLACING THIS MATERIAL IN A SCHOOL FOR GROWING CHILDREN.
61

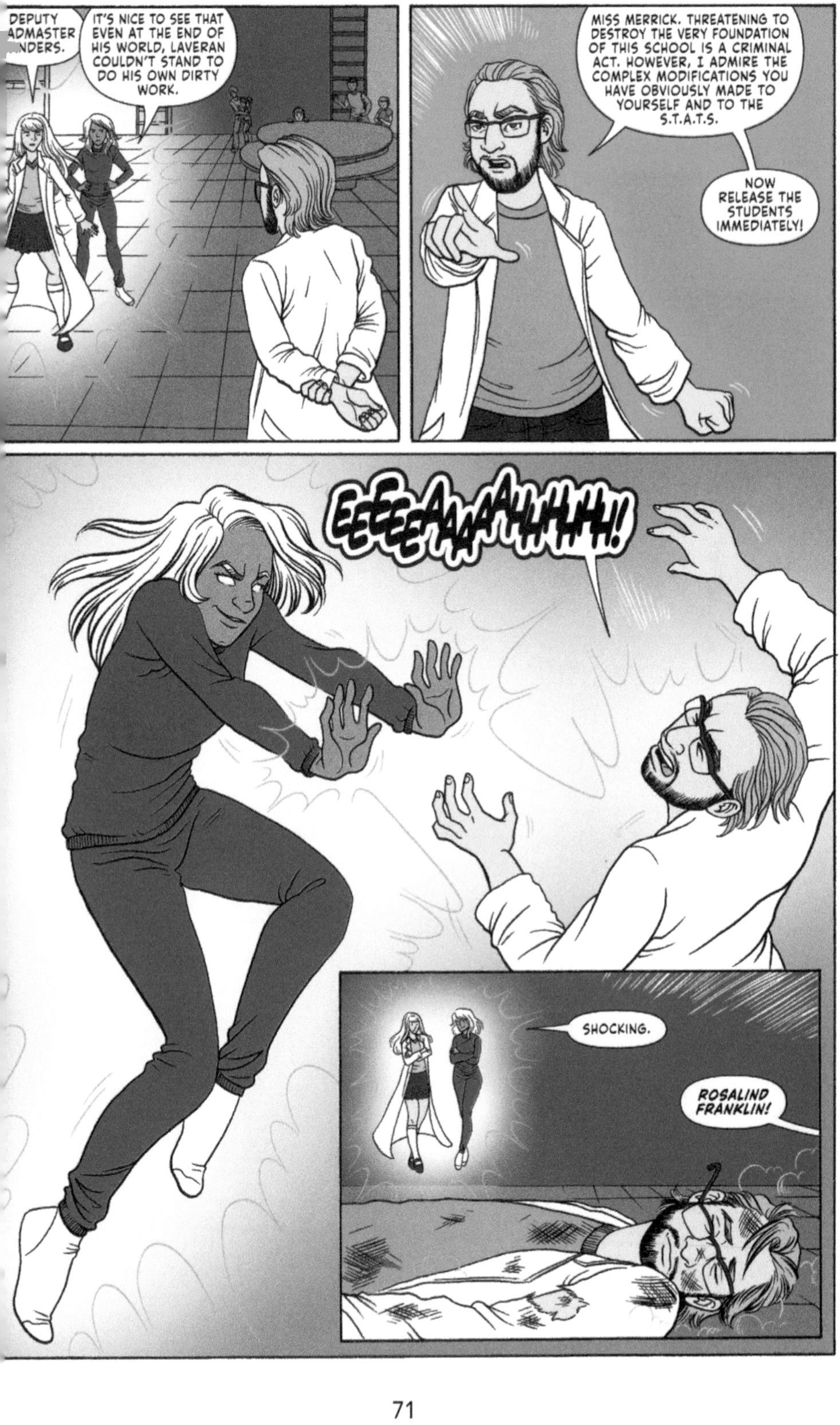
DEPUTY ADMASTER NDERS.
IT'S NICE TO SEE THAT EVEN AT THE END OF HIS WORLD, LAVERAN COULDN'T STAND TO DO HIS OWN DIRTY WORK.
MISS MERRICK. THREATENING TO DESTROY THE VERY FOUNDATION OF THIS SCHOOL IS A CRIMINAL ACT. HOWEVER, I ADMIRE THE COMPLEX MODIFICATIONS YOU HAVE OBVIOUSLY MADE TO YOURSELF AND TO THE S.T.A.T.S.
NOW RELEASE THE STUDENTS IMMEDIATELY!
EEEEEAAAAHHHHH!
SHOCKING.
ROSALIND FRANKLIN!

I AM *TWO MINUTES OLDER* THAN YOU AND I *ORDER YOU* TO *STOP BEING EVIL!*

ROSIE, YOU WANT TO BE A DOCTOR! L YOUR POWERS HELP PEOPLE

MY QUEEN. QUIET YOUR BROTHER.

FWOOSH

THUD

MY QUEEN. *KILL* YOUR BROTHER.

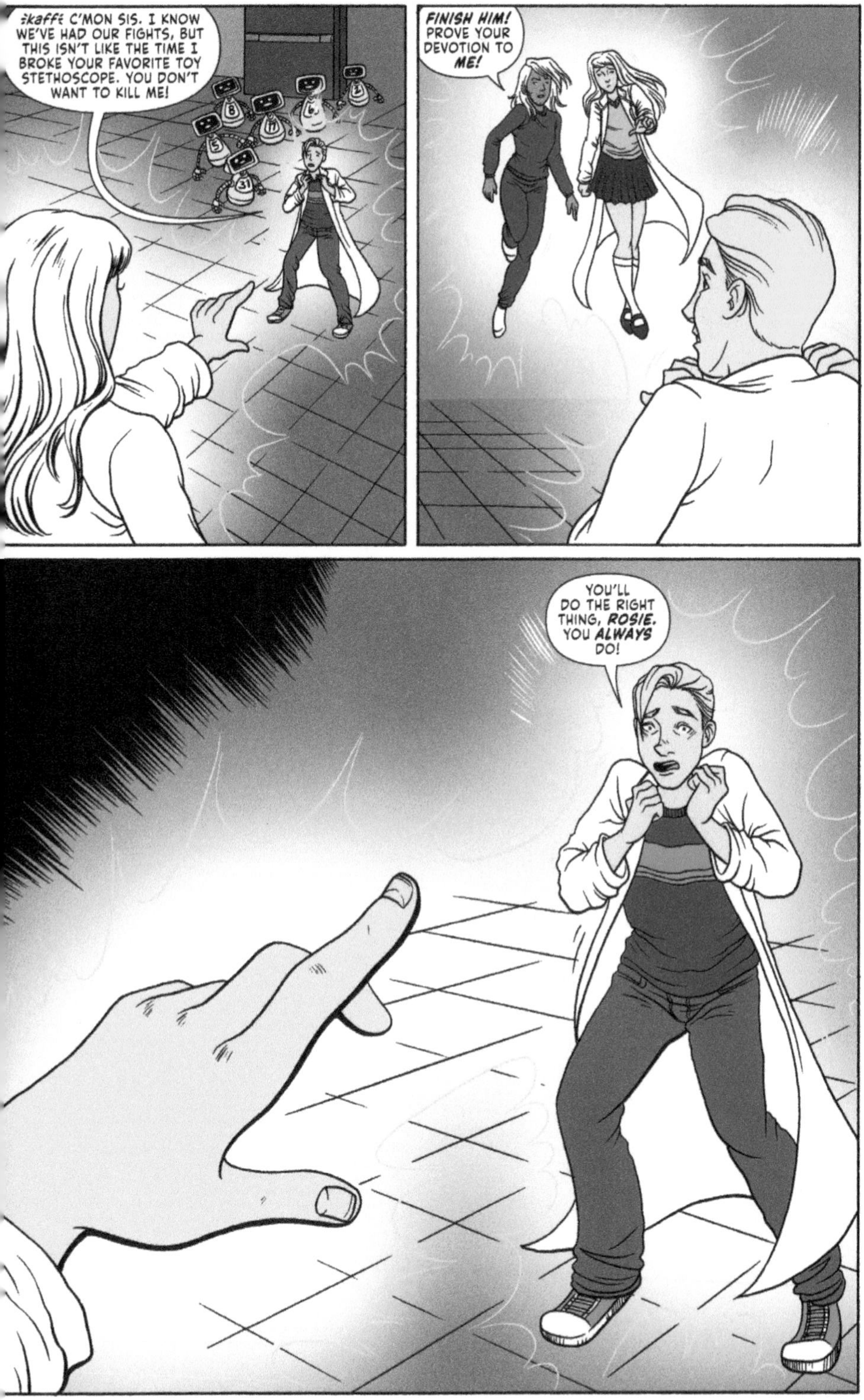

kaff C'MON SIS. I KNOW WE'VE HAD OUR FIGHTS, BUT THIS ISN'T LIKE THE TIME I BROKE YOUR FAVORITE TOY STETHOSCOPE. YOU DON'T WANT TO KILL ME!
FINISH HIM! PROVE YOUR DEVOTION TO ME!
YOU'LL DO THE RIGHT THING, ROSIE. YOU ALWAYS DO!

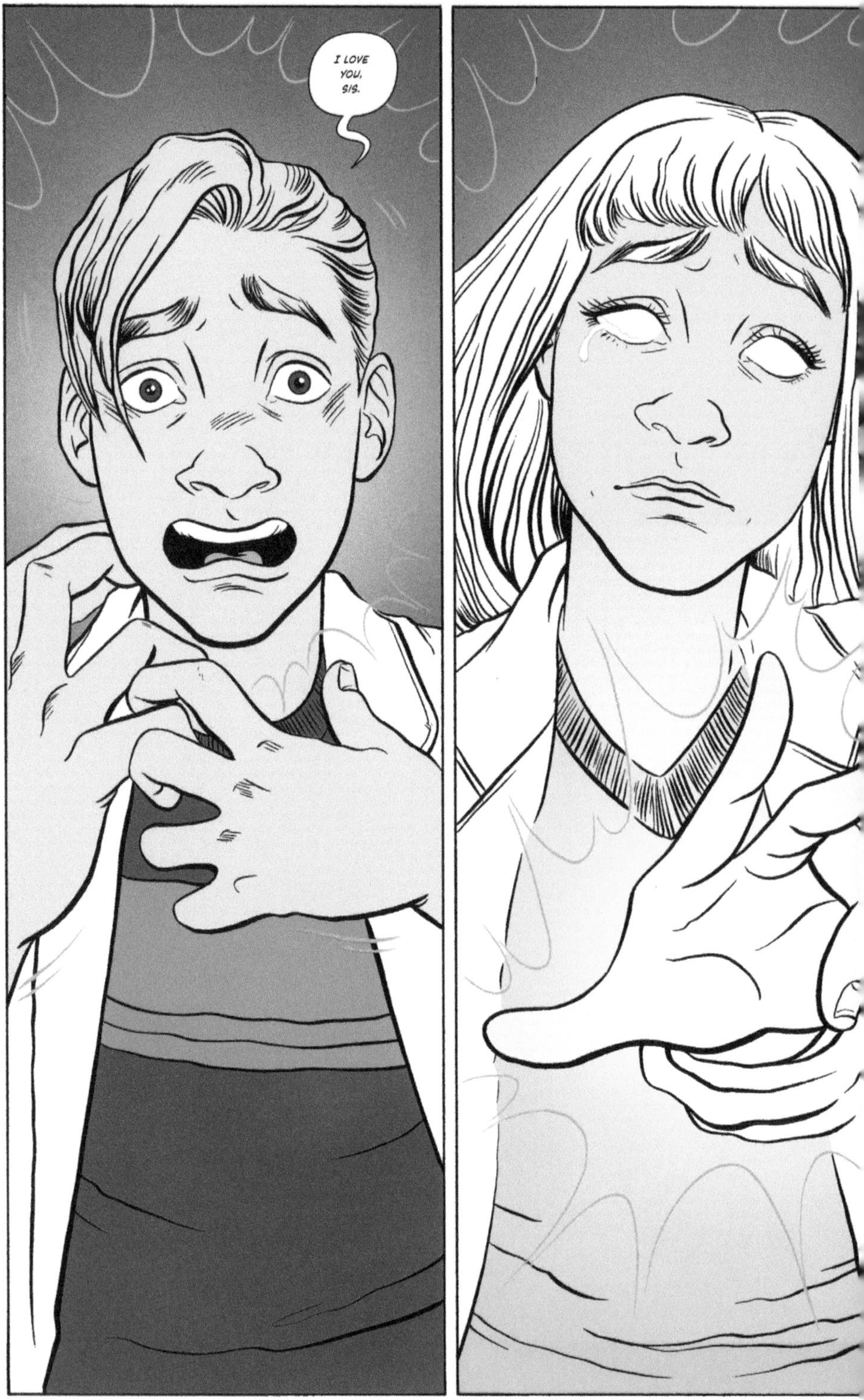
I LOVE YOU, SIS.

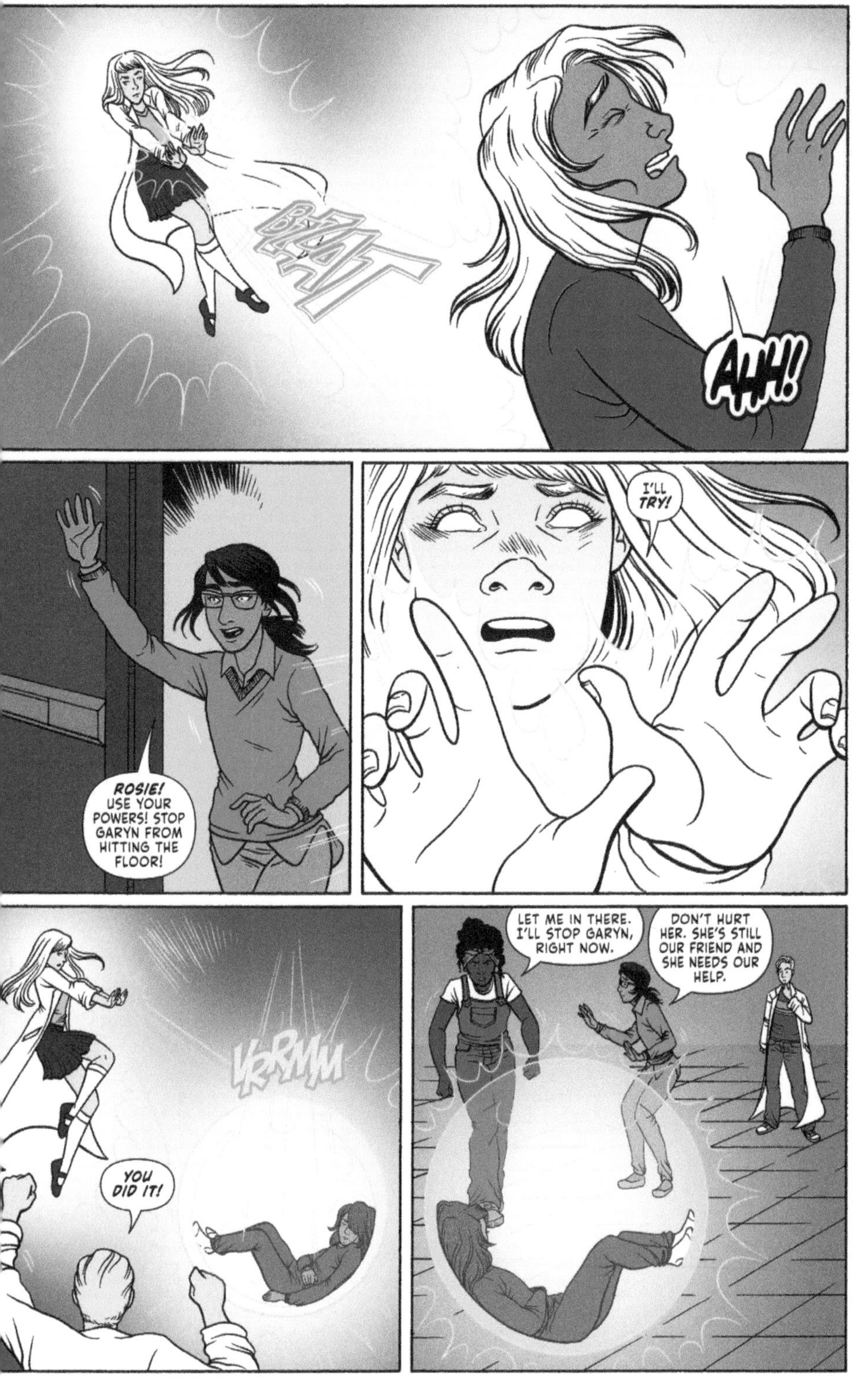
BZAT
AHH!
ROSIE! USE YOUR POWERS! STOP GARYN FROM HITTING THE FLOOR!
I'LL TRY!
VRRMM
YOU DID IT!
LET ME IN THERE. I'LL STOP GARYN, RIGHT NOW.
DON'T HURT HER. SHE'S STILL OUR FRIEND AND SHE NEEDS OUR HELP.

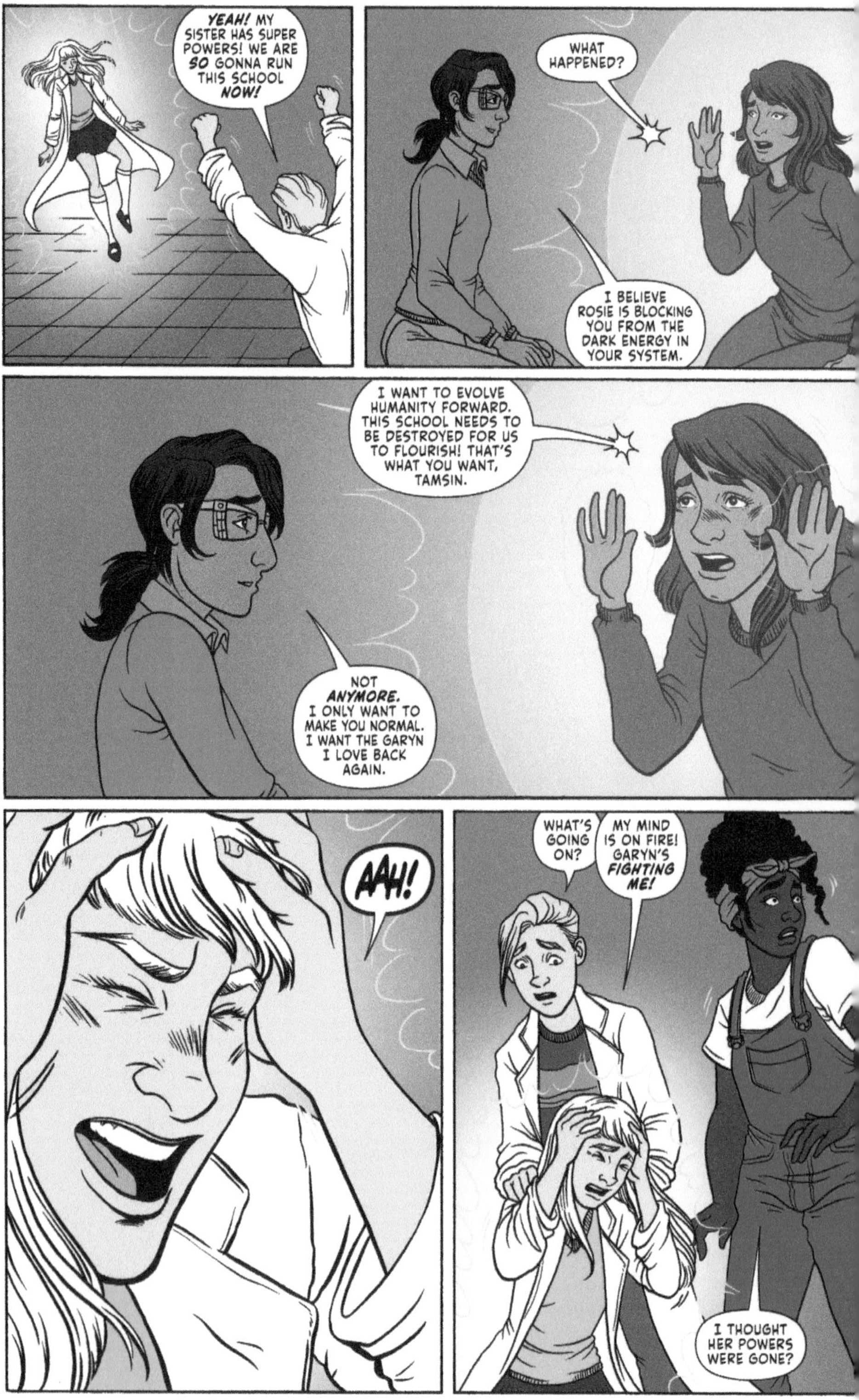
YEAH! MY SISTER HAS SUPER POWERS! WE ARE SO GONNA RUN THIS SCHOOL NOW!
WHAT HAPPENED?
I BELIEVE ROSIE IS BLOCKING YOU FROM THE DARK ENERGY IN YOUR SYSTEM.
I WANT TO EVOLVE HUMANITY FORWARD. THIS SCHOOL NEEDS TO BE DESTROYED FOR US TO FLOURISH! THAT'S WHAT YOU WANT, TAMSIN.
NOT ANYMORE. I ONLY WANT TO MAKE YOU NORMAL. I WANT THE GARYN I LOVE BACK AGAIN.
AAH!
WHAT'S GOING ON?
MY MIND IS ON FIRE! GARYN'S FIGHTING ME!
I THOUGHT HER POWERS WERE GONE?

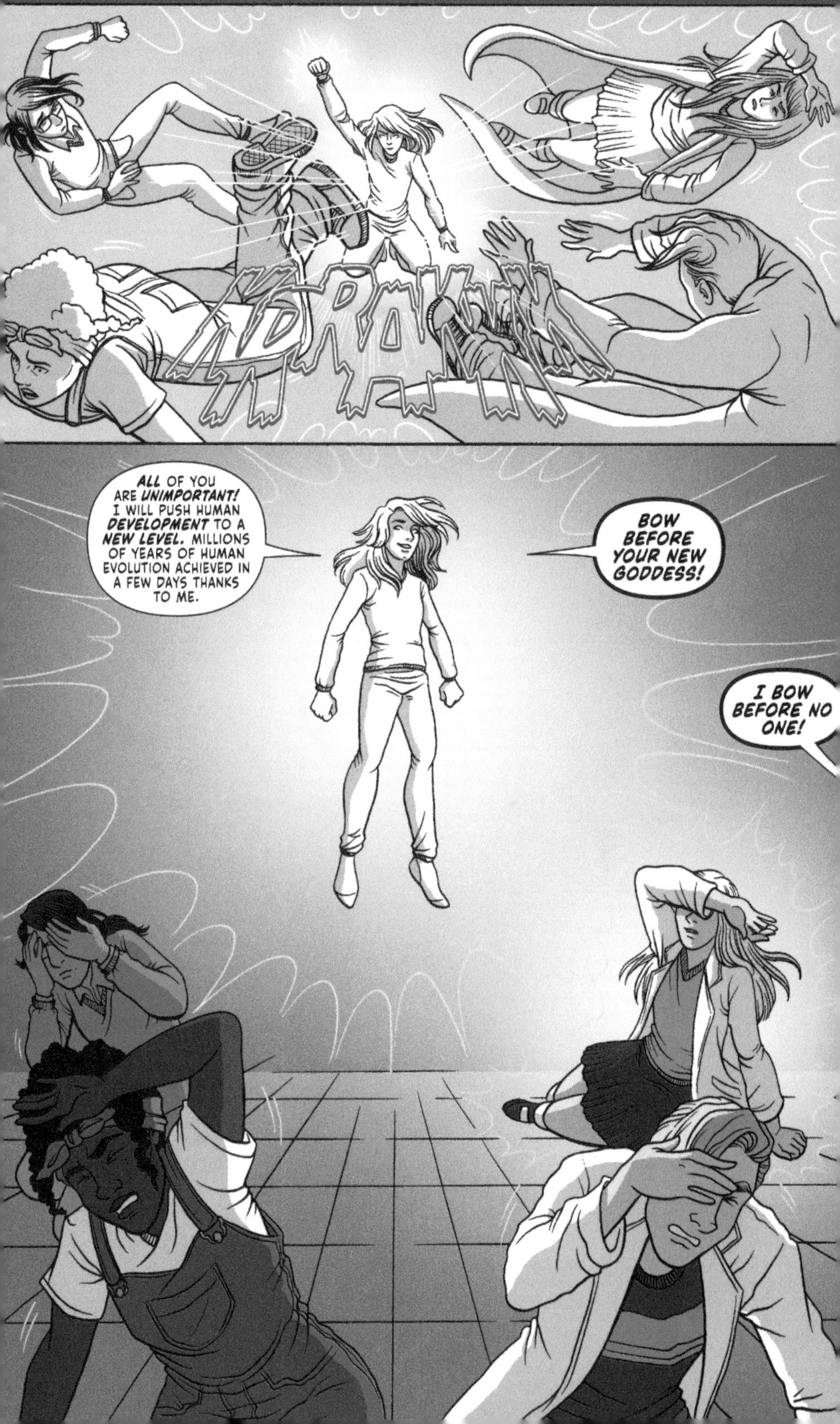

KRAKOOM
ALL OF YOU ARE UNIMPORTANT! I WILL PUSH HUMAN DEVELOPMENT TO A NEW LEVEL. MILLIONS OF YEARS OF HUMAN EVOLUTION ACHIEVED IN A FEW DAYS THANKS TO ME.
BOW BEFORE YOUR NEW GODDESS!
I BOW BEFORE NO ONE!

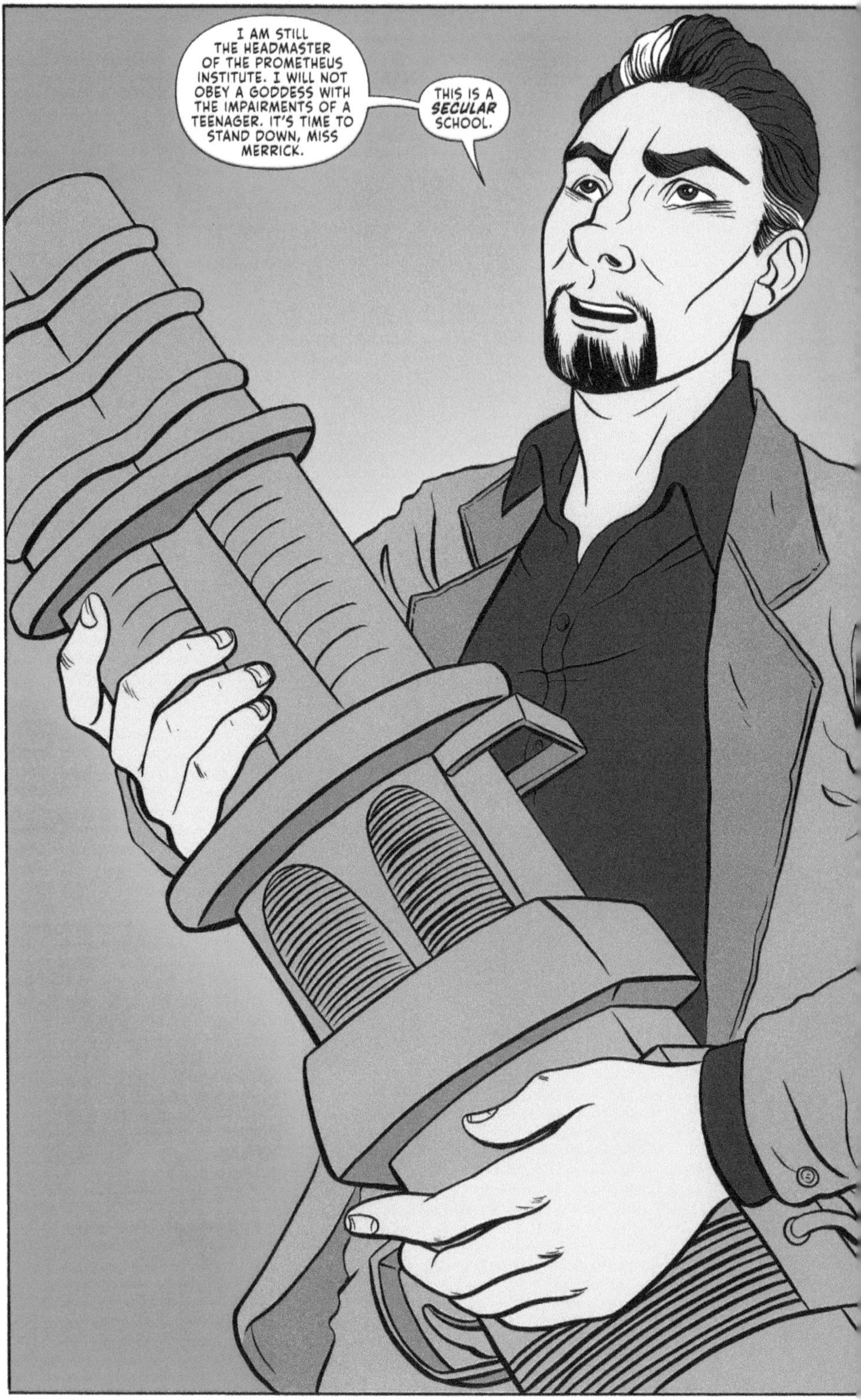
I AM STILL THE HEADMASTER OF THE PROMETHEUS INSTITUTE. I WILL NOT OBEY A GODDESS WITH THE IMPAIRMENTS OF A TEENAGER. IT'S TIME TO STAND DOWN, MISS MERRICK.
THIS IS A *SECULAR* SCHOOL.

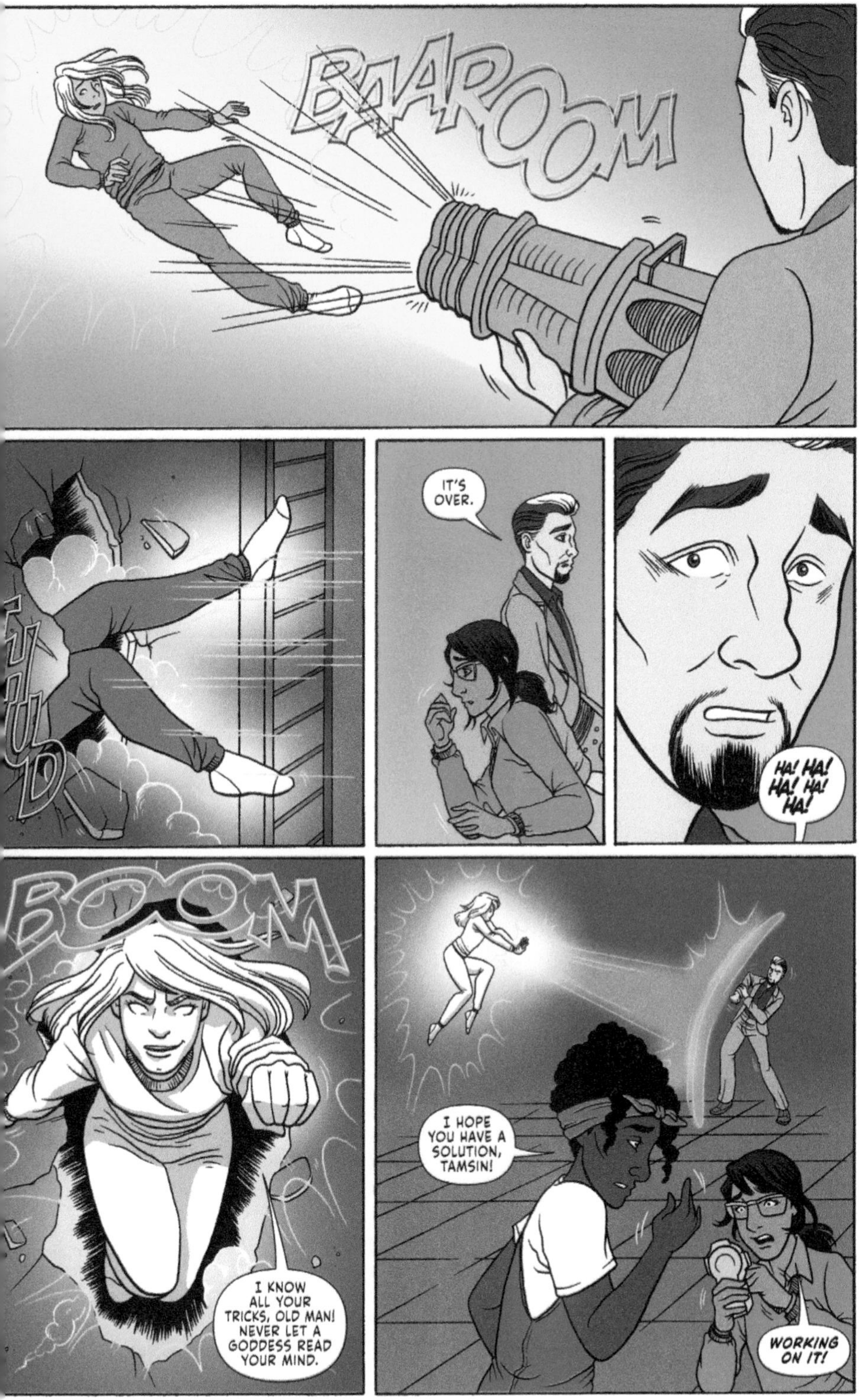
BAAROOM
IT'S OVER.
HA! HA! HA! HA! HA!
BOOM
I KNOW ALL YOUR TRICKS, OLD MAN! NEVER LET A GODDESS READ YOUR MIND.
I HOPE YOU HAVE A SOLUTION, TAMSIN!
WORKING ON IT!

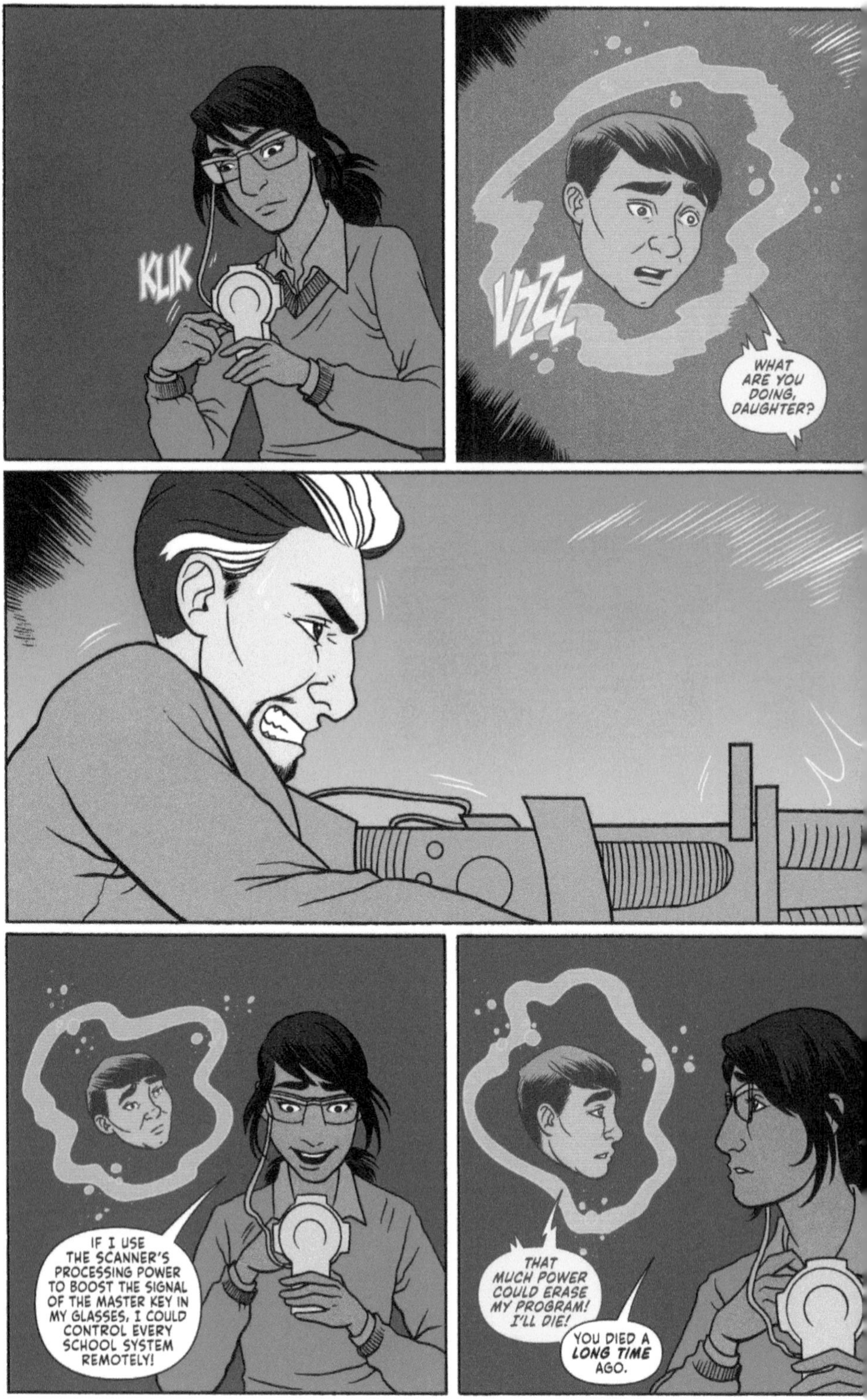
KLIK
VZZZ
WHAT ARE YOU DOING, DAUGHTER?
IF I USE THE SCANNER'S PROCESSING POWER TO BOOST THE SIGNAL OF THE MASTER KEY IN MY GLASSES, I COULD CONTROL EVERY SCHOOL SYSTEM REMOTELY!
THAT MUCH POWER COULD ERASE MY PROGRAM! I'LL DIE!
YOU DIED A LONG TIME AGO.

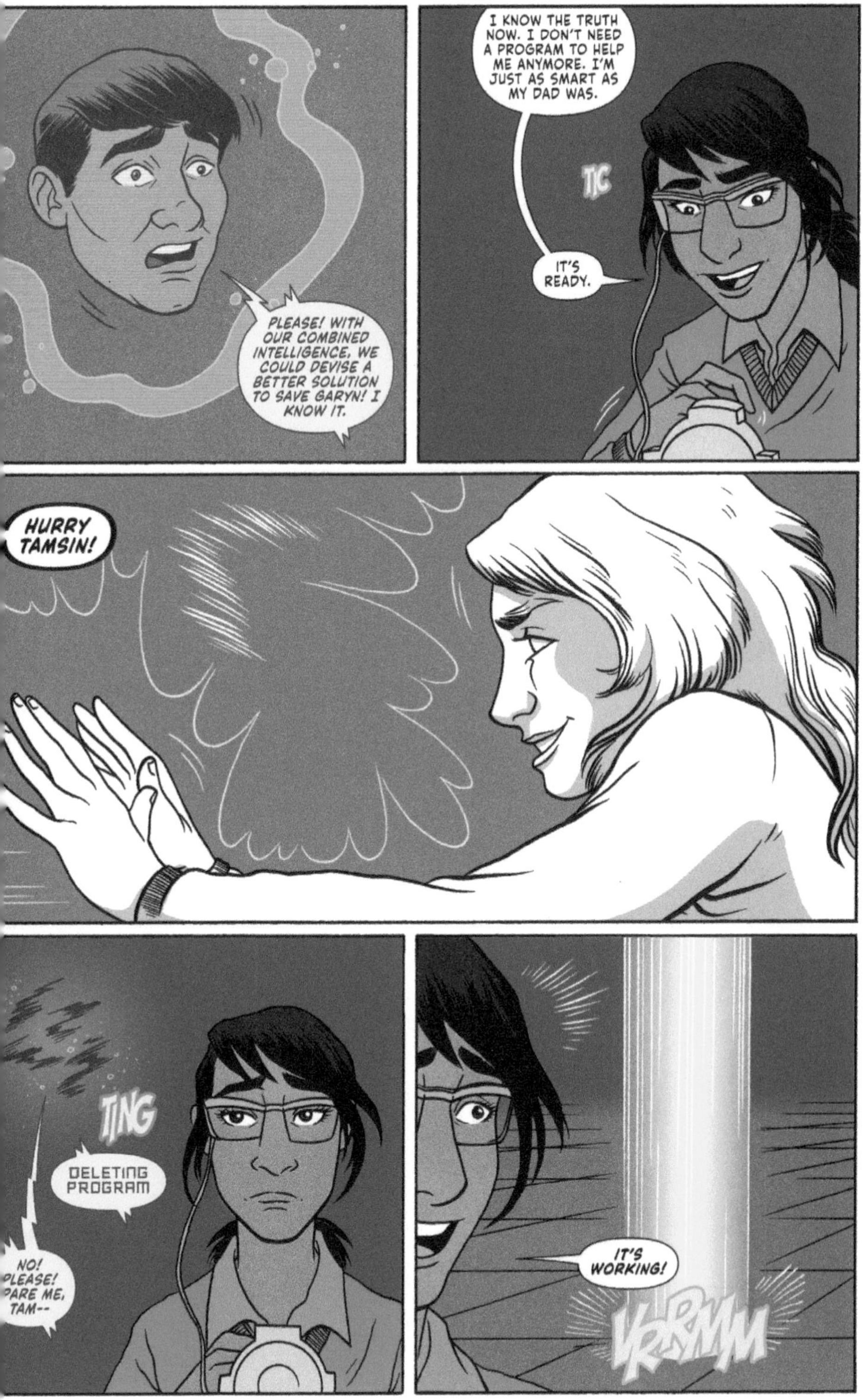
PLEASE! WITH OUR COMBINED INTELLIGENCE, WE COULD DEVISE A BETTER SOLUTION TO SAVE GARYN! I KNOW IT.
I KNOW THE TRUTH NOW. I DON'T NEED A PROGRAM TO HELP ME ANYMORE. I'M JUST AS SMART AS MY DAD WAS.
TIC
IT'S READY.
HURRY TAMSIN!
TING
DELETING PROGRAM
NO! PLEASE! PARE ME, TAM--
IT'S WORKING!
VRRMM

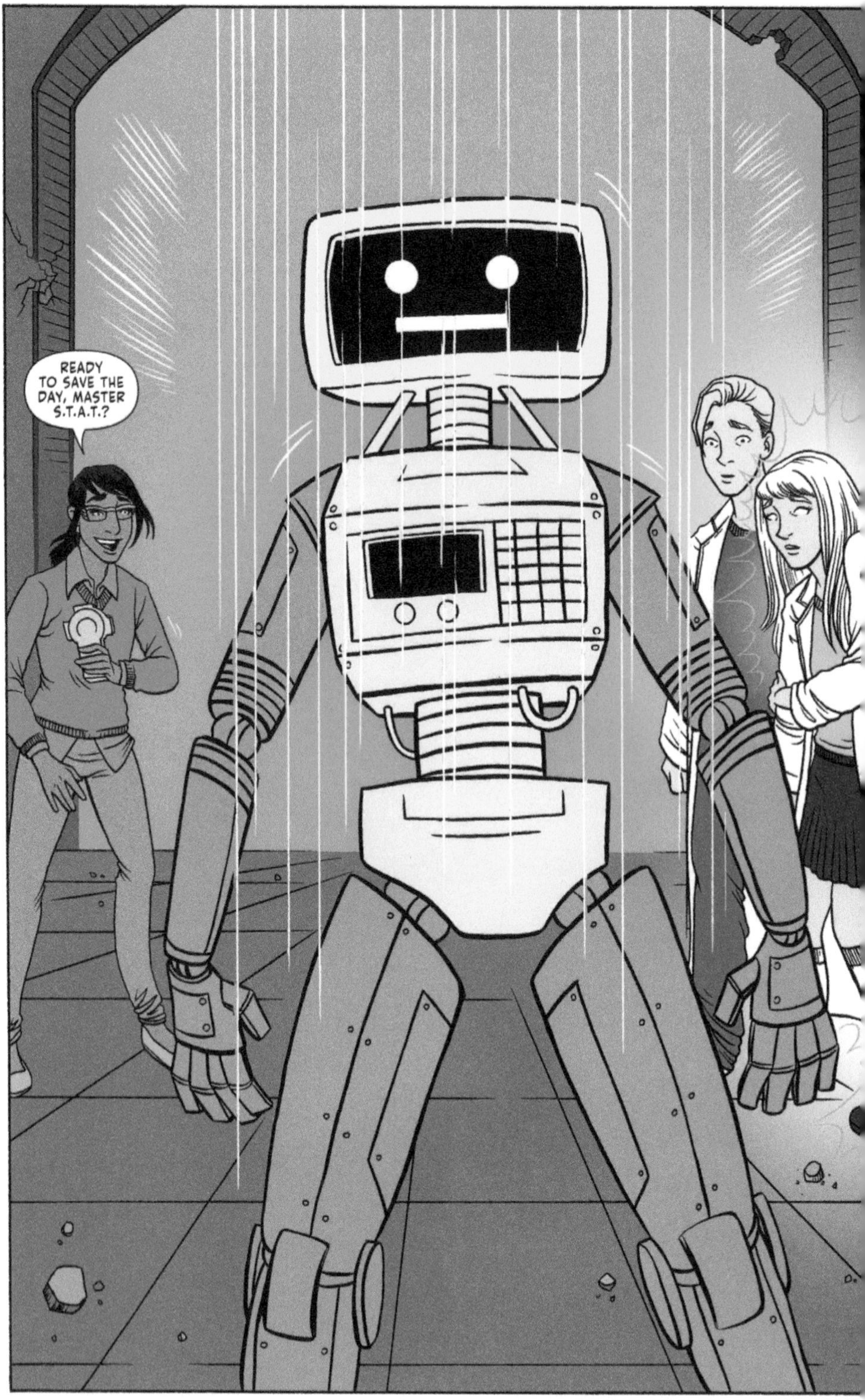
READY TO SAVE THE DAY, MASTER S.T.A.T.?

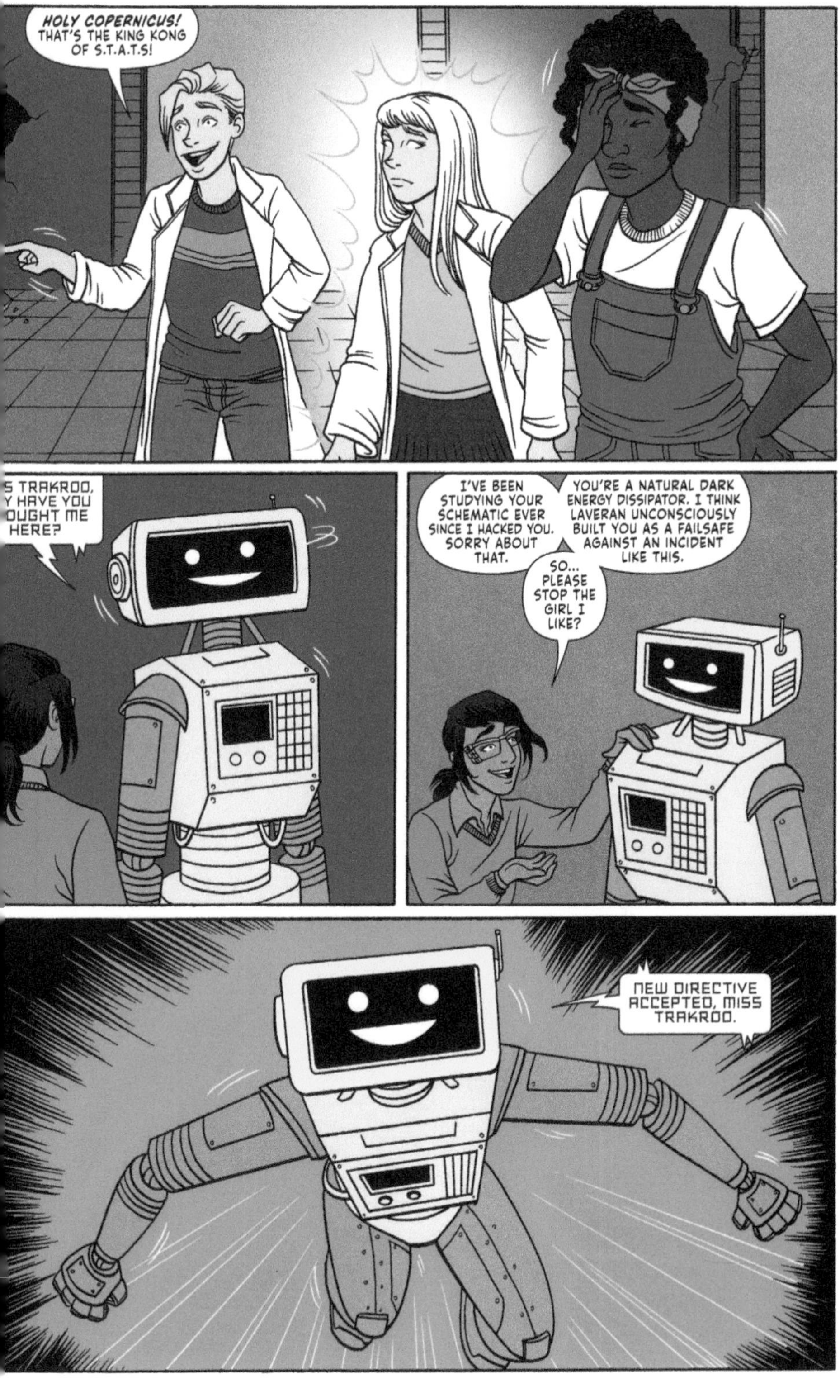
HOLY COPERNICUS! THAT'S THE KING KONG OF S.T.A.T.S!
S TRAKROO, Y HAVE YOU OUGHT ME HERE?
I'VE BEEN STUDYING YOUR SCHEMATIC EVER SINCE I HACKED YOU. SORRY ABOUT THAT.
YOU'RE A NATURAL DARK ENERGY DISSIPATOR. I THINK LAVERAN UNCONSCIOUSLY BUILT YOU AS A FAILSAFE AGAINST AN INCIDENT LIKE THIS.
SO... PLEASE STOP THE GIRL I LIKE?
NEW DIRECTIVE ACCEPTED, MISS TRAKROO.

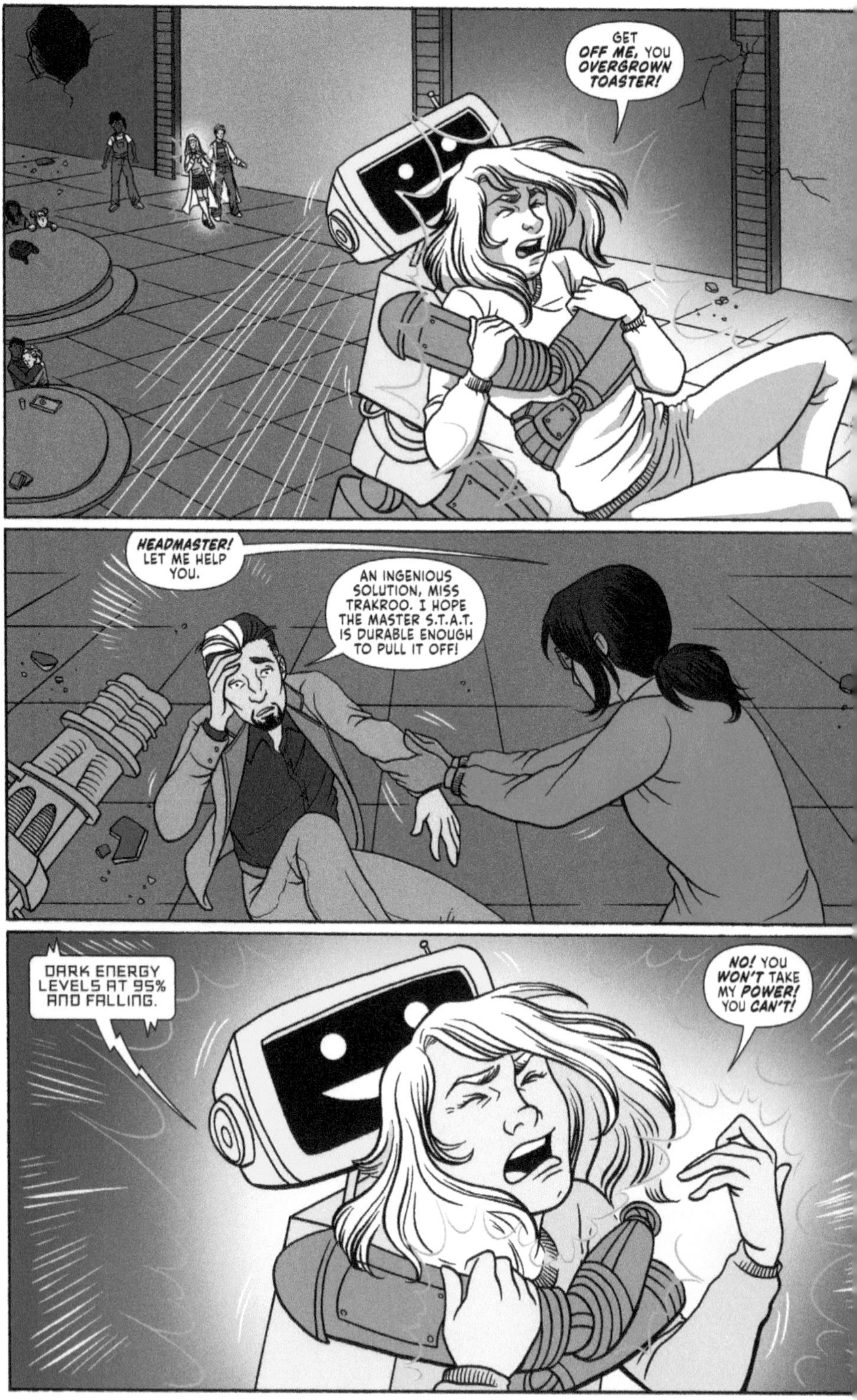
GET OFF ME, YOU OVERGROWN TOASTER!
HEADMASTER! LET ME HELP YOU.
AN INGENIOUS SOLUTION, MISS TRAKROO. I HOPE THE MASTER S.T.A.T. IS DURABLE ENOUGH TO PULL IT OFF!
DARK ENERGY LEVELS AT 95% AND FALLING.
NO! YOU WON'T TAKE MY POWER! YOU CAN'T!

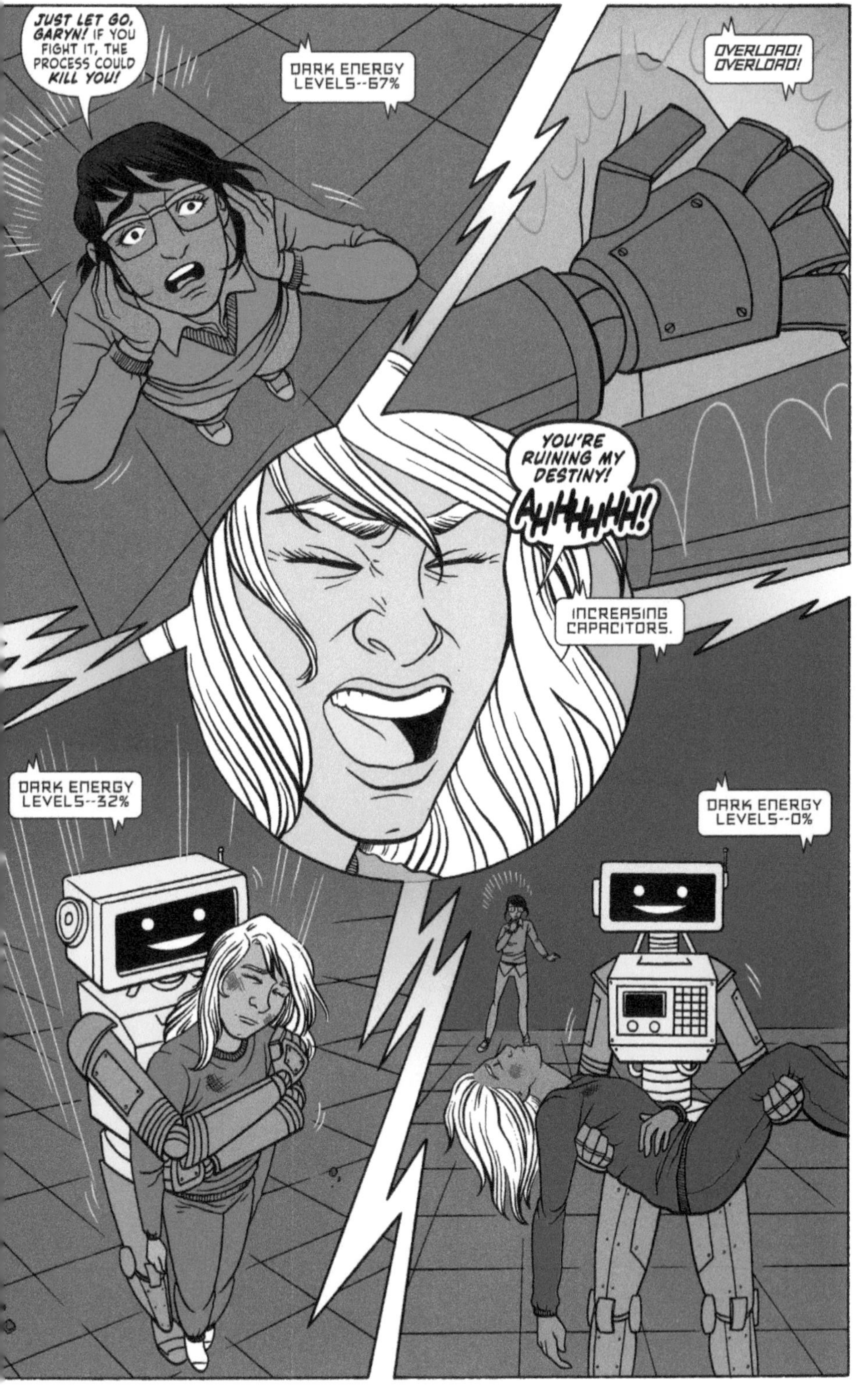
JUST LET GO, GARYN! IF YOU FIGHT IT, THE PROCESS COULD KILL YOU!
DARK ENERGY LEVELS--67%
OVERLOAD! OVERLOAD!
YOU'RE RUINING MY DESTINY!
AHHHHHH!
INCREASING CAPACITORS.
DARK ENERGY LEVELS--32%
DARK ENERGY LEVELS--0%

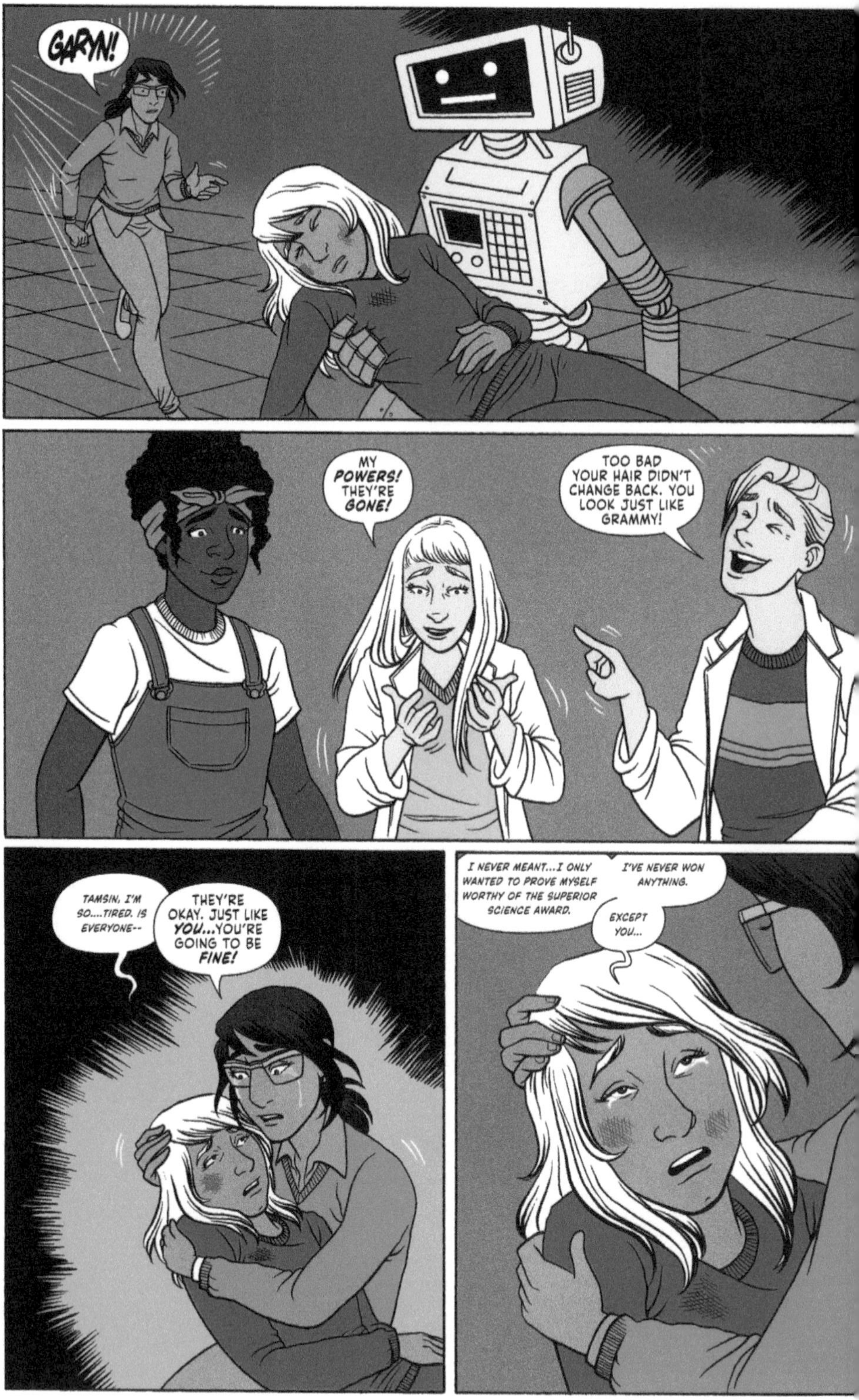
GARYN!
MY POWERS! THEY'RE GONE!
TOO BAD YOUR HAIR DIDN'T CHANGE BACK. YOU LOOK JUST LIKE GRAMMY!
TAMSIN, I'M SO....TIRED. IS EVERYONE--
THEY'RE OKAY. JUST LIKE YOU...YOU'RE GOING TO BE FINE!
I NEVER MEANT...I ONLY WANTED TO PROVE MYSELF WORTHY OF THE SUPERIOR SCIENCE AWARD.
I'VE NEVER WON ANYTHING.
EXCEPT YOU...

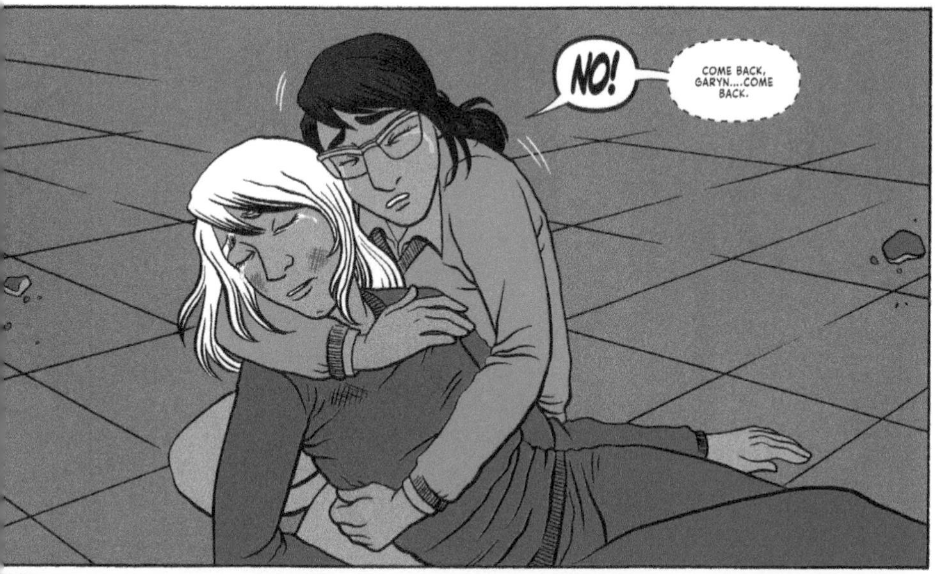
NO!
COME BACK, GARYN....COME BACK.

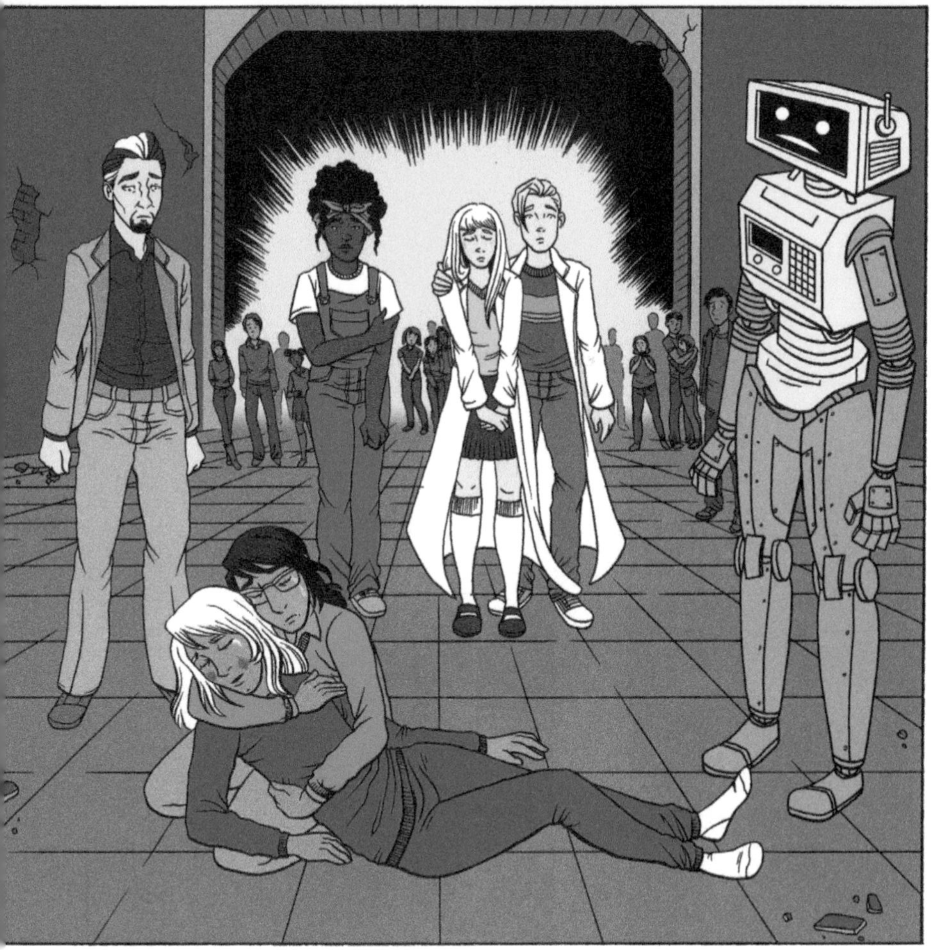

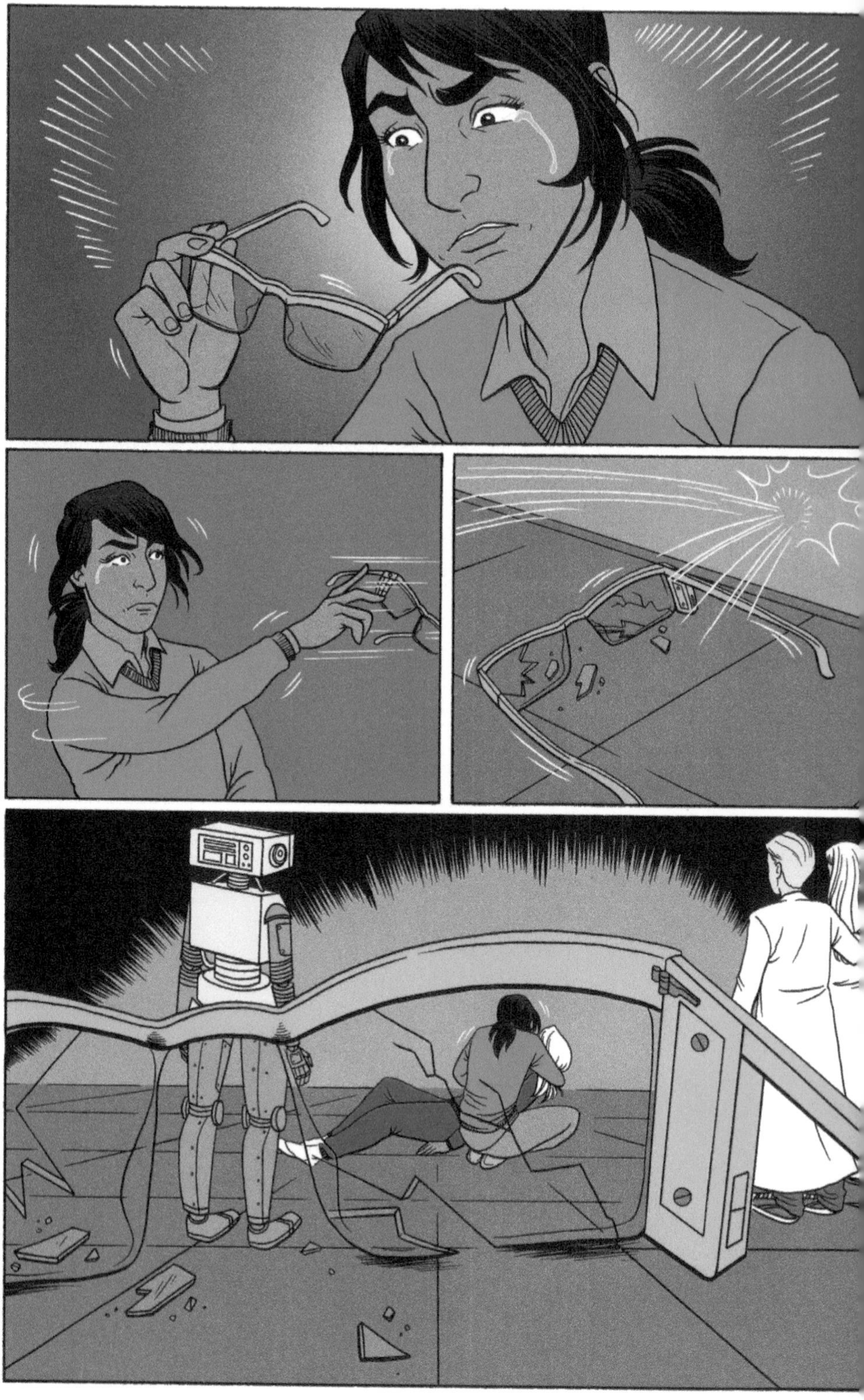

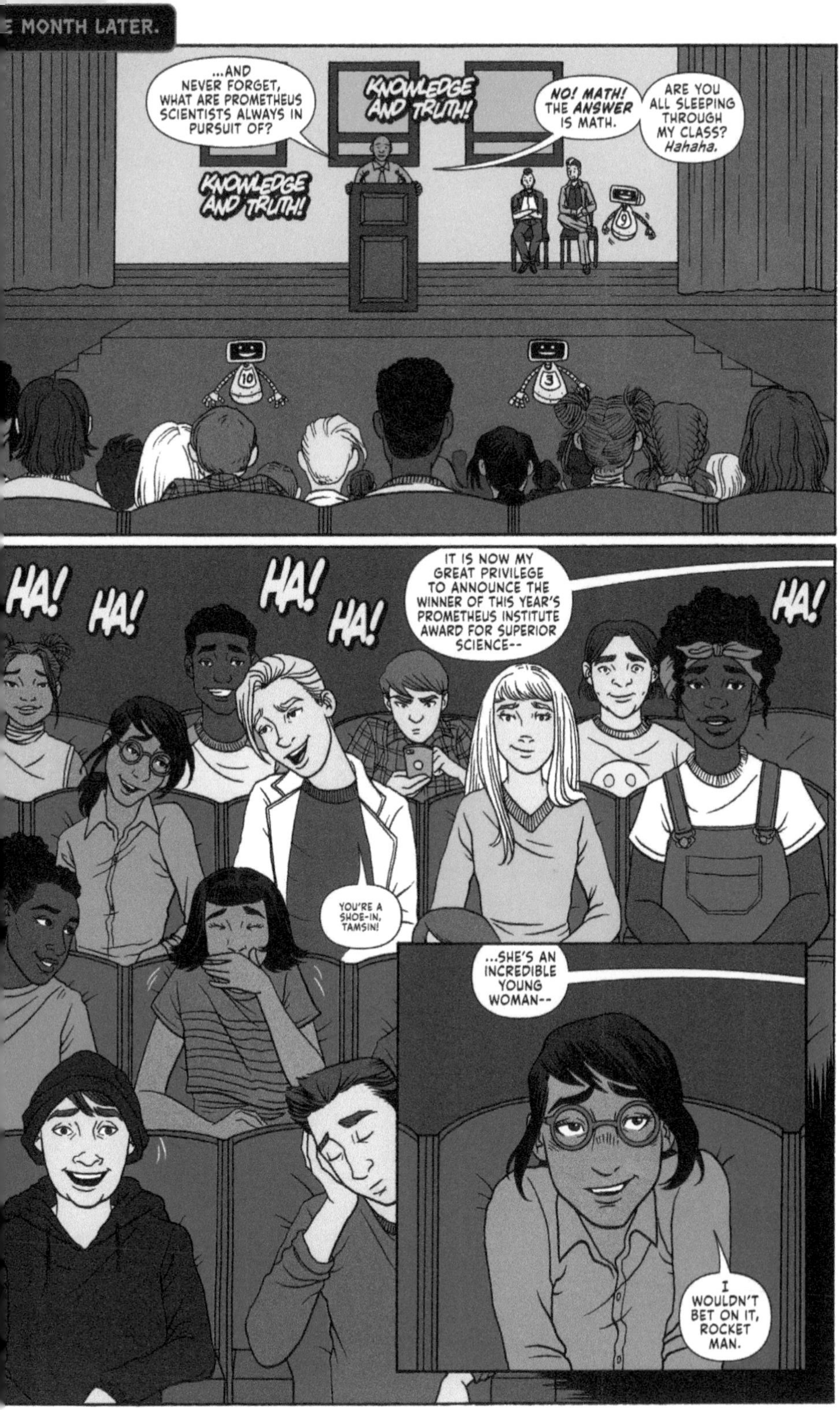
E MONTH LATER.
...AND NEVER FORGET, WHAT ARE PROMETHEUS SCIENTISTS ALWAYS IN PURSUIT OF?
KNOWLEDGE AND TRUTH!
KNOWLEDGE AND TRUTH!
NO! MATH! THE ANSWER IS MATH.
ARE YOU ALL SLEEPING THROUGH MY CLASS? Hahaha.
HA! HA! HA! HA! HA!
IT IS NOW MY GREAT PRIVILEGE TO ANNOUNCE THE WINNER OF THIS YEAR'S PROMETHEUS INSTITUTE AWARD FOR SUPERIOR SCIENCE--
YOU'RE A SHOE-IN, TAMSIN!
...SHE'S AN INCREDIBLE YOUNG WOMAN--
I WOULDN'T BET ON IT, ROCKET MAN.

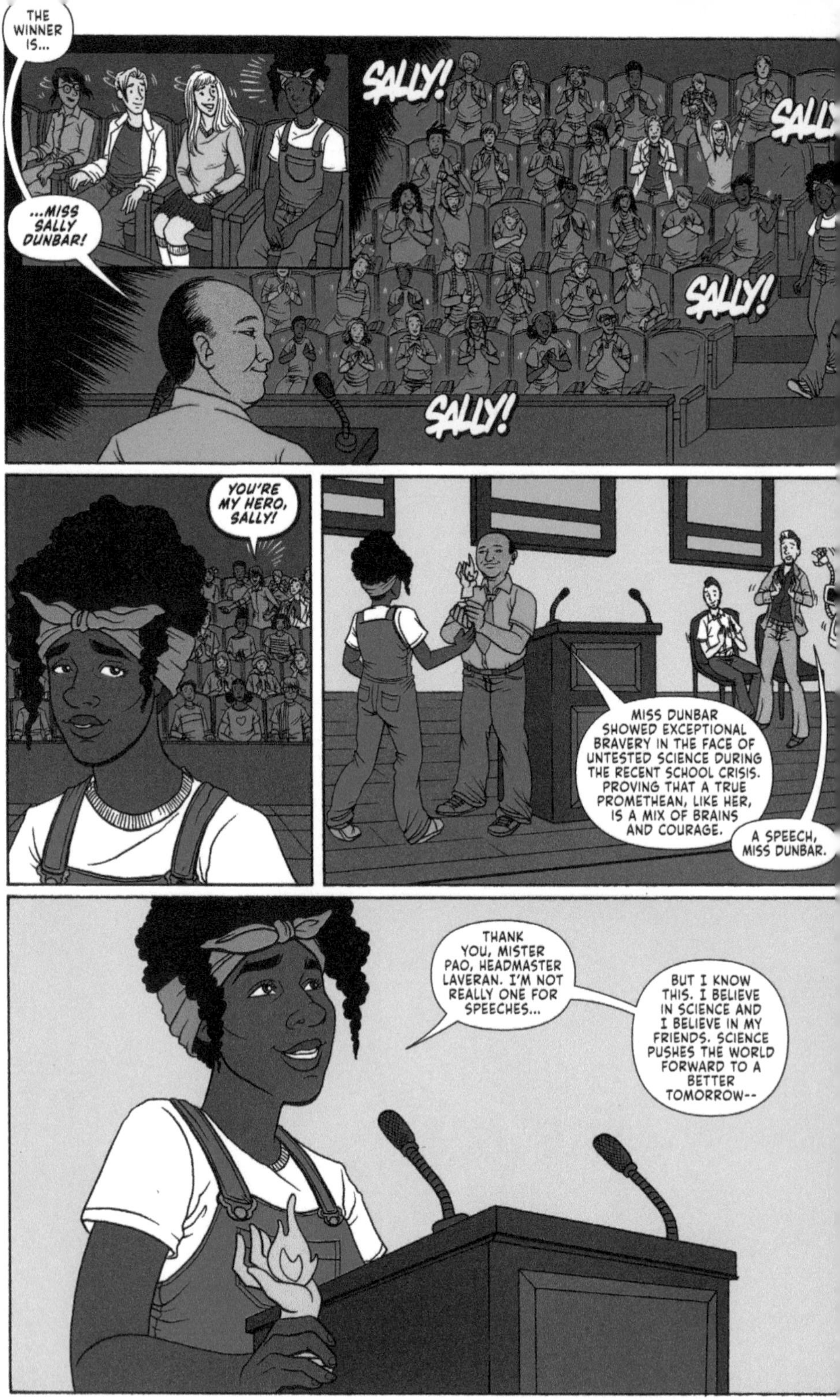
THE WINNER IS...
...MISS SALLY DUNBAR!
SALLY!
SALLY!
SALLY!
SALLY!
YOU'RE MY HERO, SALLY!
MISS DUNBAR SHOWED EXCEPTIONAL BRAVERY IN THE FACE OF UNTESTED SCIENCE DURING THE RECENT SCHOOL CRISIS. PROVING THAT A TRUE PROMETHEAN, LIKE HER, IS A MIX OF BRAINS AND COURAGE.
A SPEECH, MISS DUNBAR.
THANK YOU, MISTER PAO, HEADMASTER LAVERAN. I'M NOT REALLY ONE FOR SPEECHES...
BUT I KNOW THIS. I BELIEVE IN SCIENCE AND I BELIEVE IN MY FRIENDS. SCIENCE PUSHES THE WORLD FORWARD TO A BETTER TOMORROW--

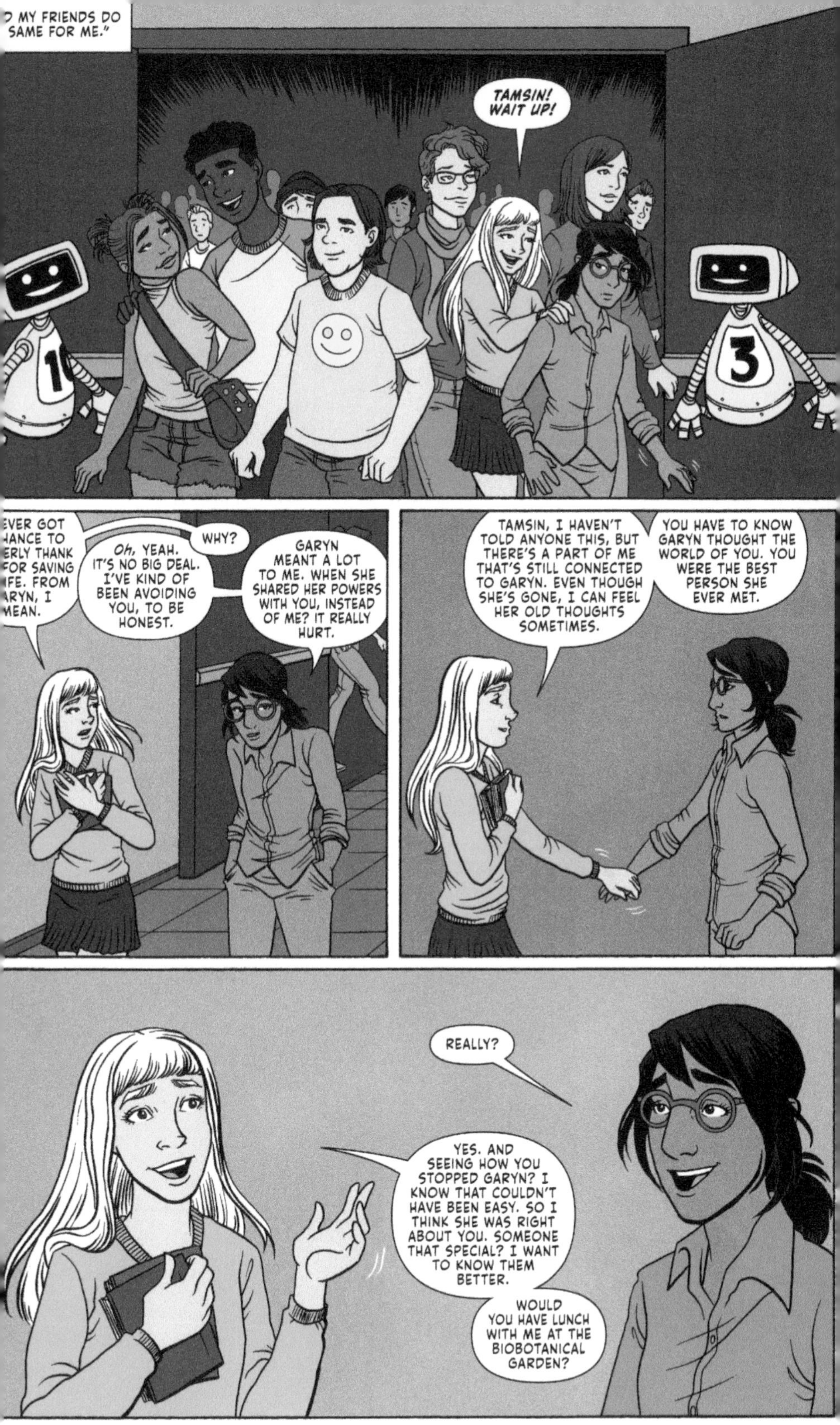

D MY FRIENDS DO SAME FOR ME."
TAMSIN! WAIT UP!
EVER GOT HANCE TO ERLY THANK FOR SAVING IFE. FROM ARYN, I MEAN.
WHY?
Oh, YEAH. IT'S NO BIG DEAL. I'VE KIND OF BEEN AVOIDING YOU, TO BE HONEST.
GARYN MEANT A LOT TO ME. WHEN SHE SHARED HER POWERS WITH YOU, INSTEAD OF ME? IT REALLY HURT.
TAMSIN, I HAVEN'T TOLD ANYONE THIS, BUT THERE'S A PART OF ME THAT'S STILL CONNECTED TO GARYN. EVEN THOUGH SHE'S GONE, I CAN FEEL HER OLD THOUGHTS SOMETIMES.
YOU HAVE TO KNOW GARYN THOUGHT THE WORLD OF YOU. YOU WERE THE BEST PERSON SHE EVER MET.
REALLY?
YES. AND SEEING HOW YOU STOPPED GARYN? I KNOW THAT COULDN'T HAVE BEEN EASY. SO I THINK SHE WAS RIGHT ABOUT YOU. SOMEONE THAT SPECIAL? I WANT TO KNOW THEM BETTER.
WOULD YOU HAVE LUNCH WITH ME AT THE BIOBOTANICAL GARDEN?

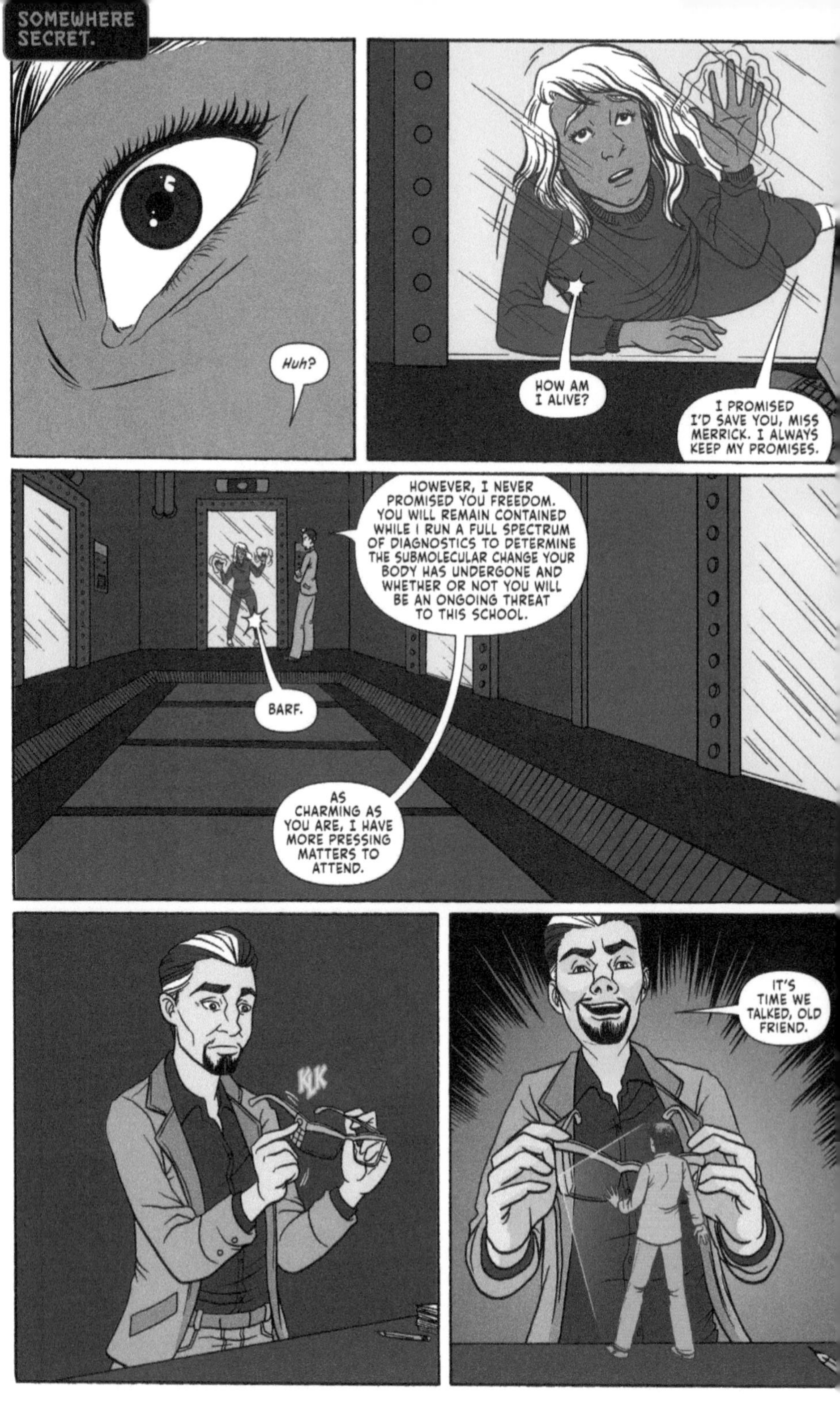
SOMEWHERE SECRET.
Huh?
HOW AM I ALIVE?
I PROMISED I'D SAVE YOU, MISS MERRICK. I ALWAYS KEEP MY PROMISES.
HOWEVER, I NEVER PROMISED YOU FREEDOM. YOU WILL REMAIN CONTAINED WHILE I RUN A FULL SPECTRUM OF DIAGNOSTICS TO DETERMINE THE SUBMOLECULAR CHANGE YOUR BODY HAS UNDERGONE AND WHETHER OR NOT YOU WILL BE AN ONGOING THREAT TO THIS SCHOOL.
BARF.
AS CHARMING AS YOU ARE, I HAVE MORE PRESSING MATTERS TO ATTEND.
KLIK
IT'S TIME WE TALKED, OLD FRIEND.

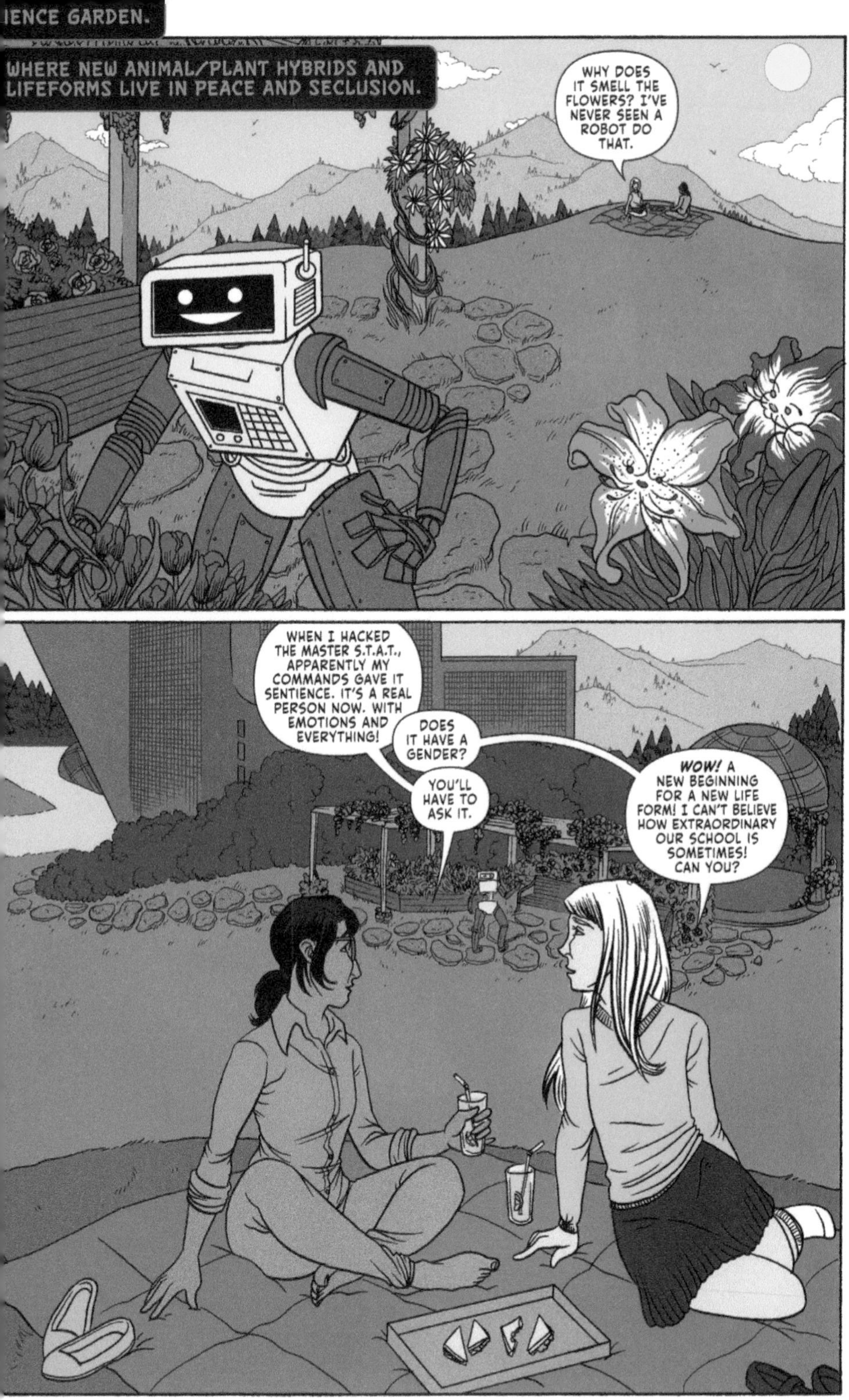
IENCE GARDEN.
WHERE NEW ANIMAL/PLANT HYBRIDS AND LIFEFORMS LIVE IN PEACE AND SECLUSION.
WHY DOES IT SMELL THE FLOWERS? I'VE NEVER SEEN A ROBOT DO THAT.
WHEN I HACKED THE MASTER S.T.A.T., APPARENTLY MY COMMANDS GAVE IT SENTIENCE. IT'S A REAL PERSON NOW. WITH EMOTIONS AND EVERYTHING!
DOES IT HAVE A GENDER?
YOU'LL HAVE TO ASK IT.
WOW! A NEW BEGINNING FOR A NEW LIFE FORM! I CAN'T BELIEVE HOW EXTRAORDINARY OUR SCHOOL IS SOMETIMES! CAN YOU?

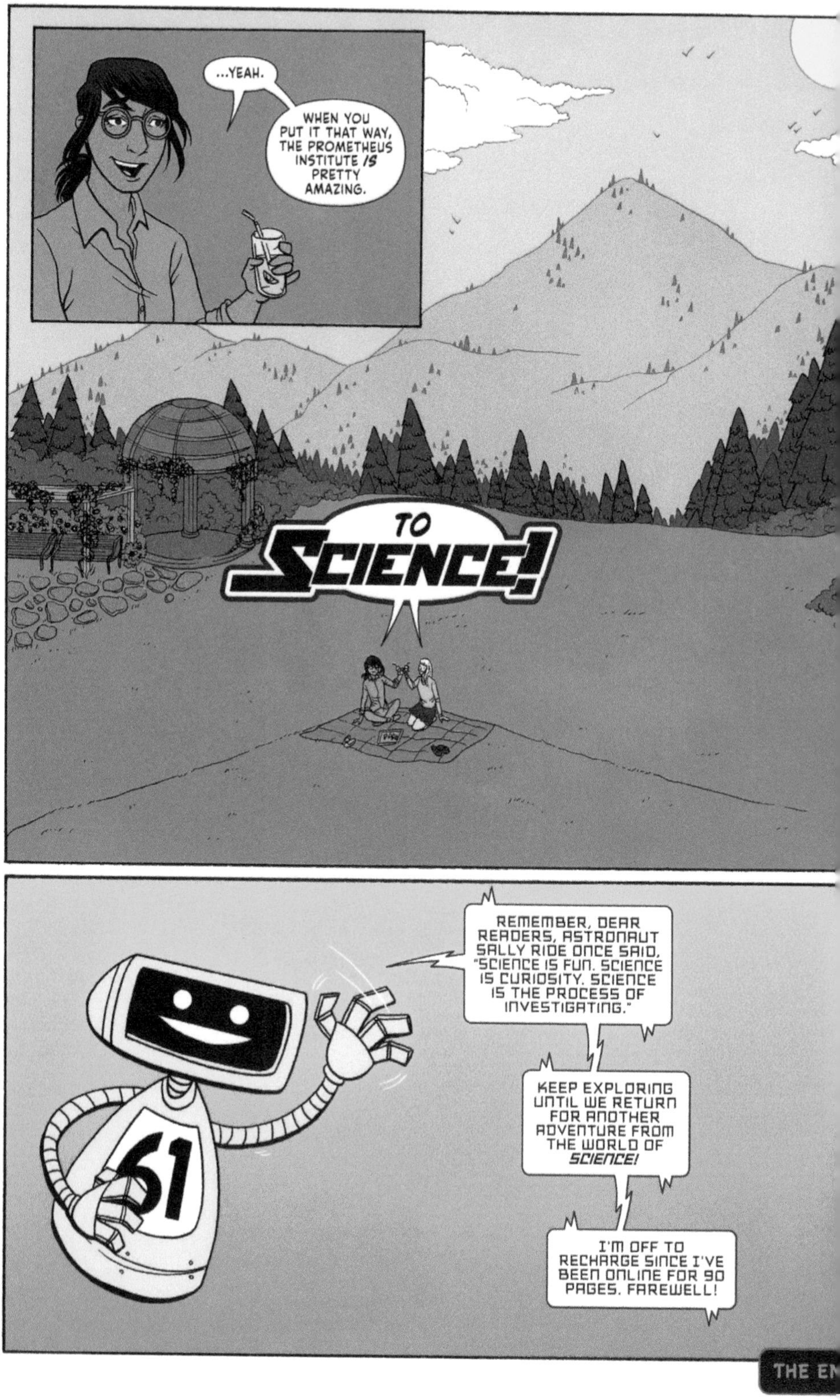
...YEAH.
WHEN YOU PUT IT THAT WAY, THE PROMETHEUS INSTITUTE *IS* PRETTY AMAZING.
TO SCIENCE!
REMEMBER, DEAR READERS, ASTRONAUT SALLY RIDE ONCE SAID, "SCIENCE IS FUN. SCIENCE IS CURIOSITY. SCIENCE IS THE PROCESS OF INVESTIGATING."
KEEP EXPLORING UNTIL WE RETURN FOR ANOTHER ADVENTURE FROM THE WORLD OF *SCIENCE!*
I'M OFF TO RECHARGE SINCE I'VE BEEN ONLINE FOR 90 PAGES. FAREWELL!
61

BEHIND THE SCENES!

Let's talk about

SCIENCE!

THE ELEMENTS
OF DARK ENERGY

Page 9

PANEL 1

A shot out of a horror movie, from the point of view of the door. Tamsin and Thomas are turned towards the noise and looking over their shoulders in fear. Off camera, the door has been slammed open.

1. **SFX (DOOR OPENING):** WHUMP!

2. **SALLY (OFF PANEL):** Tamsin, what is going on!?

3. **THOMAS:** Quick! Put me back inside your glasses!

PANEL 2 (INSERT INTO PANEL 1)

Very much like Page 6, Panel 6 an extreme close on Tamsin's temple as she pushes the switch to turn off her father's hologram.

1. **SFX (BUTTON PRESS):** BZZ

PANEL 3

Medium shot of Tamsin turning to face SALLY DUNBAR (15 – African-American, Queen Latifah at 15, wears overalls, sweet, tough, good at chess, loves LEGO and models, Mechanical Engineer). Sally's mouth hangs open in shock, but happy shocked, she thinks what she saw is so cool!

This is Sally's introduction so the focus should definitely be on her.

1. CAPTION: Sarah "Sally" Dunbar. Mechanical Engineer. Science Builder.

2. TAMSIN (OFF PANEL): Sally, I can explain –

3. SALLY: That looked rad! Why didn't you tell me this was your project for the award? I love holograms!

PANEL 4

Tight on Tamsin and beside her face is Thomas' floating head. This is an important panel because it's going to introduce an idea that will continue for the rest of the book so his head should be pink now. The same pink as her glasses. This will introduce the idea that only she can hear him. When Thomas is locked away in Tamsin's glasses he can still see, experience, and comment on everything that is going on. In moments like this he is going to appear as a floating holographic head beside Tamsin (think Firestorm: https://vignette.wikia.nocookie.net/justice-league-action/images/5/5c/Ron.jpg/revision/latest?cb=20170302045104). His head is cocked toward Tamsin, so he looks as if he is literally whispering in her ear. When he's a holograph head, he will be tinted pink like her glasses.

Tamsin has a sheepish expression on her face, one arm across her body clutching the other arm in a classic awkward posture.

1. THOMAS: Yes, Tamsin. Run with this. Convince her that she's stumbled onto nothing. No conspiracy here.

2. TAMSIN: Yeah, it's for my project, I'm not even sure if this is the one I'm going to enter.

3. SALLY (OFF PANEL): You don't have to be modest! Here, I got something to boost your confidence...'

PANEL 5

Sally has her arms out, holding a present for Tamsin. It's a mini-Tamsin, made out of Legos. Sally's blushing just a little bit. Tamsin smiles. She's surprised by this gift.

1. **SALLY:** It's a mini-Tamsin! I know you're newish here so if you ever feel lonely, you now have two best friends. Mini-Tamsin and yours truly!

2. **TAMSIN:** Thanks, Sally!

3. **SALLY:** Don't think this gets you out of a hologram talk with me, missy! You have got to show me how you made that!

Page 9 script by Ashley V. Robinson & Jason Inman

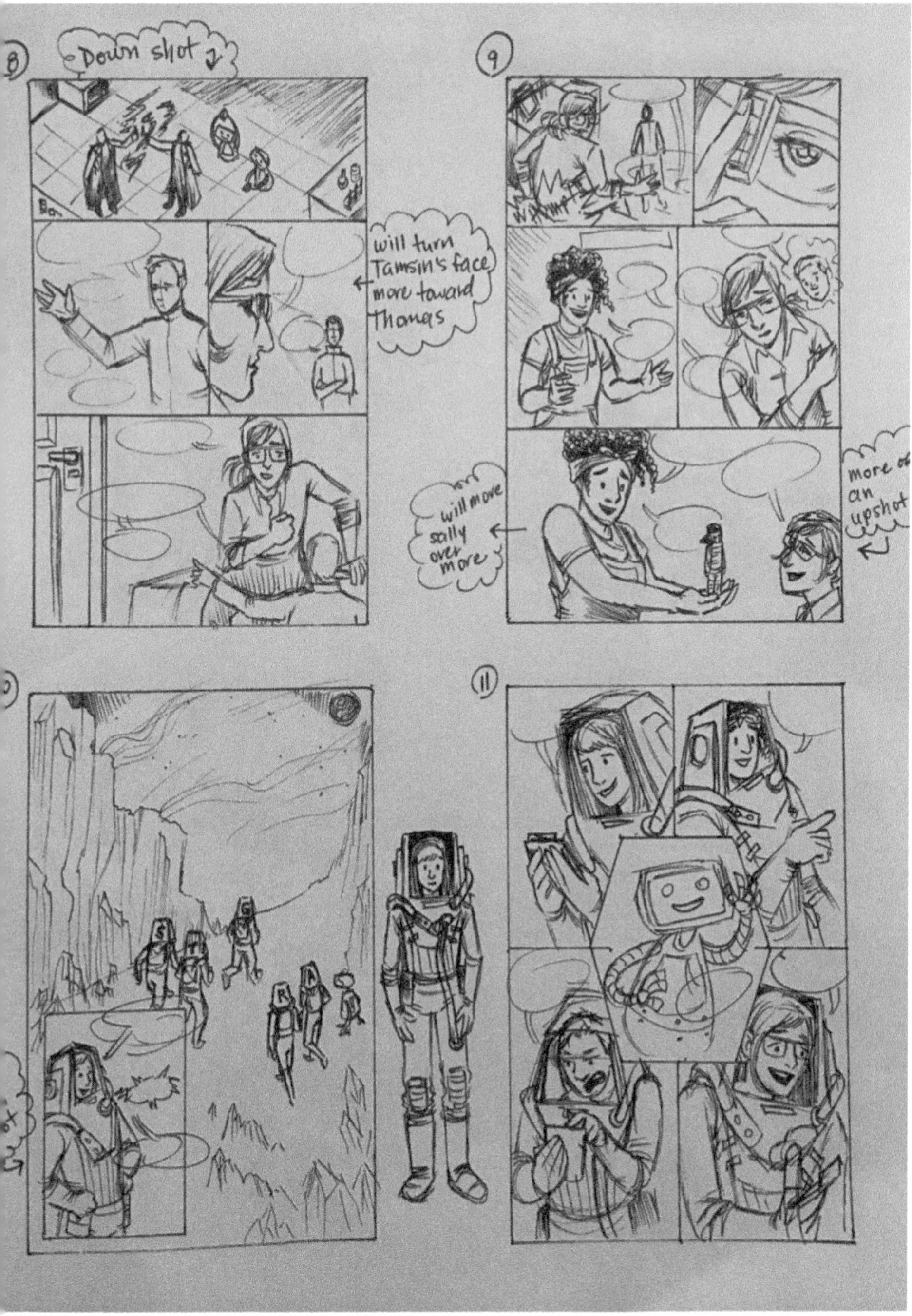
Down shot
9
will turn Tamsin's face more toward Thomas
will move sally over more
more of an upshot
11

Page 8–11 layouts/thumbnails by Desiree' Pittman

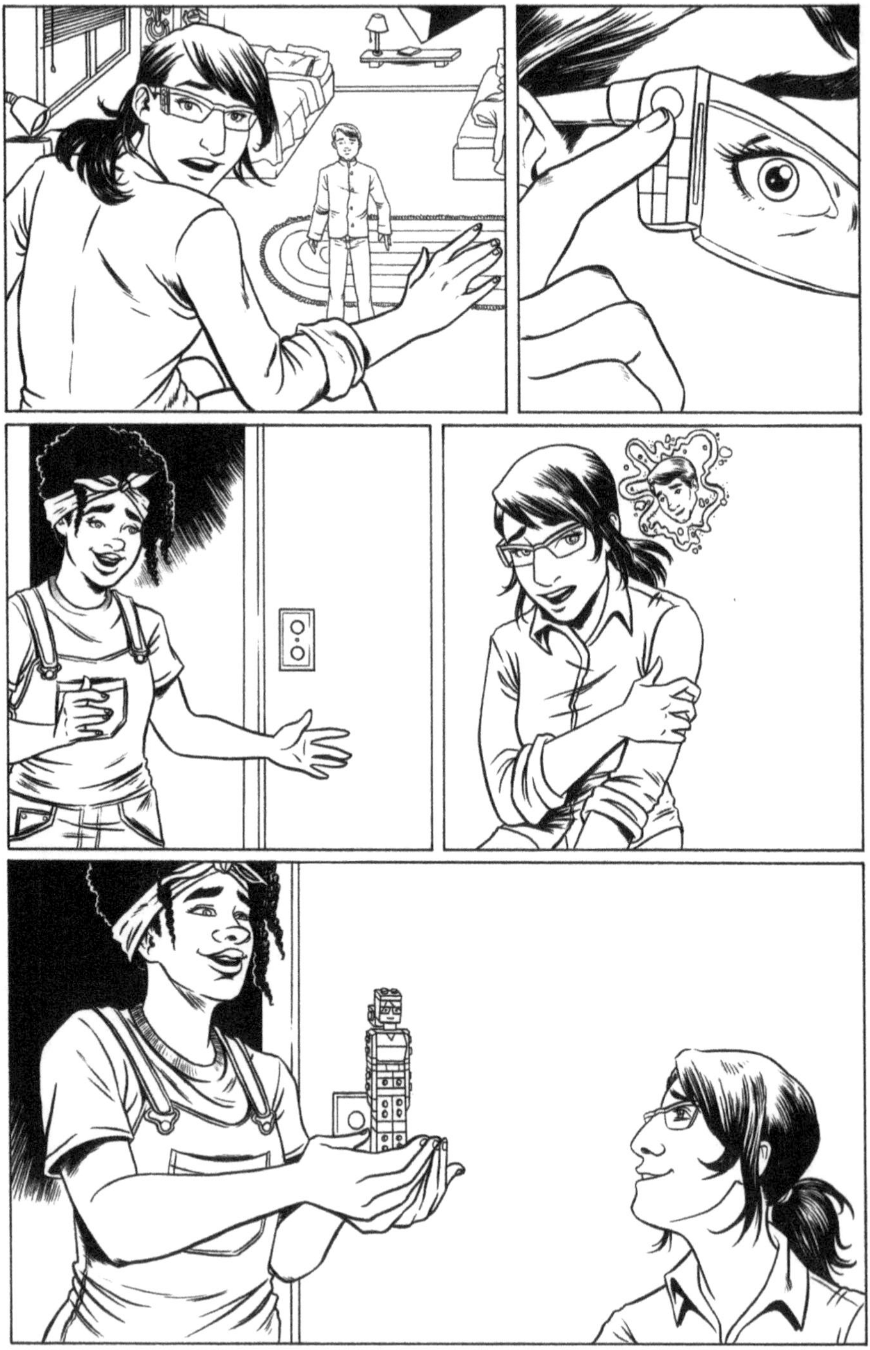

Page 9 inks by Desiree' Pittman

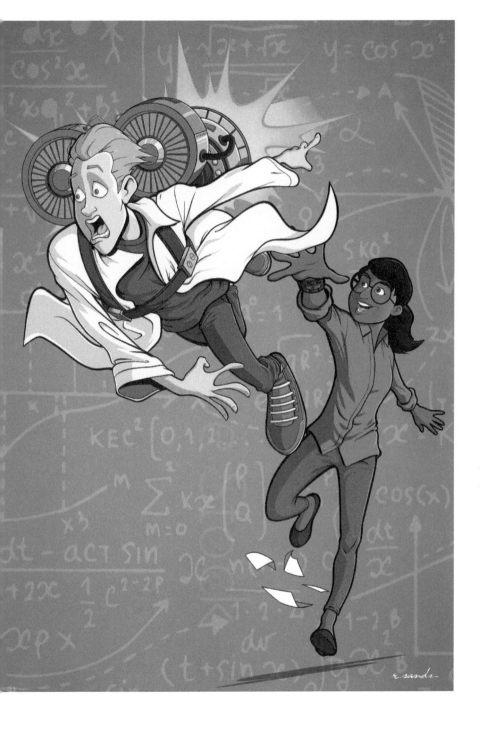

Art by Ryan Sands

Why a book about science?

It's a good question to pose to two creators of a graphic novel who both hold theatre degrees. This is a story that was a long time coming, and it wears so much of our influences in its pages. If you're familiar with our past works, you can probably spot some of our ever-loving *Star Trek* homages, but when we were crafting *Science!*, we really wanted it to be a science fiction story based in scientific facts.

Can you imagine?

But what does that even mean?

It means hours upon hours of us reading complicated articles in an effort to pull keywords which led to story inspiration. It also means learning that *Star Trek* played fast and loose with their science more often than you may initially have guessed. Warp drive? Forget about it!

When we went in search of a "mysterious power source," that's when things got really interesting, and when Jason stumbled onto the crux of the story –Dark Energy.

We won't cop to how long it took us to finally embrace the power of Dark Energy, but it took more than a single initial brainstorming session. But, honestly? We're writers! What sounds cooler than "Dark Energy"? Almost nothing!

But ... but ... what is it?

Well, according to Space.com, it makes up ¾ of the known universe and scientists still struggle to define it. That's wonderful for a pair of writers because it is both a real thing *and* undefined by the traditional scientific method, so we have a lot of room to play! If you are a fan of the new *Voltron* update, then you might be familiar with their semi-magical power source by which their entire universe is connected known as "Quintessence." Well, that's basically Dark Energy!

Fictional cosmic allegories aside, Dark Matter is the name for the force which affects the spreading of the universe.

Albert Einstein, arguably the most well-known scientist who we definitely reference throughout *Science!* (and is a personal hero of Sally's), was the first scientist to discover that space is not simply made of "space," for lack of a better word. Space is not all star stuff and planetoids, with lots of emptiness in between. What makes up the much-written-about "space"? You guessed it – Dark Energy! It is the force between forces.

In fact, according to NASA, approximately 68% of the universe is Dark Energy.

A little less than 5% of the universe is filled with Earth and everything observable from Earth (other planets, asteroids, et cetera), plus every human being, and all the copies of the graphic novel you are currently holding in your hands! That leaves about 27% of the universe made up of Dark Matter!

We don't really get into Dark Matter in this first volume of *Science!* (the subtitle probably gives it away: *The Secret of Dark Energy*), but we're definitely open to pursuing it in future stories!

In many ways, Dark Energy functions similarly to the purpose Garyn serves in our story. Tamsin, AJ, and Rosie have strong focuses and points of view. Garyn flits between every one, often with great success. It was our intention that the readers be a little put back on their heels with Garyn. Tamsin and Sally don't always know what Miss Merrick is up to, but she definitely has the power to draw everyone around her into her orbit … and sometimes slow the pursuit of their own goals in service of her own wants and needs. These shared traits made it easier and easier as *Science!* went along for our readers to discover Garyn's true nature and goals.

Over the course of the graphic novel, Tamsin learns that there is room for her heart to expand. She learns to let people into her life other than just the ghost of her father. In this way, Tamsin is also a lot like Dark Energy. Einstein actually discovered that space is able to bring more space into existence. This is what's called a "cosmological constant." What helps to fuel this expansion? Our old friend, Dark Energy.

There's a secondary theory about Dark Energy, that it's a "new dynamic energy fluid of field," according to NASA. If you've already read *Science!* (or if you skipped to the end just to read the afterword – spoilers!), then you have probably concluded that this is the characteristic we ran with in our exploration of Dark Energy in the hands of teenagers. It is specifically when potentially used or harnessed as a power source that scientists refer to Dark Energy as "Quintessence" – which you probably remember from earlier.

Again, at the time we are writing this afterword, no one knows exactly what Dark Energy is. It fulfills the idea of a Mystery Box. A Mystery Box is a popular storytelling device. It's a secret. Sometimes it is literally a box. Sometimes it's a secret lab beneath your super smart science school! If we are very, very lucky, when Tamsin is ready to have more stories told about her, we will have even more discoveries in the real world that we'll be able to port over into hers.

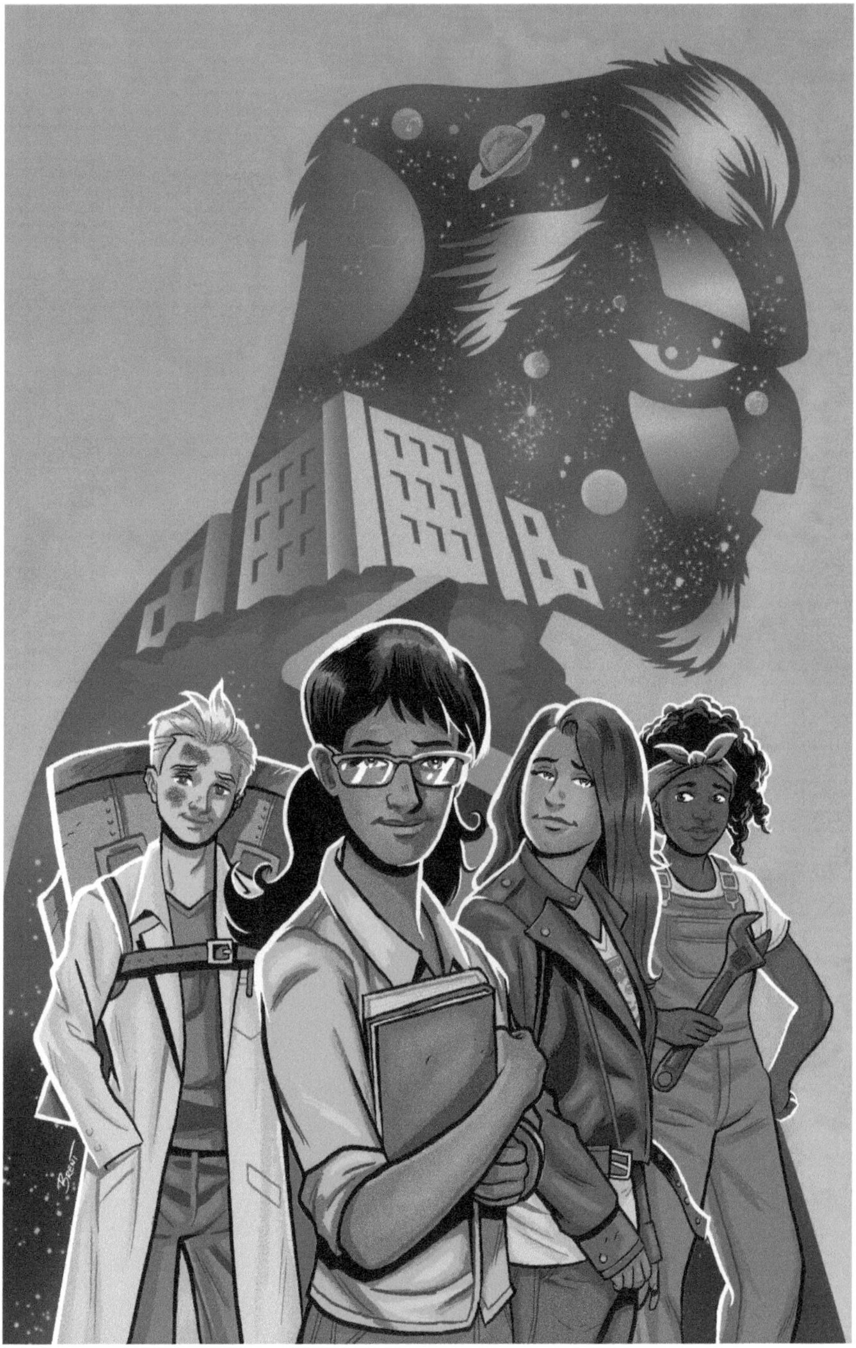
BRENT

Art by Brent Schoonover

Bios

Ashley Victoria Robinson is a Canadian hobbit now living in the United States. Her comic book writings have been published through DC Comics/IDW, Top Cow, Action Lab Comics, Not Forgotten Comics and Colonial Comics. She is the host of the *Geek History Lesson* podcast (alongside Jason), any number of shows for the youtube channels including: Jawiin, Nerd Alert, Geek Bomb, Collider, Screen Junkies, Crave Online, DC All-Access, Comicbook.com, Geek & Sundry, Hyper RPG, Major Spoilers, and many more. She is also the co-creator of Jupiter Jet and *The Red Shirt Diaries*.

She is one of the current faces of Twitter Marketing's Entertainment campaign and has been featured in several international commercials including Intel alongside *The Big Bang Theory's* Jim Parsons. Follow her antics on Twitter & Instagram @AshleyVRobinson

Together, Jason and Ashley have co-written *Jupiter Jet* (Action Lab), *The Red Shirt Diaries* (and tie-in webcomic), *Town Hall* (stage play), *Swan Story* (DC Comics/IDW's Love is Love Anthology), with more to come!

Jason Inman is a Kansas farm boy who read too many comics and science fiction novels as a child. Luckily, he was able to turn that into a career.

His newest non-fiction book, *Super Soldiers*, is about the secret connection between comic book characters and soldiers in the military. Jason is also the co-creator and co-writer of *Science!* for Bedside Press and *Jupiter Jet* for Action Lab Entertainment. You might have also seen his face when he was the host of *DC All Access*, DC Comics official web series for over three years. Besides having written for several comic and entertainment websites, Jason has produced and written for web shows including Good Mythical Morning and Screen Junkies.

Prior to becoming a writer, Jason served in the US Army and Kansas Army National Guard deploying as part of Operation Iraqi Freedom.

When not posting weekly episodes of his podcast, Geek History Lesson or content on his Youtube channel, youtube.com/jawiin, Jason can be found searching California for old cowboy towns.

Desiree' Pittman Hello there! My name is Desiree' Pittman, Dez for short. Growing up, I just wanted to create art all the time. In 2001, I attended the School of Visual Arts in Manhattan where I studied cartooning and illustration and later graduated in 2005 with a BFA.

I currently reside in Portland, Oregon with my amazing husband, Jason, who is also a very talented artist. On top of doing my own projects, I enjoy commission work and collaborations. You're most likely to see me at a Convention drawing Zombie Portraits and selling prints of my illustration work.

And just in case you wanted to know, I love food. Food is pretty awesome. And ice-cream, MAN do I love ice-cream.

Becka Kinzie is a freelance artist and colorist from Ontario, Canada. Some of her coloring work has been featured in comics such as Hacktivist (vol. 2), and the Gothic Tales of Haunted Love anthology. When not coloring, she's drawing her own horror/darkly inclined comics and art. She's currently working on her horror/sci-fi webcomic, which can be found on her website at thebecka.com.

Taylor Esposito is a comic book lettering professional and owner of Ghost Glyph Studios. As a staff letterer at DC, he lettered titles such as Red Hood and The Outlaws, Constantine, Bodies, CMYK, The New 52: Future's End, and New Suicide Squad. Prior to this, Taylor was credited on numerous titles for Marvel as a production artist. He is currently working on a new batch of creator-owned titles, such as The Paybacks and Interceptor (Heavy Metal Comics), Heroine Chic, Dents, Mirror, and Finality (Line Webtoon). Other publishers he has worked with include Rosy Press, Zenescope, Valiant, and Dynamite. He can be reached at@TaylorEspo or @GhostGlyph on Twitter and taylor@ghostglyphstudios.com

S.M. (Samantha Mary) Beiko is an award-winning author of young adult fantasy, as well as a professional editor for both books and comics. Her first standalone novel was *The Lake and the Library*, followed by The Realms of Ancient trilogy, which is comprised of *Scion of the Fox* (winner of the 2018 Copper Cylinder Award), *Children of the Bloodlands*, and *The Brilliant Dark*. Her short fiction has been published in *Gush: Menstrual Manifestos of Our Times, Parallel Prairies: Stories*, and the Disney Princess Treasury comics collections. She is also the co-editor, of the original graphic novel anthology *Gothic Tales of Haunted Love*, and the cartoonist behind *Krampus is My Boyfriend!*, a teen fantasy romance webcomic available for free online.

Find out more about her work at www.smbeiko.com.

Thanks to all of our Kickstarter backers!

.X.
@Lbutlr
A Napoleon
A Winky Face
A.D.R
Aaron Cohen
Aaron Esham
Aaron Nabus (Hall H Show
  Podcast)
Aaron Westendorf
Abf
Adam Kennedy
Adam Williams
Adelardo Fuente
Adrian Duenas
Aims Foster
Alan Blank
Albert Wiradharma
Alex "Fox" Dell
Alex Marzoña
Allan Shepherd
Alley Hennigan
Alok Baikadi
Amanda K Smith
Amanda Ryan
Anders Bolinder
Andrew Bosco
Andrew M Conner
Andrew Rawlings
Andrew Vandeyar
Andrew Vine
Andrew Zacheis Aka "Drewski"
Andy Poon
Andy R
Angela Dehart
Angela Sullivan
Angelique Mad
Angus Ladyman-Palmer
Anke
Anna S
Anne W
Anon
Anonymous
Anthony Rubin
Anthony Torres
Arianna & Laurence Shapiro
Armond Netherly
As Moss Russell
Ashley King
Aunt Barbara

Austin C. Deutsch
Austin Lohouse
B. Pressly
Barb Dunlap
Barbara Randall Kesel
Barry English
Beau King
Becky Smith
Ben Matsuya
Benjamin Akers
Benjamin E Lee
Benjamin Golub
Bernardo De Los Santos
Beth Klandrud
Big Dave Adams
Bill Brooks
Bill Looper
Bill Schweigart
Black Cape Comics
Blake Mclean
Bob Eddy
Bob Michiels
Bobbi Boyd
Borys Pugacz-Muraszkiewicz
Brad Mcalpine
Bradley "Youngyoda" Simmons
Bradley Bradley
Brandon Forsythe
Brandon Palzkill
Brandon Petrosky
Brandon T. Snider
Brandon Wareing
Brent Sieling
Brett Bennett
Brian (Aka @Brainwise)
Brian Faneuff
Brian Fried
Brian Ganninger
Brian Groth
Brian Maxwell
Brian Richards
Brian W. Sanders
Brit Wilbert
Brock E. Severson
Bryan Martin
Tommy Myers
C Sparrell
C. Gorzelnik
Caitlin Mccauley
Calvin Tonini

Cam Ostrin
Cameron Macdonald
Carey Boys
Carlos Gutierrez
Carlos M. Mangual
Casey Briggs
Catdotyi
Cfp33pfc
Chad Fopma
Chad Johnson
Chad Neary
Chaim And Tobias Steinberg
Charles Atencio
Charles Lefort
Charlie Cordes
Charlie Stickney
Chris "Amazing" Singer
Chris And Phaedra Bier
Chris Bramante
Chris Buchner
Chris Halliday
Chris Newell
Chris Villalta
Christian Juel
Christoph
Christopher A. Hoffmann
Christopher Kranz
Christopher Murphy
Clarissa Thorne
Claude Weaver Iii
Cody Dixon
Cody G.
Coleman Bland
Collector's Paradise
  (Comicsandcards.Net)
Cooper Jones
Craig Hackl
Creatively Queer Press
Cwn
Cydney Tibricël Helms
Damon Schofield
Dan
Dan Evans Iii
Dan Eyer
Dan Kosonovich
Dan Murphy
Daniel Higgins
Daniel J. Martinez
Daniel Kibler
Daniel Lin

Dan-O
Darian Lindle
Darren Duncan
David And Lexi Bovensiep
David Avallone
David Boone
David C Williams
David Galla
David M. Booher
David Moore
David Pepose
David Portnov
David Schneider
David Skelton
David Stanley
Dc Fleming
Debbie Crookston
Debra B.
Dena Burnett
Dennis Reardon
Derek Harder
Derek M
Derek Outwater
Devaughn Brown
Deven S. Payton
Devon Camel
Dfio291
Diamond Wong
Diane Clark-Sutton
Dimos Galatakis
Dina Quaas
Dj Wooldridge
Doesn't Matter Ho
Doktor Calamari
Don, Beth, & Meghan Ferris
Donald E. Claxon
Doug "Valhalar" Triplett
Dr. Anthony
Dr. Eleanore Blereau
Dr. Riordan Frost
Dresdenq
Dustin Heideman
Dusty Pearson
Dwayne Farver
Dylan Blight (@Vivaladil)
Earth-2 Comics
Eduardo "Ballinplays" Cabrera
Elaine Tryling
Elijah Mekwunye Jr.
Emi
Emi Lovell
Emily And Hannah Judkowitz
Emily Miller
Emma S
Enrique Matthew &
    Elena Chumbes

Eric A Jackson
Eric Baker
Eric Brady
Eric Matossian
Eric Michael Klein
Eric Michael Messex
Eric Rankin
Erin Subramanian
Ethan Butler
Evan Ritchie
Everybody's Hometown Geek
Facts Not Included Podcast
Foolsinc
Frank Kim
Frank Moran
Frankie Mundens
Gabi
Gaciel Acosta
Garrett L.
Gehrigan Var Dresdan
Gene Shaw 2
George Wook
Gerry Tolbert
Ggk
Gibran Graham
Gleb And His Family
Gmarkc
Grant Quackenbush
Greg Schienke
Greg Wright
Gregory Minton
Hafsa Alkhudairi
Henry Barajas
Hethukawa
Hope Mastras
Howard Fein
Matt Chitty
Ian Birchenough
Ilta T. Adler
Internetionals
Isaac 'Will It Work' Dansicker
J&D
J. Todhunter
Jack Gulick
Jacob Costelloe
Jacob Westfall
Jadexan
Jaenen
Jake Hefner
James <Bigjim> Thatcher
James Denning
James Masters
James Mellar
James Peter Lawton
Jason Anderson
Jason Blodgett

Jason Crase
Jason Pittman
Jason 'Xenophage' Frisvold
Jay Lofstead
Jdferries
Jeff Barbanell
Jeff Hamilton
Jeff Lewis
Jeff Peterson
Jeff Rowat
Jeffrey & Susan Bridges
Jeffrey Bazzell
Jenna Bushor
Jennifer Priester
Jensa 4 Science!
Jeremie Lariviere
Jeremy Kwan
Jeremy Simser
Jeremy Whiting
Jerry Ahern
Jerry Hillman
Jessa Will
Jesse W
Jillian Lambert
Jim Curl
Jim Kettner
Jim Kosmicki
Jimmy Dunn
Jimmy Palmiotti
Jlclemon
Jodi Berdis
Johl Ca
John D. Pelzer III
John L. Beall
John Lamar
John Lampson
John M.
John Matsuya
John Monahan
John Roland
John Stefan
Jolene Miller & Donna Steppe
Jonas Richter
Jonathan Bione
Jonboy Meyers
Jonelle Edwards
Jon-Paul D. Lopez
Joost N
Jordan
Jordana Greenblatt
Jordanne Wilson
Josh Elder
Josh Ghormley
Josh Medin
Joshua Lowry
Joshua-Jon

Blaise Hopkins
Andrew R. Crosby
Evan Zoller
Choppyjones
William Everall
Justin
Justin
Justin Rogers
Kaitlin Thompson
Kaleb Swenson
Kamoxl
Kar Fedosh
Karl Haverly
Kat Kan
Kat Stammers
Kate Allred
Katherine Malloy
Kathy Ebright
Katie M Cook
Keith H.
Kelly Smith
Kelsey Kirkland
Kendall Sherwood
Kent Akselsen
Kent Archie, Ph.D
Kent Heidelman
Ket Strait
Kevin Chiok
Kevin Mahadeo
Kevin Nolen
Kevin Sco
Kevin Stahlecker
Khalid Alomayri
Kim C.J.
Kim Mcclain
Kim Wincen
Kimberly Warne
Kingsley Lu
Kirk Blackwood
Kita
Konrad Kedzior
Krista Hoxie
Kristen M. Chavez
Kristian K-J-Beers
Kristyn Connor
Kurt Marquart
Kurt Moore
Kvh
Kyle Gerbrandt
Lance
Laura Burns
Laurel
Laurel Kristick
Lauren Daniels
Layla Simonsen
Ldy50

Lea Mara
Lemon Twist
Lenurd The Joke Gnome
Leo Kallis
Leokii
Lindsey Petrucci
Lisa // The Viet Vegan
Lisa Spangenberger
Lisandro Gu
Lloyd Thistle
Loren Fleming
Louis Murphy
Lucas "The Walrus" Ellis
Lynn
Mabel & Henry Alexander
Mac Lacey
Mara Knopic
Marcus Kingi
Maria Wren
Mark
Mark Byzewski
Mark Scheetz
Mark Thompson
Matt Chin
Matt Goolsby
Matt Kelly Of Horror
    Movie Night
Matt L
Matt Lazorwitz
Matt Lord
Matt Waterman
Matt Young
Matthew Cooper
Matthew Hannan
Matthew O'brien
Mendel Greene
Mesha
Mi Desbrow
Michael Abbott
Michael Curtis
Michael Feldhusen
Michael Gulick
Michael Hill
Michael Levesque
Michael Rotton
Michelle Quirk
Mike Brown
Mike Burke
Mike Gibson
Mike Kalinowski
Mike Kennedy
Mike Krug
Mike Speakman
Milena Barone
Mitch Gerads
Mitchell Cameron

Molly & Moira Featherston
Morgan Gordon
Morgan Perry
Morgan Whitlock
Ms. Debra Lovelace
Angela Laree
Nadia Bethea
Narsi Reddy
Natasha R. Chisdes
Nathan Hartwog
Nathan Marchand
Nathan Nolan
Nerd Chronic
Niall Gord
Nicholas Fenner
Nick Vega
Nicolas Izambard
Niels Minamizawa Mathiesen
Nikki Zano
Nina Frey
Edward Doubleday Jr
Norman Jaffe
Not Needed
Olympic Cards And Comics
Omar Spahi
Patrick Mcmillan
Pattie Miller
Patty Kirsch
Paul "Ilys" Symeou
Paul Bentley
Paul Chapman, Practitioner
    Of Science!
Paul Charvet
Paul Franklin
Paul Mcerlean
Paul Santos
Paul Y Cod Asyn Jarman
Peter Halasz
Peter Mazzeo
Phil White
Philip Noguchi
Phillip Whit
Pj Campbell
Ms. Nichenko
Praetorian
R.J.H.
Rachel Cushing
Rachel H Sanders
Rachel Silvestrini
Rae Larson
Ralph Lachmann
Randolph Washington Jr.
Randy Holland
Rane Wallin
Raúl Alejandro Mendoza Diaz
Ray Macdonald

Rebecca Mutton
Remick, Larkin, Mimi & Warren
Rex Thomas Baylon
Rheya Sylvia Rocks!
Ricardo Rodriguez
Richard Hansen
Rick Norman
Rico Dostie
Rob Fowler
Rob Smith
Rob Steinberger
Robert Ahn
Robert L Vaughn
Robin Feins, Mhs Ela
Robin Gonzales
Rodney Jones
Rosalia
Ross Mc
Rui M Almeida, Aka Ariamus
Russ Walker
Russell Reitsema
Ryan Clarke
Ryan Duncan
Ryan Dunlavey
Ryan Gray
Ryan Hodapp
Ryan Holder
Ryan R. Venis, Md
Ryan Raines
Sabir Pirzada
Samantha Katherine Stegemeyer
Sami Chase
Sammy G.
Samuel W. Johnson
Sarah Galletly
Saul Hymes
Sawanna Davis
Scarlett Letter
Schulman Family
Scott
Scott Garvin
Scott Niswander
Scott Schaper
Scott Steubing
Seamas
Sean Janelle
Seth
Shadowcub
Sharla K. Nolte
Shaun Watson
Shawn Dean
Shawnta Dodson
Shayne Pickett
Shoshana Sternlicht
Skyings

Smitty Werbenjagermanjensen
  (Or Paul)
Sol Foster
Sonia Lai
Sophie Mcnickle
Spiffjbug
Spoiler Steve
Stacy Fluegge
Stellar Ash
Steph Turner
Stephen Schleicher
Sterling Gates
Steve
Steve "Bob" Martin
Steve Bearfield
Steve Davis
Steve Ewell
Steve Harris
Steve Komas
Steven Cain
Steven Scott
Steven Tsai
Stuart Sti
Sune Høyer Sørensen
Sunny Chauhan
Super-Dad Charles Rashed
Supporter Or Supported By
Susan Renee Page
Suzanne Collins
Switch7350
T.R. Nordyke
Tara Samek
Tasha Sargent
Tatum Shank
Ted B
Terminal Velocity Comic
  Book Podcast
Terra Byrne
Terry Mayo
Thad Hait
Thadd Williams
Steven House Of L &
  Ryan Of Asgard
  (Geek Like Tendencies)
Kelly K.
Drew Marks
The Brugadorns
The Comic Source
The Hoffman Family
The Swain Boys
Thegreatnateo
Thom Parham
Tim Beedle
Tim Bucknell
Tim Dhanens
Tim Peters

Tim Robertson
Tim Smyth @Historycomics
Timothee Engel
T-Money
To David Zusiman
Tom Carter "Indexsonic"
Tom Duford
Tom Powers
Tom Trainor
Tony Andrews
Torsten Hoffmann
Tracey Pollard
Travis Mickey
Travis The Magic Man
Trevor D. Garner
Tricia And Lorelai Dillard
Tristan Ragan
Troytogo
Tyler Hildebran
Tyler Sex
Tymothy Peter Diaz
Uyvbjhkv
Vanessa Fontaine
Victor Rebella
Vince Bayless
Waller Hastings
Waterdragon511
Alex King
White Beard Geek
Wil Young
William Hairston
William Thode
William V. Albert
Willie Y.
Wlc
Xiong Pao Chang
Yes
Your Mind University Alumni,
  Jacob Kahnke
Zac And Momo
Zachary Presley
Zachary Schenk
Zackary Rall
Zoe Gross